This was what she wanted, what she'd dreamed about since she was a lonely little girl.

A home shared with a man she loved and who loved her, and a child to nurture and adore. Her eyes filled with tears as she realized how very close she was to having that dream come true.

Tonight she would tell Case, she decided, her heart suddenly fluttering with an acute case of nerves. Tonight she would snuggle next to him and place his big hand on the gently swelling curve of her belly. And then, when he felt the baby kicking, she would tell him that he was going to be a father.

After tonight there would be no more secrets between them. No more worry… No more fear.

Dear Reader,

I hope you've got a few days to yourself for this month's wonderful books. We start off with Terese Ramin's *An Unexpected Addition*. The "extra" in this Intimate Moments Extra title is the cast of characters—lots and *lots* of kids—and the heroine's point of view once she finds herself pregnant by the irresistible hero. The ending, as always, is a happy one—but the ride takes some unexpected twists and turns I think you'll enjoy.

Paula Detmer Riggs brings her MATERNITY ROW miniseries over from Desire in *Mommy By Surprise*. This reunion romance—featuring a pregnant heroine, of course—is going to warm your heart and leave you with a smile. Cathryn Clare is back with *A Marriage To Remember*. Hero and ex-cop Nick Ryder has amnesia and has forgotten everything—though how he could have forgotten his gorgeous wife is only part of the mystery he has to solve. In *Reckless*, Ruth Wind's THE LAST ROUNDUP trilogy continues. (Book one was a Special Edition.) Trust me, Colorado and the Forrest brothers will beckon you to return for book three. In *The Twelve-Month Marriage*, Kathryn Jensen puts her own emotional spin on that reader favorite, the marriage-of-convenience plot. And finally, welcome new author Bonnie Gardner with *Stranger in Her Bed*. Picture coming home to find out that everyone thinks you're dead—and a gorgeous *male* stranger is living in your house!

Enjoy them all, and don't forget to come back next month for more of the most exciting romantic reading around, right here in Silhouette Intimate Moments.

Yours,

Leslie Wainger
Senior Editor and Editorial Coordinator

Please address questions and book requests to:
Silhouette Reader Service
U.S.: 3010 Walden Ave., P.O. Box 1325, Buffalo, NY 14269
Canadian: P.O. Box 609, Fort Erie, Ont. L2A 5X3

Paula Detmer Riggs

Mommy By Surprise

Silhouette®
INTIMATE™MOMENTS®

Published by Silhouette Books

America's Publisher of Contemporary Romance

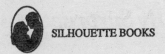 SILHOUETTE BOOKS

ISBN 0-373-07794-7

MOMMY BY SURPRISE

Copyright © 1997 by Paula Detmer Riggs

Books by Paula Detmer Riggs

Silhouette Intimate Moments

Beautiful Dreamer #183
Fantasy Man #226
Suspicious Minds #250
Desperate Measures #283
Full Circle #303
Tender Offer #314
A Lasting Promise #344
Forgotten Dream #364
Silent Impact #398
Paroled! #440
Firebrand #481
Once Upon a Wedding #524
No Easy Way Out #548
*The Bachelor Party #656
Her Secret, His Child #667
†Mommy by Surprise #794

Silhouette Desire

Rough Passage #633
A Man of Honor #744
Murdock's Family #898
†Daddy by Accident #1073

Silhouette Books

Silhouette Summer Sizzlers 1992
"Night of the Dark Moon"

*Always a Bridesmaid!
†Maternity Row

PAULA DETMER RIGGS

discovers material for her writing in her varied life experiences. During her first five years of marriage to a naval officer, she lived in nineteen different locations on the West Coast, gaining familiarity with places as diverse as San Diego and Seattle. While working at a historical site in San Diego she wrote, directed and narrated fashion shows and became fascinated with the early history of California.

She writes romances because "I think we all need an escape from the high-tech pressures that face us every day, and I believe in happy endings. Isn't that why we keep trying, in spite of all the roadblocks and disappointments along the way?"

To Beverly Beaver,
so glad I found you.

Chapter 1

"He's late! I know something's happened." Molly Grandville gnawed on her lip while peering out into the darkened sanctuary, her seal brown eyebrows pulled into a worried frown.

"Now, hon, don't get yourself into a state," her husband, Thad, soothed, patting her plump shoulder with a clumsy hand. "Case said he'll be here, so he will."

"But Pastor Lutz wants to start the ceremony at three o'clock sharp and it's almost ten till."

Standing to one side, Prudy Randolph watched the young couple with a mounting uneasiness she was trying very hard to hide. Maybe, a tumble of years from now, she might look back on this and laugh at the acute case of nerves presently turning her knees to jelly. At the moment, however, her thoughts were centered on the man they were expecting to walk down the center aisle of the big old church any minute now.

Case Randolph. The baby's godfather to her godmother. And her ex-husband.

"I specifically told Uncle Case not to be late, and he *prom-*

ised,'' Molly said plaintively, giving Prudy a quick, anxious look. Prudy took a deep breath and fashioned what she hoped was a reassuring smile, but before she could utter the soothing words that automatically came to mind, Molly rushed on. ''I know he's been on this important case, which is why he showed up at the hospital looking like a hoodlum, but—''

"Now, hon, Case explained about that," Thad reminded her with only a hint of impatience. "He was just coming off a stakeout when I called him, and he couldn't very well turn up looking like a banker when he's working undercover."

"At least he could have shaved," Molly insisted. "And covered up that awful tattoo on his shoulder. The poor nurses were scared to death when he walked in and demanded to know which room I was in."

Prudy heard the thread of hurt in the younger woman's voice and stifled a sigh. Though Molly was twenty-two and already a wife and mother, she had yet to completely outgrow her dependence on her father's little brother. But then it had been Case who'd paid for Molly's private schooling after her parents had been killed. And Case who had paid for Molly's wedding to her childhood sweetheart ten months ago. What he *hadn't* done was try to take her parents' place. Case wasn't about to become anyone's daddy. Hadn't he told Prudy that often enough?

"What if he's forgotten the baptism is supposed to be today?" Molly wondered aloud. "You know how he gets sometimes—his mind on his job and everything else on hold."

"Case has his share of faults, Mol," Prudy assured her quietly, "but forgetfulness isn't one of them."

Nor was forgiveness, she thought sadly, returning her gaze to the tiny face of the peacefully sleeping infant in her arms. Casey Randolph Grandville was three weeks and two days old, as sturdy and solid as a little brick with his uncle's glossy black hair and square jaw. Though relaxed now in slumber, little Casey's mouth had the same obstinate line as Case's and the same intriguing comma at one corner. He was all male, this little one, with the promise of his uncle's fierce temperament stamped on his miniature features.

Deep inside, Prudy felt a familiar throbbing, like the first twinge of post-op agony pushing past the blessed numbness of a general anesthesia. She closed her eyes for a millisecond, grabbing frantically for her self-control or, if not that, for numbness.

A baby who looked like Case, she thought with a rush of emotion. So much like the baby she'd lost a lifetime ago. The little boy who would be ten years old now.

If only he had lived, she thought, her mind slipping far too easily into the same worn grooves. *If only...* What had some-one called those words? A fool's lament?

Yes, foolish is exactly the word for the woman she'd been all those years ago. Foolish and in love with a man who had never once lied to her about his unwillingness to father a child. Take it or leave it, he'd said. Everything else in their relation-ship was negotiable. But not that. And God help her, she'd agreed.

No babies. Not ever.

For four years, she'd been sublimely content with her lusty, sexy husband. Happy with her job as a maternity nurse at Portland General Hospital. Thrilled with the little cottage by the river Case had bought for her. Wonderfully, ecstatically in love. Then, one by one, her friends started having babies. And each time she'd attended a baby shower, she'd ached a little more until she'd found herself desperately unhappy. Taking care of other women's babies in the nursery was no longer enough for her. She'd wanted to hold a baby of her own to her breast and feel the greedy little mouth begin to suckle.

She'd been so sure Case would change his mind once he realized the baby was already on the way. All of her friends had told her that same thing. They'd all been dead wrong. By the time she'd realized what a terrible mistake she'd made, the damage had been done. Through a tangled weave of de-ception, she'd conceived Case's child, and fate had taken it from her before it could even be born. An unfortunate mis-carriage, her doctor had said. Nature's attempt to correct a mistake. In this case the mistake had been hers, a mistake that had ultimately lost her the man she loved.

A soft sigh escaped her lips. Just one lie. Not a host of them. Not even a handful of them. Just *one* little lie—one deception—and he'd never been able to forgive her for it.

She'd been very young then. So very, very young. Everyone was allowed one mistake. She'd made hers. And she'd paid, she thought as she watched Molly rush over to greet the minister who had just entered by a rear door. Oh, how she'd paid. It had taken Case a long time to stop loving her, and even longer to end their marriage. But eventually he'd done both.

Now, eight years after he'd walked out of their place on Mill Works Ridge for the last time, she was about to see him again. She straightened her spine at the thought, aware that Molly was leading the beaming minister toward the baptismal font.

Stubby and round with wisps of snowy hair feathering over a bald head, the cleric had a kind face. And the promise of humor in his eyes, she decided as she watched him shake Thad's hand with both of his. "Haven't seen you look so pleased with yourself since I married you to your sweet bride," Pastor Lutz said with a chuckle that set his little potbelly jiggling under the sober black shirt.

Thad actually blushed. Prudy had already noted the young father's shy pride in his new family and liked him all the more for showing it.

"Pastor, I'd like for you to meet Casey's godmother, my aunt, Prudy Randolph," Molly murmured, reclaiming the minister's attention.

"Ms. Randolph. Welcome to Willamette Avenue Community Church." His blue eyes twinkled into a smile that radiated warmth, and Prudy felt some of the tension seeping from her rigid spine.

"Thank you, I—"

She was interrupted by the sound of a heavy door banging shut. All eyes turned toward the sound as Case came striding out of the gloom at the rear of the sanctuary, still tugging on a suit jacket over the wide expanse of white shirt molding his impressive chest muscles. He moved like a man with a mission, his walk part swagger, part power, the muscles bunching in his thighs with each step he took, drawing the sharply creased cloth of his trouser legs taut.

Watching him with hungry eyes, Prudy remembered the last time she'd seen him naked. How tempted she'd been to run her fingers through the softly curling chest hair. How fast her heart had beat when she'd realized the prodigiously savage strength he'd been hiding beneath the conservative clothing of a civilized man.

A part of her ached to feel that hard chest pressed against her breasts while his arms tightened around her and his mouth came crashing down for a hard, possessive kiss.

"Uncle Case!" Molly's smile was rainbow bright. As bright as Prudy's own had once been at the sight of her handsome husband charging through the door, his arms already reaching for her.

Prudy sucked in a breath, and waited for the moment she'd dreaded for weeks to be over and done with. To get through this with some semblance of control was all she wanted. If she could retain at least some of her pride and dignity while she was at it, that would be nice, as well. Surviving this was the main thing on her agenda, though. With a start, she realized she had a death grip on the baby and relaxed her hold.

"It'll be okay," she whispered to her godson, who didn't stir. In spite of his inner toughness and sometimes blunt manner, Case was a gentleman at heart. No matter what kind of resentment he might still harbor against his ex-wife, he wouldn't let that bleed over onto a sacred ceremony. His sense of propriety and decency was nearly as strong as his will.

Still, she couldn't prevent the sudden fluttering in the pit of her stomach. It was the same feeling Case had aroused in her the first time they'd met. She'd been a year older than Molly, a brand-new RN who'd just moved to Portland to take a job at Portland General. Case had been twenty-seven and gorgeous in his cop's uniform, with a body honed to a lean toughness by the physical work he'd done to put himself through college and a wickedly sensual gleam in his midnight blue eyes.

He'd gotten himself cut up on a fence while chasing a four-teen-year-old kid who'd stolen a souped-up Camaro, then, like a jackass, rear-ended Case's patrol car while pretending he could drive.

Determined to be big-city blasé instead of small-town awed, Prudy had ordered Patrolman Randolph around like a drill sergeant, then giggled when her big tough cop had displayed an endearing terror of needles. She'd fallen in love between the first and second sutures the trauma doctor had been stitching into Case's injured shoulder.

"Sorry, little bit," Case said to Molly as he reached the front of the church. "I had trouble getting away." He leaned closer to kiss his niece's cheek, and sunlight caught the inky silk of his hair, finding traces of silver among the thick strands. Though he'd always worn his hair longer than fashion, it was now long enough to fall past his shoulders without the restraint of the rubber band that pulled it back into a ponytail. The blatant mark of a rebel, she thought. Even at forty-five, Case was marching to his own drummer. Though he'd dressed in a conservative suit, snowy shirt and tie, there was something earthy and raw and untamed about him. As though he tolerated the constraints of polite society on his own terms. No doubt about it, she thought with a sad pang, her ex-husband was still a seductively attractive—and intimidating—man.

"Thad." The two men shook hands, one of those thrusting, hard-gripped, brief handshakes that males seemed to take such pride in.

Molly introduced her uncle to the minister, who lifted his snowy eyebrows at the mention of Case's last name. "Oh, then you and this lovely lady are married?" the pastor said, beaming paternally from one to the other.

"Not anymore," Prudy informed him, finally finding her smile as she met Case's gaze. His eyes were still the color of midnight, with smudges of obsidian around the irises. Predatory eyes, she'd once called them—until they warmed with an inner fire. And then she'd lost the ability to form a coherent thought.

Seasoned by time, his face was ruggedly hewn, more angles than curves, with a lack of symmetry that she'd always found irresistible, even as it hinted at the dark complexity of the man himself.

Though her brain noted changes—a tiny gold earring winking at her from his left ear, added lines of stress in his broad forehead, deeper grooves framing his hard mouth, a sharper edge to the cynicism in his eyes—her heart smiled at the memory of those unsmiling lips brushing hers on that first magical night when she'd started falling in love.

He'd smiled at her then, a lopsided, endearingly restrained, involuntary invitation that had enchanted her. *I've been waiting for you all my life, sweet Prudy,* he'd said in that smoke and steel voice of his. *You don't know it yet, but you're mine.*

"Hello, Prudy. Nice to see you again." His voice was cool, his gaze impersonal before it dropped to the child in her arms, and Prudy felt a stab of pain going all the way to the quick.

"He looks like you, Uncle Case," Molly said, beaming down at her son.

"Poor kid," Case all but growled. "Maybe he'll get over it."

Molly punched him, and he grinned at her, revealing a flash of deep male dimples.

Remember the arguments and the anger, Prudy reminded herself as she inhaled the familiar scent of his aftershave. Remember the loneliness after he left, and the hours spent waiting by the phone. Squaring her shoulders, she lifted her chin and forced calm into her expression. When she met Case's gaze, he lifted one black eyebrow in mocking salute.

Bastard, she thought, her temper sparking.

"If you'll take your places around the font, we'll begin," the pastor ordered with a brisk note of anticipation. "Godparents on my left, please. Parents on my right."

As Case took his place next to the woman he'd never figured to see again, he decided he needed a stiff drink. At least a double. Hell, no, a triple, he amended as the minister opened a small black book and cleared his throat.

The baby hiccuped, and Prudy smiled. Late-afternoon sunshine spilled from the triangular window in the soaring facade behind the altar to bathe her in a golden glow, and for an instant, he felt his breath dam in his throat. Her heart-shaped face was radiant beneath the coppery halo of her hair as she gazed down at the baby cradled in her arms. A shaft of pain shot through him, slicing neatly and efficiently through the chains he'd put around his emotions.

She looked so right, standing there. So serenely happy. Only someone who knew her very well, or loved her with all his heart, would notice the subtle curve of sadness at the corners of her smile.

He told himself he was neither—just a cop trained to notice the tiniest details. Like the fact that her profile was as fragile as ever, a heart-tugging combination of sensitive slopes and impish curves. She had a pixie's face, he'd teased her once. With lush brown eyes that took on a subtle gleam of golden warmth when she laughed and a wide, expressive mouth. Pensive, sad, even trembling with anger, her mouth had once driven him crazy, just as her lush shape had once robbed him of good sense.

She was thinner now, he noticed, but the curves under the clinging material of her dress were generous enough to excite a dead man to life. Her derriere was sweetly rounded beneath the graceful folds of her skirt, and her breasts filled the bodice to perfection. In spite of her short stature, she had a ripe figure, as perfect now as it had been the first time he'd coaxed her to bare it to him.

Gritting his teeth, he dragged in a lungful of air, then let it out slowly. Did God punish a man for lusting after his ex-wife in church? he wondered as the solemn words of the ancient rite rolled over him. Because, if He did, Case was pretty sure he'd just been sentenced to the fires of hell.

By the time the minister finished and little Casey was bawling for all he was worth, Case was ready to chew nails. Thanks to a scum-of-the-earth dope dealer by the name of Felix Cardoza, he'd had a grand total of four hours' sleep in the past thirty-six, and his bum shoulder was aching like a sonofagun. He figured to hang around for a few minutes, then split for the nearest watering hole and the triple Jack Daniel's he figured to order as soon as he hit the door.

"Here, I'll take him—" Molly said before giving Prudy a teasing grin "—Godmama."

Case ground his teeth as he took a careful step backward. Prudy bent to press a gentle kiss to the baby's silken forehead before relinquishing him to his mama. "There you go, sweet-pea," she murmured.

"Is he okay?" Thad directed his question at Prudy, who was smoothing the baby's frilly christening gown over his sturdy little legs.

"He's fine," Prudy assured him. "And wet."

Molly rolled her eyes while Thad looked helpless. "Get my bag from the front pew, will you, sweetheart?" Molly asked when Thad continued to hover.

"Uh, oh, sure. Right away."

Molly glanced around, her eyebrows drawn. "What's wrong, my dear?" the minister asked with obvious concern.

"Is there someplace where I can change him?" Molly asked in a hushed tone. "Someplace besides *here,* I mean. Somehow it doesn't seem right to change a diaper in a church."

Chuckling, the pastor gestured toward a rear door. "In that case, why don't we step into my office? You can use my couch as a changing table while I fill out the baptismal certificate."

Molly nodded and looked relieved. Case figured it was time to head out and said so, only to have Molly's blue eyes widen into twin circles of dismay. "But Aunt Prudy has made a buffet lunch."

"Honey—"

"Uncle Case, you promised!"

Case had forgotten how persuasive Molly could be when she turned those big blue eyes on a guy. He shifted his feet and braced for the inevitable flood of tears. From the corner of his eye, he caught the minister's commiserating grin.

"I *promised* to attend the kid's christening and I did. But—"

"You promised to attend the *celebration,* and the celebration isn't over."

Case felt frustration ladder down his spine, but he was determined to be reasonable. "Honey, I have a pile of paperwork on my desk about a mile high."

Molly's lips trembled. "I thought you cared about your nephew."

Noting that Prudy was watching with one of those you-don't-have-a-prayer smiles had him biting off a curse.

"I *do* care, but Sunday's the only day I have to catch up." He kept his tone mild and his expression calm. Inside, however, he was contemplating Molly's plump little neck and imagining how satisfying it might be to wring it. As for her big ox of a husband, who thought every word that came from her mouth was golden, life itself would eventually shake that dumb-looking grin off his face. Thad had yet to learn what Case had discovered a long time ago—a man who allowed himself to fall in love was heading for a whole mess of trouble.

"You can spare an hour." Molly punctuated her words with a determined nod.

Prudy saw Case's jaw harden. He was being grimly patient, which was a bad sign. Next came the inevitable explosion. And Case in a temper was exactly what they did *not* need at this particular moment.

"Molly, why don't you change Casey's diaper before it starts to leak all over your new dress and let me negotiate with your uncle," she suggested, mustering her most persuasive smile.

Molly looked abashed. "Promise you won't let him yell at you. He does that when he's being stubborn."

"The hell I do," Case muttered, then scowled when he remembered where he was and realized his voice had, as predicted, already gone up an octave.

"Sorry, Reverend," he muttered, his face heating. Not with embarrassment, he knew, but fury that he'd felt obligated to apologize in the first place—or allowed himself to follow through on the urge.

"Not to worry. I understand." The cleric gave him a sympathetic look before stepping back and indicating that Molly should precede him. Thad offered Case a supportive shrug before following his wife. Poor guy had better develop some gumption, or his life was going to be hell, Case decided with a mental scowl.

Prudy waited until the others had disappeared before turning to face him. "She loves you a lot," she said with a smile.

"She's a good kid." He took a swipe at his hair, feeling it tug at the thong he'd tied around the ends, then resettled his shoulders. His shirt collar was as stiff as a shackle against his gullet and the tie he'd bought especially for today was cinched noose tight. He ran a finger under the brutally tight collar band and worked his jaw to stretch his neck.

"I see you still hate to wear a suit." Though Prudy spoke quietly, Case could see a laugh lurking in the soft curve of her lips. Knowing he shouldn't, he let his gaze linger on the tiny clutch of golden freckles just a kiss away from one corner of that enticing mouth. Her smile faded, even as her tongue made a nervous swipe over her lower lip, leaving it glistening with moisture. The urge to blot those soft lips dry with his own snuck under his guard like a sucker punch in the dark. Dammit, no woman just heading into her forty-second year should look so...well, tempting, he thought as his stomach muscles slowly twisted into knots.

"Molly should know better," he grated, his temper lashed tight.

A frown pleated tiny creases in the smooth skin of Prudy's brow. "Better? I don't understand."

"You and me. Godparents." He shot an uneasy glance at the altar. "I knew this was a dumb idea."

Prudy took a deep breath and hoped Case wasn't planning to do something that would spoil this special day for Molly and Thad. And her.

"Why is it dumb?" she asked quietly.

When he looked back at her, his expression had changed. From controlled to brooding. "Because, dammit, you're still the sexiest woman I've ever met."

Prudy opened her mouth, then shut it again. Heat surged from a spot between her breasts until she felt scorched.

"You don't have to sound so angry about it."

"Angry? Hell, I went past angry right about the time I got a good look at you in that dress."

"My dress?" she repeated, glancing down at the champagne silk shirtwaist. It wasn't fancy, and it certainly wasn't immodest. It wasn't even new.

"What's wrong with it?" she challenged, meeting his gaze head on.

"It makes me feel like I'm sixteen and tripping over my feet, that's what's wrong with it." He sounded so outraged Prudy burst out laughing.

"I'm sorry, Case. Really."

One side of his mouth curled into a mocking smile. "No, you're not, you little witch. Otherwise, you would have worn something that didn't show off those world-class legs quite so well."

"I...thank you—I think."

"Don't gloat. It's not becoming."

His eyes had darkened to a rich navy blue, and one eyebrow was cocked at a suggestive angle. It didn't take a genius to discern his thoughts. Memories tumbled down on her, images of the two of them wrapped together, their bodies slick with passion.

She felt longing run like a bolus of adrenaline through her veins. It felt like the first spike of a fever, this sudden need to have his hands on her again. It wasn't going to happen. Neither wanted the pain a renewed intimacy would arouse. But with one fast jolt of the old electricity, her body was already humming anyway, traitorous as always.

In the distance she heard the muffled crying of a baby and remembered then why she and Case were standing face-to-face after eight long, empty years. Not because he had sought her out to renew acquaintances. And not because he hadn't been able to forget her, or because he still loved her. If she started building castles in the air again, she was destined to be crushed when they came crashing down.

Case had been enjoying the confusion in her eyes and the blush on her cheeks. He wasn't as smooth with the ladies as his partner, Petrov, but he'd been around the block a few times in forty-five years of living. In spite of the history between him and Prudy, most of it bordering on rotten, she was still attracted to him. And God help him, he wanted her so much he was damn glad the front of the church was bathed in shadows.

And then what? Let her rip him open again so he could bleed out what little blood she'd left him with?

"Nice to see you again, Prudy," he said, deliberately cooling his voice. He let his gaze roam the length of her body with an insolent slowness before he returned it to her face. "For a minute I forgot why that surprises me."

For an instant she looked as though he'd just slapped her. And then she blinked away the hurt and offered him a beautiful smile.

"No matter how thick you pile on the ice, Sergeant Randolph, I'm not going to let you make me feel small again. What I did was wrong. I've admitted that. And I've asked you to forgive me. But I'll be damned if I'll play victim to your wounded martyr for the rest of my life."

She turned on her heels, as graceful as a ballerina, her skirt swirling around her sleek legs as she headed for the rear door. He stood rooted, methodically calling himself every filthy name in his considerable lexicon. When he found himself starting over, he moved, catching up to her just as she was reaching for the doorknob.

"I'm sorry," he said when she rounded on him. "I'm a foul-tempered jerk—"

"What you are is an unforgiving bastard," she muttered, holding herself stiffly away from him.

He realized then that he was still holding her shoulders and told himself to let her go. Instead, he began rubbing his palms over the soft curve of her upper arms. Under the slinky sleeves, he knew her skin was warmed silk and lightly dusted with tiny golden freckles. His palms tingled with the need to roam and explore, to mold the curve of the small, perfect breasts under the seductive lines of the dress, to rub those thrusting nipples until they went deliciously hard for him.

He felt his body swell and swore under his breath. "When

the hell are you having this *celebration?*'' he all but growled, his gaze on her mouth.

She drew a shaky breath. "Right away."

Before he could think better of it, he leaned forward and took her mouth for a hot, hard kiss. "I'll be late," he said before letting her go. "Save me a place."

Chapter 2

The steaming July sun was already casting long shadows across the quiet access road leading to Mill Works Ridge as Case parked his dusty, gas-guzzling '69 Charger behind Thad's gleaming new minivan. With a low curse at his own stupidity at agreeing to this damn party thing, he cut the engine and jerked the key from the ignition. After putting in an hour at his desk, hacking a good two inches off the stack of paperwork that had all but threatened to bury him, his mood bordered on foul.

He was also as hungry as a hibernating bear who'd just opened its eyes, no doubt because he hadn't eaten since noon when he'd bolted down a fast-food hamburger before changing into his suit and tie for the christening. Consequently, the gallon of coffee he'd consumed while wrestling three weeks of daily reports into submission was giving his stomach fits.

Unless Prudy had suddenly developed restraint, which he figured was damn close to impossible, she would have enough food prepared for a dozen celebratory dinners, most of it exotic and foreign. Fancy, pretty dishes with names he couldn't pronounce.

He remembered a lot of nights longing for a greasy hamburger with fries soaked in catsup and chased down by a beer instead of vintage wine.

Oh, yeah, gourmet cooking had been only the first of a long string of Prue's hobbies. His least favorite had been interior decorating, which had resulted in his getting more bruised shins than he could count from stumbling over rearranged furniture when he crept in late at night.

He'd cheered silently when she'd moved on to gardening, only to find himself spending what little free time they had together with a hoe in his hands and dirt under his fingernails.

Along about their third anniversary, she'd bought herself a sewing machine with more dials than a jet cockpit and set about taming the sucker to her will. After she'd made curtains for every damn room in the place, she'd turned her hand to dressmaking.

He scowled at the car door as he twisted the key in the lock, his mind already forming an image of her small, lush body draped in a long, slinky robe the color of wild violets she'd made out of sinfully sheer material. Like purple cobwebs, he recalled with mixed emotions. For lounging, she'd told him with one of the pleased-as-punch smiles that had always tied him into knots. For driving her poor, hardworking husband out of his mind had been more like it, he corrected as he stalked up the walk.

As he gained the porch, he missed a step. Damn, if she hadn't painted the front door a deep pink. The woman had the color sense of a demented gypsy, he thought, taking an angry stab at the doorbell.

Molly opened the door and gestured him in with the half-eaten brownie in her waving hand. "Aunt Prudy's in her bedroom changing Casey's diaper," she said when he stopped inside and glanced around warily.

Not one damn thing in the room was familiar. Not the furniture or the color of the walls, which were now as blue as the sky on a good day. Not even the overhead light fixture. He also noticed that a huge new sofa sat dead center in what any normal person would consider to be a traffic path. He told himself he didn't care one way or the other that she'd wiped out all signs of their life together. Hell, why should he? Hadn't he done the same thing?

"'Bout time you showed up," Thad called out from his place on the couch. "Darn women have been talking nonstop about having babies and feeding babies and Lord knows what else about babies all damn afternoon."

"Oh, hush up, you big lummox." Molly took another bite and swallowed. "What would you like to drink, Uncle Case? There's beer and wine and Aunt Prudy made a spare pot of extrastrong coffee just for you."

Case thought about the black sludge already sloshing around in his gut and decided he could wait a while for his next hit of caffeine. "Beer's fine."

"Good man," Thad muttered, saluting Case with a bottle of imported lager.

"*If* Thad hasn't drunk it all by now," Case added, winning him a giggle from his niece.

"Be nice to him, Uncle Case. He's not handling fatherhood very well."

"The hell I'm not," Thad muttered before tipping his bottle to his mouth for a long, soothing swallow. Case figured the kid for six-six, two hundred fifty pounds of henpecked putty. A slave to his hormones, a victim of his own illusions. Unlike his nephew-in-law, Case no longer believed in fairy tales and happy endings, just one of many reasons why he'd remained a bachelor after his divorce.

"It's okay. Aunt Prudy warned me that some men resist paternal responsibility," Molly declared before padding in her stocking feet into the kitchen.

Thad watched her go with brooding eyes. As soon as she disappeared from sight, he let out a low, growling sigh. "I swear, Case, I managed to hold it together in the church, but between you and me, all those damn milk-making hormones rocketing around in that woman are testing my patience big time."

Case scanned the room with a professional eye, reacquainting himself with the exits and windows, then headed for an ugly-looking chair in pea-soup green near the fireplace where he'd have a clear view of the goings-on and a wall at his back.

"I hate to tell you this, kid, but Molly didn't get pregnant all by herself," he said as he stretched out his legs.

He'd missed a spot when he'd polished his loafers this morning, he realized, then shrugged it off. It had been a long time since he'd been a lovesick teenager on his first date, eager to impress the prettiest girl in the freshman class.

A damned lifetime.

Thad took another swallow, then leaned forward to roll the green bottle between his big palms. "I wanted to wait to start this family stuff. Hell, I wasn't even used to being married. But Molly kept talking about how all her friends were having these cute little babies." He lifted his head and gave Case a sheepish look. "Guess I'm not made of steel like you."

Case lifted one eyebrow. "No man is made of steel, kid. Especially when he's got a woman's soft backside snuggled up against him in the dark."

Thad grunted. "Guess it's no good worrying about it now."

"Worry about what, honey?" Molly asked as she crossed between the two men to hand Case a beer.

"College," Thad said a beat too quickly. "For Casey."

"Oh, that's already settled. Our sons will go to Harvard and our daughters will go to Wellesley. Like me."

"Son, singular, and no daughters," Thad declared in a stern voice. "We agreed, remember?"

"I was in hard labor at the time, so it doesn't count," Molly dismissed with an airy wave of her hand.

"The hell it doesn't!"

"Now, Thad—"

"Don't 'now, Thad' me. We made a deal and we're sticking to it." He swiveled his head toward Case, clearly looking for support.

"Right, Case?"

Shifting focus, Case caught the flash of champagne silk from the corner of his eye and knew that Prudy had returned to the living room. Even as he steeled himself against the sexual tug he knew now to expect, he felt the muscles of his belly contract. At the same time adrenaline jolted into his bloodstream, preparing him for fight or flight. He'd done both in the past. Neither had worked for long.

"Wrong, kid," he told Thad with a humorless smile. "You can't make a deal with a woman. Even if they agree to the rules at the beginning, they have a way of changing them in the middle of the game."

"Uncle Case, that's not fair!" Molly cried, glaring in his direction.

"Isn't it?" Case offered his niece a bland look before shifting his attention to the other end of the room. "What's your take on this discussion, Prue?"

Her gaze met his with steady calm, but her lips were slightly curved. And her eyes were sad. "You don't discuss, Case. You give your opinion, then jut out that stubborn chin and dare anyone to disagree."

Case saluted her with his beer, a reluctant grin tugging at his mouth. "I seem to remember that never worked with you."

While he drank, he kept his gaze on hers. For almost twenty years this woman had wandered in and out of his life, and though she no longer held his heart, he hadn't been able to rid himself of the nagging thrum of desire she inevitably aroused in him.

He was honest enough to admit that was one of the reasons he'd done his darnedest to weasel out of today's festivities. He should have known Molly would turn mule-stubborn on him. Hell, she was a Randolph. What else could he expect?

His jaw turned hard as he watched Prudy glide past him, the baby nestled against one slender shoulder. Golden sunlight filtering through the miniblinds turned her hair a rich, soft copper and added the luster of rich satin to her complexion. He knew all too well how soft and warm her skin would feel beneath a man's hands, just as he knew how wonderfully lush her lips would be under his.

He shifted, took a long swallow and listened to the grandfather clock in the corner chime the quarter hour. The hell with family obligations, he decided, scowling at the gently

swinging pendulum. The instant that old clock started to an-
nounce the hour he was outta there.

"Would you like to hold him, Uncle Case?" Molly asked
when Prudy started to settle little Casey in his mother's arms.
Fear shot through Case like a jolt of adrenaline.

"Maybe later," he hedged. Molly's eager smile faded, and
he felt like a jerk.

Prudy saw hurt shimmering in Case's niece's blue eyes and
sighed. Poor Molly loved her big, impossible uncle so very
much, and though he would never admit it, Case loved his
brother's only child dearly.

Summoning a smile, she perched on the edge of the ottoman
near the hearth and crossed her legs. This was a stupid idea,
she decided as she watched Molly settle next to her husband.
Even under the best of circumstances, Case was unpredictable
in social situations, especially when he'd been all but black-
mailed into attending. Even under the best of circumstances,
that was enough to have her nerves jangling, but it was her
own muddleheaded, adolescently dopey reaction to seeing him
again that worried her the most.

Biting her lip, she was suddenly aware that the room had
fallen silent and all eyes were on her. But then, she was the
hostess, wasn't she?

Okay, fine, she thought. She'd made a fool of herself before.
Plenty of times. It was in the genes. All the O'Gradys had a
tendency to speak first and think later.

So, say something profound, Prudence, she heard a voice in
her head command. Unfortunately, it sounded exactly like her
mother's voice, and in the eighteen years during which she'd
lived under her mother's roof, she'd never done one single
thing right. Or so Kathleen O'Grady had told her at least once
a day until Prudy had left home for good on the morning of
her eighteenth birthday.

"Well…" She heard her voice trail away, and for the life
of her, she couldn't think of anything else to say. She
smoothed her skirt, then toyed nervously with the hem. "I
thought it was a lovely ceremony, didn't you?"

Molly nodded. "Oh, yes. Beautiful. And Casey was such a good little boy."

"He bellowed like a bull," Thad contradicted with a proud grin.

Case made an unintelligible sound that held a ring of agreement.

"You'd bellow, too, if someone threw cold water in your face," Prudy declared with a fond glance at her godson who was now busily chewing on his fist.

"Kid better get used to it," Case said, his gaze holding hers for an instant before drifting lower. The look in his eyes told her that he was undressing her in his mind, and she scowled. Yet, even as she wished him in Hades, she felt her breasts begin to tingle.

"What do you think, Aunt Prudy?"

"What?" Prudy jerked her gaze around, only just now aware that Molly had been speaking to her. "I'm sorry, sweetheart, what did you say?"

"I asked what you'd think about having a girl named after you?"

Thad groaned and took another swig of beer. "Help me, Case."

"You're on your own, kid," Case said with a slow grin that told Prudy he knew exactly what kind of an effect he was having on her. In response, she lifted her chin higher and deliberately pinned her gaze on Molly.

"I'd be honored," Prudy replied. "Although, I must say I've never liked the name much. Half the time, people shortened it to 'Prude.'"

"Which I can testify you're definitely not," Case said just loud enough for her alone to hear. Memories zigzagged through her mind—of his demanding mouth closing like hot, wet silk over a nipple, of his teeth grazing nerve endings until they screamed. Damn the man, she thought grimly, her stomach churning nearly as painfully as it had during last week's bout with the flu. Even after eight years of distance, he could still make her squirm.

Determined to resist, Prudy shot to her feet. "I don't know

about everyone else, but I'm ready to eat." She gestured toward the kitchen. "Shall we fill our plates and eat in here, or would you like to settle outside on the patio?"

Thad was out of his seat in a wink, his hand extended toward his wife. "Don't have to ask *me* twice. Not when I've been sittin' here for a good hour smelling all those good smells coming out of the kitchen."

"I'll just put Casey down on your bed, if that's all right with you, Aunt Prudy," Molly said as she let Thad help her up. "He'll probably be okay for another half hour or so before he needs to nurse again."

"I'll take him," Prudy offered, eager to feel the baby's warm little body against her shoulder again, for protection from those smoldering looks from Case, if for no other reason, but Molly was already moving toward the door leading to the hall.

"Don't you dare hog all the salmon mousse," Molly warned Thad over her shoulder before disappearing.

"Bossy," Thad muttered through a doting grin as he headed toward the kitchen, leading with his nose.

Prudy started to twist her hands together, then realized what she was doing and smoothed her skirt instead.

"Molly isn't kidding about Thad's passion for my salmon mousse," she told Case with a cool smile. "Or aren't you hungry?"

His blue eyes took on the shimmering depths of a midnight in high summer. "Yeah, I'm hungry. Eight years hungry."

Her indrawn breath whispered between them. Run, her mind ordered, but she couldn't make herself move as he drew up those long legs, then unfolded from the chair in one lithe, continuous motion that seemed to go on and on. Though Case was physically a few inches shorter than Thad's towering six and a half feet, he seemed bigger, somehow.

Wider.

More intimidating.

A magnificently fashioned male with enough strength to be gentle if he chose and enough power to send heavily armed men running for cover.

Case had added bulk to a frame that had once been whip-cord thin, most of it hard-packed, sinewy muscle, she realized, mentally measuring the width of the strong male chest an arm's length away with the memories she'd shelved with such care eight years earlier.

"Case—"

Somehow the beer bottle was on the table by the chair and the hand that had been wrapped around it was in her hair, pulling her closer.

"Tell me to get lost, Prudy. Or God help me, I won't leave until morning."

"Case," she began again, then found herself at a loss. "I didn't...I don't—"

"I do," he grated when she ground to a halt again. "And I *will*, if I'm still here when Molly and Thad take off."

His hand was firm on her chin, nudging her head back until his mouth was poised over hers. "Cards on the table, Prudy. I want to make love to you, and I think you want to make love to me."

Prudy felt her breathing stuttering in her chest, and her stomach was suddenly upside down. Between her legs, she felt a lashing of heat, and her ears were ringing. She felt soft inside and so terribly empty. A longing to be filled with his hard, thrusting possession raged through her.

"Prudy?" His voice was a low, throbbing command that seemed to race through her bloodstream. "No bluff. Call or fold."

She drew a breath, another and then forced her lips into a smile. Inside she was quaking, but her voice was calm when she answered.

"Call."

Chapter 3

Prudy's feet hurt. Mostly she wore sneakers at work, the kind with air pumped into the soles to cushion the hard pounding her size fives took on a daily basis. At home, she invariably went barefoot to give her poor tootsies a well-deserved break. Consequently, she wasn't used to wearing heels, especially the new spiky ones she hadn't been able to resist buying to go with her dress. Worse, she had a headache. A real whopper, brought on by six feet plus of muscle-packed male with a sexy, lopsided grin that made her blood pressure go berserk.

"This is the last damn dish I could find," Case informed her with a wry grin as he carried an empty plate to the sink where she was loading the dishwasher. He'd removed his jacket and tie and rolled up his sleeves, revealing the brawny, darkly burnished forearms she'd always loved.

The three Grandvilles had left nearly twenty minutes ago. In that time she'd dealt with the leftovers, what few there were, and tried not to think of the rash words she'd flung at Case an hour earlier.

Stifling a sigh, she cast a furtive glance at the green bottle of over-the-counter painkiller on the kitchen windowsill, wishing she could shake a couple of tablets out onto her palm and down them with a brimming goblet of wine.

She hauled in a deep breath instead, desperate to save face. So far she'd come up with only one plan—to plead temporary insanity. Which was completely true. Obviously, she'd been out of her mind. Of course, she wasn't going to go to bed with Case.

Not that the idea didn't have merit. Considerable merit, honesty forced her to admit to her utter disgust. But then what? Start an affair for old time's sake? Or take a stroll down memory lane? It was a lane that had held nothing but heartbreak for her—and if she walked along it again, she'd only be asking for more of the same.

"I think I had too much champagne," she muttered as she pushed her hair away from her throbbing temple.

Case offered her an amused glance that had her teeth snapping together. "Won't work, honey."

She glared at him before snatching the dish from his big hands. "You provoked me into agreeing."

"Yep."

His grin was unrepentant. It also folded a crease into his right cheek, adding charm to his already darkly handsome face. She could berate herself from now until doomsday for accepting his outrageous proposition, but it wouldn't change the hold he had over her.

"What if I told you I'd changed my mind?" she challenged, her breathing growing more rapid with each breath she took.

"I wouldn't believe you." Before she could respond, Case braced his hands on either side of her hips, caging her in his arms. "Kiss me, Prudy. Now."

"Why?" Her voice came out breathless and just a little hoarse.

"Because we're good together. Very, very good."

She felt her defenses slipping and hastened to shore them up. "There's more to life than good sex."

"Yeah, but at the moment I can't think of one single thing." His grin slanted. "Can you?"

Prudy stared into his dark eyes, searching desperately for a shimmer of the love he'd once felt for her, but she saw only heat. Disappointment turned her blood cold and she tried to edge away. But Case only smiled as he folded her into his arms.

"No more talk," he grated before covering her mouth with his. In direct contrast to the tension she felt in his sinewy embrace, his kiss was undemanding, even gentle, a soft brushing of his lips across hers.

She shivered, and he drew back to capture her gaze with his. "Your face is turning pink, honey."

"I must have put on too much blush."

One side of his mouth curved as he brushed the callused pad of his thumb over her cheek, leaving a trail of scorching heat.

"You looked like an angel this afternoon, standing there in church with the baby in your arms," he whispered in a thick voice. "A very sexy angel."

Her headache forgotten, Prudy felt her pulse racing, each furious beat adding to the anticipation building inside her body. She was about to make a serious mistake, and yet she didn't seem to care. Not when a sweet, tingling lethargy was taking charge of her body.

"I'm not sure that's a compliment," she managed to utter through suddenly dry lips.

"A sexy angel with fire in her hair," he went on, his voice rumbling deep.

He slipped his hand into the soft thickness curling back from her temple, his fingers sensuously gentle against her scalp, and it took all of her will to keep from leaning into his touch like a pampered and well-loved kitten.

"Relax, angel," he urged, his mouth poised over hers.

"I...can't," she managed. "It's been such a long time. I'm afraid I'm terribly out of practice."

A smile softened the stern lines of his bronzed face, the same smile that had once lured a shy student nurse into falling head over heels in love with a hell-raising cop. She felt her heart turn over and knew she was lost. Again.

"Just follow your instincts," he ordered gruffly a split second before touching his mouth to hers in a caress so light and fleeting she felt herself straining to taste more of him.

Instead of deepening the kiss, however, Case continued to tease her with gentle, tasting kisses, his mouth as soft as a whisper against hers. Eager, ready, she parted her lips, inviting his tongue to penetrate. In answer to her unspoken plea, he traced the line of her lower lip with the tip of his tongue, wringing a frustrated whimper from her throat.

His arms tightened, yet he waited, tempting her. Denying her, even as he let her feel the hard bulge of his own need pressing against the junction of her thighs. Needing more, all but trembling from impatience, she pushed to her toes and wound her arms around his neck, drawing him closer until her breasts were nestled against the hard barrier of his chest.

She felt his body tense a split second before his mouth turned hard and hungry. Her senses sharpened, turned equally wild, and she clutched at his strong neck, desperate to return his kiss. Doubt, guilt, fear faded into the need to surrender, to exult. To love.

Her mouth took his freely as her hand stripped the thong from his hair, allowing the rippling ebony thickness to slide through her fingers. How she loved his hair. So black and silky, with a tendency to wave in places, curl in others.

"I love your hair long," she whispered when he drew back to offer her a quizzical look. "It smells like sunshine."

"Yours smells like flowers," he murmured, nuzzling the curls at her temple with his face. "And your skin smells like woman."

He nosed aside a cluster of coppery waves to find her ear, then gently nipped her earlobe, sending little needles of pleasure through her.

"Feel good?" he demanded.

She murmured an affirmation, and his arms tightened as he took her mouth again. One of his hands slipped to her bottom, urging her closer until she was barely balanced on her toes, her breasts teasing his chest.

She moaned and rubbed against him, feeling a feverish need to ease the hot urgency already building inside her. Instead, her instinctive movements served to increase the throbbing ache.

"That's the way, baby. Let it happen."

He moved his hand from her derriere to her breast, kneading gently, skillfully, through the thin silk until she felt her flesh swelling in response. With the pad of his index finger, he massaged the nipple into a pebbling hardness.

"Maybe we'd better discuss protection before I get too far gone to care," he grated, drawing back to look into her eyes. She met his gaze directly, her chest rising and falling furiously.

"I'm on the pill. Menstrual problems."

It was embarrassing to admit to being premenopausal, but she knew Case would refuse to make love to her if there were the slightest risk of pregnancy.

He nodded, relief clearly evident in his eyes. "In case you're worried about catching anything, I've been…careful."

She managed a smile in spite of the jealousy ripping through her. She hadn't just been careful. She'd been celibate.

"Is the bedroom in the same place, or have you moved that, too?" he teased, his mouth brushing her warm skin.

"Same place, different bed," she managed to get out before a shiver of pleasure shook her. She felt the hot, moist flick of his tongue and a moan slipped from her lips as she arched her neck.

Instantly, he lifted his head, his mouth finding the sensitive spot just below her ear in a tender kiss that had her blood singing.

"Hang on," he ordered before suddenly swooping her into his arms. Letting out a little squeak of surprise, she grabbed for his neck, even as his mouth found hers. He carried her easily, making her feel delightfully feminine, and the urgency in his step aroused her smug female pride. Her self-contained, hard-edged ex-husband still wanted her—wanted her so much he'd forgotten the vow he'd made to never see her again.

She closed her eyes and let her senses take over. Tomorrow she might regret the moments in his arms. But right now, she was willing to pay any price to be with Case again.

Her bedroom window faced west, and the setting sun bathed the room in an amber glow that added luster to the vivid colors of the quilt she'd made the summer Case had left her. She'd kept it, unlike the rest of the things they'd accumulated during their marriage, to remind herself of the tears she'd shed while making it, as many tears as there were stitches. Tears of remorse and shame. Tears that had changed her from a foolish girl to a woman whose own mistake had given her a greater tolerance for the weakness of others. At the moment, however, she was also a woman delighting in a sensuality she'd thought dead and buried.

As he let her slide down his body, she felt reborn, alive to the quick. Her body tingled and yearned. It was like the first time he'd taken her, she realized as she found her footing, her hands braced on the impressive girth of his biceps. The first time she'd realized how much she wanted this man to be a part of her.

For eight years she'd been careful and prudent, keeping her heart safe, living the life of a nun. But now, she no longer wanted to be safe. Here, in her prim room with the memories still lurking in the corners, she wanted only to feel, to exult in sensations she'd denied herself for so long. To give and receive.

Driven by needs she now accepted, she tore at the buttons of his shirt, greedy to feel his warm, vibrant chest under the pads of her fingers. It no longer threatened her that he was bigger, stronger, more powerful. A man capable of crushing her body and her spirit.

Her man.

"Help me," she ordered, tugging his shirt from his trousers. "Hurry."

"God, I love a bossy woman," he said as he let her push the shirt from his shoulders. Even as it was falling to the floor, her hands were fumbling with his belt, her breath coming in soft little gasps.

He felt his sanity slipping as she jerked open his belt buckle and tugged down the zipper of his fly. He felt his body jerk and forced himself to gulp air.

"Slow down, honey, or we'll be done before we get a good start," he warned, his voice hoarse. His hands covered hers and together they stripped the tailored wool over his muscle-thick thighs. The slacks joined his shirt on the floor, and he kicked them aside.

She inhaled, her gaze shimmering as she kissed the scar on his shoulder. Molly was right, she realized. He had a tattoo on his arm, a wicked-looking pictograph that looked Oriental.

"What's that mean?" she asked, running her nail around the unusual design. Beneath her fingertip, his muscle bunched to granite.

"Nothing I can mention in polite company."

"When—?"

"A few years back. I was drunk and thinking about…old times." His grin was seductive and slow as he reached for the top button of her dress.

The material was as light as air beneath his big hands, and he scowled, trying not to tear it to shreds in his hurry to see her again. Her unabashed eagerness was driving him insane, his body engorged to the point of acute pain.

Her breath caught in gasps as she pushed his hands aside, slipping the tiny buttons free so easily he felt as clumsy as an ox. With a step and a wiggle, she was free of the dress that had driven his imagination crazy.

As he'd hoped—prayed?—she wore lace beneath the silk, a froth of pale peach that barely covered the firm flesh of her breasts. Had she known how this day would end? he wondered, then sucked in a breath as he pictured another man's eager hands, in another place and time, stripping her from the sexy wisps.

"Over my dead body," he muttered as he helped rid her of the panty hose he considered God's punishment on a sinful male population. Her panties were of the same devil's design, mere strips of peachy lace connecting triangles of thin silk.

Once he would have used finesse to free her. Now, he simply tore away the last barrier between them. At the same time, with the same frantic need, she was tugging at his briefs, her soft whimpers fueling the hunger raging inside him.

He kissed her hard, inhaling harshly at the way she arched into him, her body quivering. Still kissing her, he kicked off his loafers and tore off his socks before taking them both to the bed.

Holding on to her tightly, he rolled her on top of him. One of her legs tangled with his, and he groaned at the slide of her satiny flesh against his skin. Instinctively, he tightened his thighs until she was pressed against his throbbing arousal.

He kissed her throat, then turned them again until he was on top. His mouth found her breast, and he feasted on the taste of warm flesh. She jerked, then whimpered and dug her nails into his naked shoulders.

Prudy was drowning in pleasure. His body was so hot, his need so evident, his raspy breathing out of control. When he began to suck on her nipple, she felt herself coming apart as wave after wave of sweet torment shook her.

She expected him to enter her, his urgency more than evident in the thick, hard ridge stabbing at her thigh. Instead, he lapped at her nipple, then trailed slow, moist kisses along the groove bisecting her midriff. His lips were soft, his tongue bold and demanding as he left a damp trail on her skin that had her writhing with pleasure.

He kissed her navel, then moved lower, inching down her body until his shoulders were stretching her thighs, and his legs were extended between hers. She moved her slender thighs restlessly against his, sensation bunching and building inside her.

His tongue plowed a trail in the soft curls below her navel, and she cried out. Her hands left his shoulders to grab fistfuls of the quilt and she moaned incoherently.

"Sweets?" His question rasped, shimmered, and she cried out.

On a groan, he lowered his head and kissed the throbbing flesh between her legs. She dissolved, buried in pleasure, her cries coming from the depths of her soul.

"Now," she pleaded, her voice nearly gone, her hands tearing at his shoulders.

When Case rose to straddle her, he found her face flushed

and her eyes glazed with desire. His blood was pounding, and his arousal was stretching him to bursting.

"Tell me if I'm hurting you," he managed to get out coherently.

Her hands shook as she reached for him. It was the only answer he needed.

Prudy held her breath as he thrust into her, a slow inch at a time. He was thick and hard. She was tight, yet yielding, taking him snugly, yet willingly.

When he was fully buried inside her, every hot, hard inch of him, he looked into her eyes and smiled. She felt her heart expanding, as she returned his smile.

"So sweet," he grated out between tight jaws. The distended tendons in his neck testified to the restraint he was exercising.

His body took over then, driving into her with long, sure strokes that excited her to a furious rhythm of her own. They moved together, faster, harder, until the frenzy exploded in a shower of pleasure. Her cry echoed an instant before his.

Drained of even his prodigious strength, he collapsed against her and buried his face in her hair as he felt her body trembling with sweet little aftershocks.

"Okay?" he managed to ask between gulps of air.

"Very okay," she returned, her hand now stroking through his hair.

With a sigh, he moved so that he wasn't crushing her, then, still buried to the hilt inside her, he let lethargy carry him into sleep.

Prudy surfaced slowly, as was her custom when she was working a shift that didn't require the use of an alarm clock to wake her. Mornings were to be tolerated, nothing more. But, as she felt sleep loosen its warm hold, she remembered that this morning was different. Case was here.

Smiling dreamily, like a bride after her wedding night, she opened her eyes and turned her head, only to utter a tiny groan of disappointment. Only the rumpled covers and the dent in the pillow remained to prove he'd spent the night in her bed.

Or part of it, she realized as she heard the always dependable old clock striking six. She lay perfectly still for a moment, listening for movement in the house. The silence told her Case had indeed already left, probably to pull an early shift he hadn't mentioned last night.

Still, he *had* stayed with her, she rationalized as she stretched the kinks from her legs. And made glorious love to her. In spite of the definite tenderness between her thighs, she felt fantastic, ready to take on an entire menagerie of difficult patients this afternoon when her shift began at three.

Reaching out, she pulled the pillow he'd used closer, inhaling the clean male scent that still clung to the linen. Part citrus aftershave, part soap, it was a combination that was uniquely Case.

Her heart lurched, then settled into a faster rhythm as she let her mind linger over the possible avenues the future might take. Certainly Case would call again. A man didn't make love to a woman with such tenderness and fire unless she meant more to him than a casual lay.

The rose, she thought suddenly, sitting up quickly to look around, her lips parted in an expectant grin. A beautiful, glorious, wonderful paper rose, Case's quixotic, irresistible signal that he'd abandoned her reluctantly, and that he'd think of her throughout the day. A rose made from tissues and a paper clip or, sometimes, if he'd been up long enough to start the coffee for her, a paper towel secured with a twisty tie. Over the years he'd gotten very creative, ruffling the edges, or sometimes putting two together to make a giant tea rose.

He'd left the first one for her the morning after they'd made love the first time. A snowy white rose with a note that told her how special the night had been. It had been even more precious to her because she'd once told him of the pain she'd felt when her father had walked out on her mother and her when she was only six. Without even a note or a few dollars to help with the rent. As happened to so many children abandoned by a parent, Prudy had reached adulthood still carrying the emotional scars and harboring deep-rooted insecurities that undermined her self-esteem, making her fearful that any person she might choose to love would eventually walk out on her and never look back.

Case hadn't said much then, but he'd held her as she'd cried. He would never leave the woman he loved that way, he'd told her with a fierce sincerity. And then he'd left the rose and a note promising to call.

Her smile widened at the memory of his crooked grin the first time she'd thanked him for such a thoughtful gesture. Still struggling to make ends meet on a patrolman's pay, he'd promised her real ones someday, long stemmed and dewy, and like all his promises, he'd eventually kept that one, with one single red rose on the day he'd received a much-needed raise. And then, over the years, with more. Though she'd enjoyed the hothouse blossoms, she preferred the ones he made with those long, clever fingers.

What color were the tissues in her bathroom? Pink? Or had she gotten yellow to match the watercolor she'd just completed for that long narrow spot by the window?

Pink, yellow, it didn't matter. Case made world-class roses. Though she'd made herself toss out the roses themselves after the divorce, she had a mental scrapbook of them, each one precious. The first one of virginal white, others of blue and peach and aqua. Not once in the days before their marriage had he ever left her asleep after a night of loving without leaving her a rose.

Even after they'd married, he had occasionally surprised her with his own special hand-wrought bouquet. A dozen yellow ones for their wedding night. Lavender ones for their first anniversary.

Where had he put it this time? she thought as she searched under the pillows and rumpled bedclothes. Sometimes he'd left it in the kitchen, on the counter next to her coffee mug or by her place at the table. Once he'd tucked it into the shoes she wore to work.

The Mexican tile on the kitchen floor was cold against her soles, but she scarcely noticed. Her gaze went first to the coffeepot, which was just as she'd left it last night. She looked next at the table and then at her chair. No rose.

A knot began forming in her throat as she stood in the center of the kitchen and carefully scanned every available surface. Nothing.

Surely he hadn't forgotten. No, of course he hadn't.

Still, her heart thudded as she returned to the bedroom, more slowly than she left it. Though the sun was streaming through the curtains in the familiar lacy pattern, her bedroom suddenly seemed cold and lifeless. The bright spread that had glowed with such life last night seemed drab and silly.

No, she thought a little frantically. Case wouldn't just leave. He knew how special those roses were to her, knew what they'd come to symbolize. Moving with great deliberation, she made another search of the bed and the dresser, then slowly bent to poke her fingers into her sneakers lying next to the closet door.

Her chest aching, she sat down on the bed and stared at the curlicues of light on the peach carpet. Tears welled in her eyes, but she refused to let them fall.

Think, Prue. Reason this out before you jump to the wrong conclusion. Case wasn't a cruel man. No matter how angry or hurt he might have been in the past, he'd never used sex as a weapon. Never treated her with anything less than complete respect.

No, he wouldn't deliberately use her to slake his sexual hunger, then just toss her aside. He simply forgot, that's all. Or perhaps, he'd been in a rush and had had no time.

Today, when he called, she would tell him she'd missed finding a rose—and him—when she'd awakened. And he *would* call, she decided, her spirits perking up. When he did, she needed to be prepared. This time they would take things slow and easy, testing their new awareness of each other. Developing a relationship based on mutual trust and respect this time instead of raw sex.

Still, she couldn't very well deny the importance of the chemistry between them. After all, it was that volatile mix that had drawn him back to her.

She touched the tips of her fingers to her still-swollen lips and let her mind linger on the memory of his hard mouth claiming hers with an almost savage possessiveness. Her lips curved into a smile as her gaze drifted to the clothing now neatly piled atop an old blanket chest at the foot of her bed—her dress, her bra and panties, even her panty hose, folded with Case's usual geometric precision.

He was a careful man, with careful habits, a man who avoided acting on impulse. A man who had never before wanted her enough to tear off her clothes. Or his own.

Oh, yes, he would call, she affirmed, laughing softly in anticipation.

All morning long, Prudy hovered by the telephone, When the grandfather clock struck twelve o'clock noon, an aching lump had lodged in her throat that no amount of coffee could wash away. By one-thirty, when she had to start getting ready for work, her hands were shaking and the lump in her throat had expanded to an ache that filled her whole chest. By twenty past two, she'd begun to accept that the phone wasn't going to ring.

Before she left the house, Prudy took one last walk through all the rooms, searching every possible niche where Case might have left her a rose, a symbol of his regard. There was nothing—just a film of dust that had accumulated since her last cleaning spree.

Having come full circle through the empty rooms, Prudy stood at the front door, her hand on the knob. One more minute, she thought, glancing down at her watch. She'd wait just one more minute. She stared down at the second hand with the well-trained precision of a nurse, each moment that slipped away breaking her heart a little bit more. And finally, when the minute had elapsed, she turned the knob and stepped out onto the porch, glancing around even there for a small tissue rose.

As she drew the door to the house closed behind her, Prudy felt her hope fading. Case hadn't called.

Chapter 4

Two Months and One Week Later

Prudy had just wrestled the zipper of her jeans into a reluctant surrender when her gynecologist, Luke Jarrod, knocked once on the door to the examining room, then stepped inside. Squaring her shoulders, she forced a smile and tried to level her rocketing pulse.

"Congratulations, Prue, you're pregnant," he announced with one of those mischievous cowboy grins of his. "About nine weeks, I would estimate."

Shock rendered her speechless for a dozen heartbeats before joy exploded in her. Still, she refused to accept that such a wonderful miracle could possibly be happening.

"Are you sure? I mean, the symptoms…my age. I was so sure it was menopause."

Tall and rangy, his long legs encased in worn jeans, Luke leaned against the wall and folded his brawny arms over the starched white coat that was his only concession to the ordinary strictures of his profession. Though he had a waiting room full of patients, he gave the impression of a man who had all the time in the world to give her.

"Forty-one is too young for menopause in an otherwise vibrant woman like you, precious Prudy. And the symptoms are all consistent with the first trimester of pregnancy." He shot her his rogue's grin. "Besides, I'm rarely wrong."

Feeling her knees begin to wobble, she groped behind her for the examining table, the tissue-thin layer of paper covering it crinkling under her rigid fingers.

"But I'm on the pill," she said as she climbed awkwardly onto the table's padded surface. "You prescribed it yourself, nearly a year ago. For my menstrual irregularity, remember?"

Luke's blue eyes smiled indulgently. "Sugar, you know very well there's a two percent failure rate on that particular medication."

Failure? More like success, she thought through a sudden daze. A dazzling, incredible success.

"I thought, if it wasn't menopause, it was the flu," she said in a shaky voice. "Coming back again. The stomach flu. That I had the week before Casey's christening…oh, my God, Luke, that's why I'm pregnant. I had trouble keeping anything down for a few days—including my pills!"

Confusion swept the smile from Luke's eyes with such force she burst out laughing. "I know, I'm not making sense. Case used to say—" She froze with her mouth open, her thoughts arrowing straight to the night of the christening. That impossibly sweet night when Case had made love to her.

"Prudy? Are you feeling dizzy?"

She drew a much-needed breath and realized Luke was now hovering over her, his gaze narrowed and filled with concern. "More like scared," she whispered. "Very, very scared."

"Perfectly natural, given the miscarriage you suffered, but I promise I'll take very good care of you."

Prudy couldn't help smiling at the low growl of determination threaded into his Arizona twang. "I know you will, cowboy. That's not what I mean."

He grinned at the pet name she'd coined for him at their

first meeting a little more than eight years ago. "Then what's got you so spooked?"

"Case."

"Your ex-husband?"

"The one and only." She drew another long breath before forcing a smile. "He's the baby's father."

Prudy sensed his shock a split second before it was mirrored in his eyes. Luke had come to PortGen a scant two months before Case had walked out on her. Though she had tried valiantly to hide her misery, everyone had soon learned the sad details of their breakup.

"Don't look at me like that, Luke. Things…happen."

"You don't have to explain 'things' to me, Prue. I'm an obstetrician, remember? I deliver the results of those 'things' all the time."

Prudy couldn't help laughing. "What a romantic guy!" she teased, sliding off the table onto legs that still felt a bit shaky. Grinning, Luke supported her with a big hand under her forearm until she steadied.

"Want me to break the news to your cop?"

"He's not mine, and no, I'll tell him." She pressed the flat of her hand against her midriff, a smile blossoming in her mind. "Once I'm safely through the first trimester." Another month to go, she thought, before she would allow herself to plan and dream.

Luke looped a long arm around her shoulders and gave her a quick squeeze. "Walk with me to my office. I've got about five pounds of prenatal instructions and information to lay on you, Mama."

Afternoon sunlight came through the lace curtains at the window, dappling the bright quilt on her bed with whimsical patterns of golden filigree and shifting shadows. After a grueling ten-hour shift in the ER, Prudy wanted nothing more than to stretch out across the bed and let the blessed silence massage the tension from her electrified nerve endings.

As she slipped out of her sneakers and unbuttoned the top three buttons of her work smock, she gazed at the telephone on the nightstand, tempted to call her neighbor, Stacy MacAuley, and tell her she wouldn't be coming over for a cup of tea, after all. The invitation, issued by Stacy from her back porch when Prudy had gotten home from work, had seemed like a good idea at the time. Anything to take her mind off the nonstop argument raging in her head. But now she really wished she'd had the good sense to decline.

One of the few drawbacks of having a best friend who lived next door, she decided, was a lack of privacy when you wanted to end your workday by vegetating in silence or being depressed to your heart's content.

One hand clamped over her waist in a useless attempt to settle her queasy stomach, Prudy headed for the spare bedroom where she kept her desk to check her answering machine for messages, knowing, even as she stuck her head inside the door and saw the green light, that he hadn't called.

The rat, she told herself as she headed for next door. Three months was long enough to feel sorry for herself. From now on, she simply wouldn't think about him. Or miss him.

"I'd like to meet the idiot who called this morning sickness," she grumbled as she opened the MacAuleys' back screen and stepped into the cheerful kitchen. "Come to think of it, *idiot* isn't the word. Lunatic is more like it. And my guess is, it must have been a man."

Stacy flashed an understanding smile. A kindergarten teacher by profession, currently on summer vacation and a mother by inclination, she was slightly taller than Prudy's five foot nothing, with a wealth of long brown hair usually piled haphazardly atop her head and an innate cheerfulness that Prudy envied. Especially now, when life seemed to be throwing her one curveball after another.

Stacy was four months along with her second child. And glowing. Prudy envied her. Not only for the easy time she appeared to be having with her second pregnancy, but because her handsome, drop-dead sexy husband, Boyd, clearly adored her.

"The nausea will soon pass, I promise."

Prudy pulled out a chair and sat down. "I guess that depends on whose stomach is rolling. I feel like I'm taking a nine-month ride on a roller coaster, minus the thrills.''

Stacy added sugar to the herbal tea she'd just brewed for Prudy, her expression properly somber as she gave it a brisk stir. "Try a saltine, honey. It'll help.''

Prudy eyed the crackers her friend had artfully arranged on a saucer at the center of the pine table. "Once this baby is delivered, I'm never eating crackers again.''

Stacy made a funny little noise that sounded suspiciously like a stifled giggle as she leaned across the table to move the saucer of crackers closer to Prudy. Holding up a hand, she said, "Nothing from then on but brownies, I promise.''

"Oh, please, don't say the word *brownie*.'' Prudy flattened a palm over her diaphragm. "I never would have believed it, but the thought of chocolate makes me feel sick.''

"Now that *is* a scary thought.''

Stacy slid the tea a little closer to Prudy's clenched fist before taking a chair across from her. Without missing a step, the bright yellow cat approaching the breakfast nook suddenly launched herself into the air, landing an instant later in Stacy's lap.

"Hi, there, Sunshine,'' Stacy crooned to the plump feline as she scratched behind its ear. "How's Mama's baby, hmm?''

"In another month that beast is going to be bouncing off your tummy if she tries that trick,'' Prudy grumbled before stuffing another cracker into her mouth.

"Boyd is convinced that Sunshine is pregnant, too,'' Stacy said with a resigned sigh. "As of this morning, he was threatening to shoot both Sunny and her suitor, once he figures out who 'did the deed.'''

"Who's the prime suspect?''

"Chester.''

"You're kidding? I thought for sure Mrs. Makepeace would have had her darling neutered long ago.''

"Darling, my sainted aunt! That old black tom is the meanest animal in Portland, bar none. He had Sunny in hysterics the first time they met.'' Stacy glanced down at her now-purring pet and frowned. "My poor gullible sweetheart. It's all my fault. I should have taken you to the vet for spaying months ago.''

Prudy wrapped her trembling fingers around the warm mug and leaned forward to inhale the steam. Her stomach lurched in violent protest, and she stifled a groan.

"Don't blame yourself, Stace. The way things are going around here, Sunny probably would have gotten pregnant, anyway."

"Do you think it's the water?" Stacy asked, grinning.

"If it is, we're missing a huge bet by not bottling it for sale to desperate want-to-be moms.''

Stacy plucked a grape from the fruit bowl in the center of the scrubbed pine table and popped it into her mouth. Though she was ten years Prudy's junior, she'd had her share of trouble, especially in the past two years. They'd met in the emergency room where Stacy had been brought after an auto accident in which her ex-husband had been killed. Pregnant with her first child which had been conceived during an aborted reconciliation attempt, Stacy had fallen in love with the man who'd pried her from the crumpled wreck and kept her calm until the ambulance had arrived.

Boyd MacAuley had been a desperately wounded man in those days, a surgeon who'd left medicine after the death of his wife and unborn child. It was one of life's ironies, Prudy thought, that it had been an auto accident that had taken Boyd's family from him, only to have another accident three years later bring another woman and child into his life.

Prudy suspected that Stacy had fallen in love with Boyd on sight, but then, who wouldn't, given the man's sweet nature, hidden from all but the most discerning by a gruff exterior.

It had taken Boyd a lot longer to come to grips with the inner demons that had kept him from opening his heart. In the end, though, his love for Stacy had brought him full circle, into a terrific marriage and back to medicine.

Currently chief surgical resident at PortGen, he had one more year to complete before taking over the practice of one of Portland's most respected surgeons.

"Have you decided how you're going to break the news of your pregnancy to Case?" Stacy asked after she swallowed.

Prudy shook her head. "I had this fantasy that he'd call me, maybe suggest dinner or a movie." She bit her lip, embarrassed now by her naiveté. "Funny thing, it didn't feel like a one-night stand at the time. Not to me, anyway. But then, come to think of it, I'm not exactly an expert."

Case had been her only lover. She had a feeling that wasn't going to change.

Stacy smiled slightly. "You're still in love with him, aren't you?"

Prudy opened her mouth to deny her friend's softly spoken words, only to find her eyes filling with tears. "Oh, hell," she muttered as she swiped the moisture from her lashes. "So much for being in charge of my emotions."

"Is that a yes?"

Prudy offered a watery laugh. "Yes, and I hate it."

Stacy sipped her tea and stroked the cat's thick fur. Sunshine's throaty rumble filled the silence, vying with the chirping of the birds and the distant drone of city traffic. Mill Works Ridge was a quiet neighborhood bordering the Columbia River. A great place to raise a child.

Prudy pressed her fingers against her belly. Though she was eleven weeks along now, there was only a slight thickening in her waist to indicate the wonderful changes taking place inside her. Glancing up, she caught Stacy's sympathetic smile.

"It's amazing, isn't it?"

Prudy nodded. "Astounding. A part of me can't believe it yet."

"I know how you feel. I was the same way when I found out I was pregnant with Tory." Stacy grinned. "And with this one, too."

"And you were never sick?" Prudy couldn't help but marvel. For her, pregnancy was beginning to feel like a fatal disease. "Not even once?"

"Nope. The only trouble I had was right after the accident, especially when I started having contractions. But Luke, bless him, worked another one of his patented miracles."

Prudy reached for another cracker, than decided not to push her luck. "Luke wasn't the only one who worked a miracle. You've worked one for Boyd, as well. He's one of the few doctors at the hospital who always seems to be smiling. He's so nauseatingly happy, in fact, that some resentful soul tacked his picture up in the lounge to use it for dart practice."

Stacy laughed. "You little fibber!"

Prudy managed a weak smile. "He really is a changed guy, Stace. I wish you could be a fly on the wall and see it for yourself."

A dreamy glow came over Stacy's face. "Is he really that happy?"

"Are there bears in the woods?" Prudy asked. "You've worked magic in his life, Stacy. You really have."

"It isn't magic. It's love. Although I sometimes think he's as much in love with Tory as he is with me."

"Is he still obsessing about your pregnancy?"

"Lord, yes. I can't even hiccup without him asking me if I'm okay. He's not going to relax until this baby is safely born." Stacy's expression turned pensive for a moment. "Maybe that's why Case never wanted to father a child. Because he was afraid of losing you."

Prudy waited out a slow slice of pain before shaking her head. "It's not that simple, Stacy. I wish it were." She paused, searching for words to make her friend understand. "Believe it or not, Case never actually explained *why* he was so hell-bent on never becoming a father."

"But you must have asked."

"About once a month, actually," Prudy admitted sheepishly. "Case is a master at stonewalling, but from the few things he let slip, I have a hunch it has something to do with his childhood."

"Is he close to his parents?"

Prudy shook her head. "He hasn't seen them in years. All I know for sure is that he grew up in San Francisco, left home when he was eighteen and hasn't been back."

"A man with secrets. No wonder you found him so irresistible."

Prudy sighed, then pushed back her chair and got to her feet. "Thanks for the tea and sympathy, Stace. I appreciate the friendly ear."

"You listened to me often enough when I was breaking my heart over Boyd. I just wish I could do more."

"Okay, you can call Case and tell him he's about to become a father. And then duck."

Stacy laughed. "Anything but that. Although I will dial the phone for you."

Laughing because she didn't dare cry, Prudy carried her cup to the sink and rinsed it. When she turned back to face her friend, she'd made up her mind.

"It's a deal. You dial, I'll talk. And then you can pick me up off the floor after Case has torn my heart to shreds."

Case was desperate. He slammed his desk drawer shut and scowled at the voluptuous woman detective sitting at the next desk.

"Hey, Markovitch, you got a cigarette?" he called over the din of ringing telephones, purring fax machines, clattering typewriters and indistinguishable voices.

Panning the top of Case's cluttered desk with one sleek eyebrow raised, Detective First Grade Andrea Markovitch smiled slightly. "Yeah, just got a new pack from the machine. Why?"

"Because I want to bum one, that's why."

Markovitch cocked her head and offered him a smug look. "No way, Sarge. When you quit, you ordered me to refuse to let you near my smokes, no matter how mean you got."

Case ground his teeth. "You haven't seen mean, Markovitch, but you will, if you don't give me a cigarette."

"Sorry, friend. I'm not about to disobey an order, not even for you."

"Fine. I'm *ordering* you to give me a smoke."

She shook her head. "Sorry, no can do."

Case drew a careful breath and decided to play on her sympathy. After all, he was desperate, wasn't he? "Have a heart,

Andy," he pleaded, offering her a grin. "I've had a rotten week."

Markovitch leaned back and crossed her arms over her world-class chest. "You've had a rotten *month*, and I for one am thinking seriously about kicking you in your studmuffin buns if you don't lose that lousy attitude."

"Sounds kinky," Don Petrov chimed in from the desk abutting Case's. "I'd take her up on that, partner."

Markovitch tossed Petrov a disgusted look. "In your dreams, old man."

Petrov's lantern jaw dropped before he gathered his wits sufficiently to reply with a succinct obscenity. Markovitch merely snorted before returning her gaze to the report she'd been typing.

Resigned to suffering through another nicotine fit, Case shoved back from the desk and got to his feet. "C'mon, Don, let's take a shot at earning that huge salary the city forces on us every two weeks."

Petrov groaned, but pushed up from his chair. He was a shambling bear of a man, with startling green eyes and a brilliant mind hidden behind a homely face. Case would die for his partner and consider himself privileged, but he'd take a beating before he would ever admit it aloud.

"You drive," Petrov all but growled. "It's my turn to sleep."

Markovitch snorted. "This place is gonna be a whole lot more professional once you old guys put in your papers."

"Don's not old, Andy," Case drawled as he hooked his jacket from the back of his chair. "He's just seasoned."

"Seasoned, my butt. I taught you everything you know, sonny boy, and don't you be forgetting it." Glowering, Petrov lumbered between the desks, trailing the scent of lime aftershave an elderly neighbor lady bought him each Christmas.

Case exchanged grins with Markovitch before heading for the front of the squad room where he picked up the chalk to sign out.

"Phone call for you, Sergeant Randolph," the civilian receptionist called over the clatter of typewriter keys and the shouts of a drunk being escorted in by two uniformed patrolmen. "A Ms. Prudy Randolph."

Case felt his gut twist, but he managed a bored look as he marked a check by his name and Don's. He'd lost count of the number of times he'd stalked to the phone in his apartment, intending to offer Prudy the apology he owed her for leaving her bed in the middle of the damned night without even telling her goodbye.

It should have been cut-and-dried. A couple of sentences, no more. Maybe a teasing remark or two. Then, *adios, muchacha.*

Only he couldn't seem to get the words straight in his head. It was hell not knowing what he wanted. No, that wasn't exactly accurate. He knew what he wanted, all right—Prudy, naked beneath him, her body warm and sweetly welcoming as he sank into her. He just hadn't figured out how he could continue to make love to her without losing his soul to her again. Until he figured it out, he wasn't about to rekindle that particular fire. He knew from experience how badly he might get burned.

"Tell her you couldn't catch me," he called over the familiar din. Ignoring Petrov's speculative look and raised eyebrows, Case headed for the door before he could change his mind.

Case pulled stakeout duty with about as much enthusiasm as a man facing a year of solitary confinement. He hated the cramped quarters and the stale air inside the car, especially when the humidity was high and the rain pelted the roof overhead with a clattering fury. Even without his jacket and his sleeves rolled up, it was damn hot. He thought about shucking the bulletproof vest that department regulations required of detectives sitting stakeout. If he got caught, he'd be reprimanded, nothing more. No real sweat, except he'd managed a clean record for more than twenty years. He hated to mess that up now. So he sat and sweltered. And scowled. Even his partner's wry sense of humor, which Case usually enjoyed, stopped being funny after hours on end.

"You want another jolt of caffeine, partner?"

Case opened one eye to give the rumpled man in the passenger's seat a glum look. "Not unless it comes with a double slug of sour mash."

Don Petrov chuckled while he poured steaming black sludge into the cracked mug he kept under the seat for this kind of duty. In the dull light from the street lamp across the soggy street, his graying hair had taken on the dull sheen of old steel, and his wrinkled clothes would shame a beggar.

"I figure you got a reason for being such lousy company," he said, "but I gotta tell you my patience's wearing damn thin."

"Tough." Case closed his eyes again, shutting out his buddy's disgruntled frown.

"I admit I've been givin' some thought to possible reasons." Petrov paused to slurp coffee, while Case gave some thought to throttling the man who'd been his best friend, big brother and surrogate father for more years than he wanted to count. Petrov had been a thirty-year-old beat cop assigned to San Francisco's red-light district when he'd stumbled across fifteen-year-old Case and his kid sister's eighteen-year-old druggie boyfriend brawling in a dark alley.

The others had run. Case had hesitated a split second too long, and before he could move, Petrov had had him slammed up against an abandoned warehouse with his arms cuffed behind his back. In his pocket was a Baggie of party dope he'd taken from his sister less than an hour earlier. Enough to convince a hard-line judge to send him to the juvenile detention unit at the state prison at Chino until his eighteenth birthday.

"Two things come to mind," Petrov resumed in his good-old-boy voice. "Either you need to get laid, or you're in love."

Case snorted. Petrov was right about the first, wrong about the second, but Case wasn't about to admit to either.

"You ain't been yourself since that morning I stopped by to pick you up for the early shift and caught you comin' home just before dawn, like a tomcat with his tail draggin' and a smug look on his face."

"Get stuffed, Petrov."

A siren wailed in the distance, and Case stiffened. Instead of growing louder, however, the sorrowful sound faded into the clatter of the rain, and he allowed himself to relax.

Damn, but he was tired. Worn slick.

Nothing had gone right since he walked out of Prudy's front door in the early hours of a gloomy dawn with the taste of her still sweet on his tongue. He hadn't wanted to leave her arms, which is why he'd forced himself to walk out while she was still sleeping like his own sweet angel.

It was only sex, he'd told himself. Good sex, yeah. Hell, maybe the best sex he'd ever had. But still, it was purely physical. He was too savvy now to let it be anything else.

"Heads up, Case. Arturo's just turned the corner."

Case opened his eyes and lasered his gaze at the circle of light half a block ahead. "Bastard's high as a kite."

"So what else is new?" Petrov muttered, his disgust all but palpable.

"You gotta figure Felix for a fool for keeping the guy around."

"A fool he ain't. Which means he's got another reason for playing candy man to his baby brother."

"I figure Arturo's his errand boy, running messages to *El Hefe*'s goons down in the barrio. Hell, scuzzy as Arturo looks, he fits right in with the deadheads hanging out down there."

"Whatever the reason, Arturo's gonna be our Judas goat, leading Felix right to us." Case eased erect, his nerves humming and his mind clicking into well-worn grooves. After three tedious, frustrating months trying to scare up enough hard evidence to arrest the man suspected of being a prime mover in Portland's growing drug ring, he had a feeling they were going to get lucky tonight.

Chapter 5

Prudy swiped the sweat from her brow with her forearm before directing a hopeful look at the clock behind the ER admitting desk. The hands had scarcely moved since her last desperate look, she realized glumly. She had another hour and a half of this hellish night before her shift ended.

It was Friday, and the moon was full, though its brilliance was presently hidden by the thick rain clouds. In spite of the rain, the waiting room and treatment cubicles had been jammed all day *and* night with a steady stream of wackos, party animals run amok and "moonies," those unfortunate street people who were drawn to the wide double doors of the emergency entrance every twenty-eight days like moths to a bright light.

Some of the other trauma team leaders were strict about turning them away, but Prudy customarily allowed them to linger in the waiting room for an hour or so, sipping coffee from the nurse's urn. What harm could they do?

Prudy had just finished with the last of their regulars, a sweet, bald-as-a-grape accountant named Leonard who had come in for his monthly dose of werewolf antidote. After carefully measuring exactly twelve cc's of sugar water into a beaker, she'd ordered Leonard to drink it down slowly, then go directly home to bed. By the time the moon reached its zenith, the medicine would have taken effect, she'd promised.

Leonard had been effusive in his thanks, as always, and dutifully went home to do as she'd ordered, the spring back in his step and his slightly addled mind at rest. Prudy, on the other hand, felt lousy. Her stomach was even more queasy than usual, and the constant din of the trauma wing had given her a headache. Prudy had never been to a rock concert, but she had a feeling it would seem restful after the maddened frenzy of PortGen's ER on a full-moon weekend.

"I never should have gone to nursing school," she muttered to the redheaded man as big as a mountain who had just returned one of the ER's wheelchairs to its proper parking place behind the desk.

Hollis Royden had been an orderly at Portland General for twenty years. Once a navy corpsman, he had the look of a prizefighter gone to seed. Because of a truly obscene tattoo on one beefy forearm, the nurses on his shift invariably insisted he wear long-sleeved whites, no matter what the season or temperature. He was also completely professional and utterly dedicated to his patients. Prudy never worried about slipshod care or careless mistakes when Hollis was on duty.

"You are looking a mite green around the gills, Miss Prudy," he said after a long, intense look at the small, freckled face turned up toward his. "A real pretty shade of chartreuse."

"Don't try to get on my good side, Hollis," she said, shaking her head in refusal at his offer of a peppermint candy.

"'Spect you've come down with the PortGen flu. Damn bug's got half the staff on their...backsides."

Prudy smiled. "Which is exactly where I intend to spend the next forty-eight hours."

Hollis wagged his Neanderthal eyebrows as he leaned closer. "Sounds interesting," he rumbled in an insinuating tone. "Need some company?"

"Now, Hollis, you know Babycakes would skin both of us if I said yes."

The big orderly ducked his head, but not before she saw the flash of pride in his dark eyes. For all his bluster and tease, Hollis was a devoted and faithful husband to the tiny, fiery-tempered wife he adored.

"Me, maybe, but not you. Not after you stood godmother to little Hollis."

"How is the little darling?" she asked, trying to focus on the effusive answer. It was difficult, however, and she found herself nodding woodenly as Hollis recounted another of his adored four-year-old's brilliant sayings.

"Which reminds me, Babycakes wants to know if you can make it to dinner a week from Sunday. She has this guy from our church she wants you to meet. A banker come down from Seattle."

Prudy drew a tired breath. "Tell her thanks for thinking of me, but—" She was interrupted by the paramedic communications radio crackling to life behind her.

"PortGen, Medic Four, en route to your location with two male gunshot victims," a clipped baritone announced before giving an estimated time of arrival of five minutes.

"Vitals?" demanded the middle-aged admitting clerk, her fingers poised over her computer keyboard.

With bored precision, the paramedic read off a series of readings before adding with more urgency, "Get ready for a media circus on this one. We got us a cop and a drug dealer on board. One dead at the scene."

"Hope the live one's the cop," a medications nurse muttered as she circled around Prudy's desk.

"Amen to that," Hollis said.

Prudy's stomach turned, and this time it wasn't a symptom of morning sickness. *There are a lot of cops in Portland. It can't be Case,* she assured herself as she spurred the skilled trauma team into action. Case was too tough to die. Hadn't he once told her that very thing in the early days of their marriage when he'd suffered a bullet graze to the temple?

After ordering herself to set her fears aside, Prudy snapped out orders to get a treatment cubicle cleared and prepared. As she grabbed a clipboard from her desk, another call came in over the radio. There had been an automobile pileup on Interstate 5, three casualties, all of which were being brought into PortGen.

"Perkins! Get on the horn and get our people back from their breaks, then roust Dr. Hamilton out of the sack! Nap time's over!" As the nurse raced away to awaken the physician who'd only just lain down after eighteen hours of nonstop emergencies, Prudy heard the distant wail of ambulance sirens.

"Triage team, on the double!"

Half the team remained in the ER to finish preparing for the influx of patients while Prudy and two subordinates raced to the ER doors. Through the sliding-glass panels, Prudy saw that the first red-and-white had already backed up to the unloading deck. Two paramedics were pulling a gurney from the ambulance, their movements rapid, but controlled.

One minute, Prudy was running. The next, she couldn't feel her feet, or even her legs. Feeling as though she were looking through heat waves, she saw the patient, his big body lying motionless on the tightly stretched, blood-soaked white sheeting. A pressure bandage wrapped around his left thigh was already soaked through, and his buff-colored slacks were crimson from his hip to his knee.

In spite of the mid-September chill that had settled over Portland, Case was in shirtsleeves. His left wrist had been splinted and lay awkwardly across his chest. The medics had already hung plasma and removed Case's bulletproof vest, which was lying next to his feet.

White as the thin pillow beneath his dark head, his face was pinched with pain, his teeth bared, his eyes closed, his brows drawn in pain.

No! her mind screamed. Not Case. *Please don't let it be Case.* But it was. The hallway seemed to turn abruptly upside down, then crazily sideways. Prudy staggered, dropping the triage clipboard as she grabbed the wall for support.

Case was going to die in bed a very old man, he'd promised her once when she'd been worried about the hazards of his job. From a heart attack in the midst of a spectacular orgasm, he'd said. And for all his other faults—and she had them memorized, starting with his obstinate bullheaded pride—Case didn't lie.

But he did *bleed,* she realized with a shaft of brutal pain when the paramedics raced past her with Case on a gurney. One wheel caught the metal clip on Prudy's triage clipboard, flipping the board into the air and sending papers flying.

"Hey, Prue? You okay?" one of her nurses called.

Prudy couldn't answer. Her stomach lurched, and she felt a wave of clammy cold run through her. She forced her gaze to the clipboard, willing herself to pick it up, to do her job. She gulped for air, made herself move.

"Don't waste your time on this one, Prudy," another of the paramedics called from her right. The man on the gurney he was pushing had already been zipped into a body bag. Another lousy, stinking drug dealer, she thought with a momentary flash of rage. Scum. No doubt she'd met some of his "customers" up close and personal in this same hallway. Some dying, some wishing they could. Others with their brains hopelessly fried.

Those thoughts had no sooner crossed Prudy's mind than she gave herself a hard mental shake. All lives were important, and she hadn't become a nurse so she could set herself up as anyone's judge and jury. Just because Case had been wheeled past her and she suspected the man in the body bag was responsible for his injuries was no reason for her to forget that.

Bending to snatch up her clipboard, Prudy said, "Take him to the morgue."

The next second, she was running. Funny, how nightmarishly long that hallway seemed when the patient at the end of it was Case.

"Cubicle one," she ordered as she fell in step next to the gurney that carried him.

Needing to touch him, she rested her palm against his wide shoulder. His eyes snapped open, glazed for an instant with pain, before finding focus.

"Hiya, sweets," he murmured, his grin crooked and all too brief.

"Hi yourself." She managed a halfway decent smile, in spite of the fear spiraling through her. "Looks like you forgot to duck."

His thick black lashes flickered. "Didn't have a chance."

Prudy gave his hard muscular shoulder a gentle squeeze before reluctantly stepping back to allow the paramedics to transfer him to the treatment table. Later, when Case was out of danger and her job was done, she would fall apart, she promised herself as she squared her shoulders and took a deep breath.

"Call the lab and get a tech up here, stat," she told Marge Malcolm, the team "floater." "Also, best have Dr. MacAuley paged and find out which OR is available."

"Right away," Malcolm replied as she spun around and left the cubicle.

"No way," Case muttered, his eyes open again and trained directly on her. His big chest was rising and falling far too rapidly, and his color had gone from chalky to a sickly gray beneath a sheen of sweat.

"Now, Case—"

"No surgery," he grated, his voice hoarse but still surprisingly strong. "Not if they have to put me out."

"Fine, I'll tell the anesthesiologist to bash you on the head with a hammer whenever you start to yell too loudly," Prudy teased as she sidestepped one of the paramedics who was removing the pressure cuff from Case's arm. Prudy stood ready to slap a hospital cuff in its place, and another nurse was wheeling over a machine so they could start tracking his vitals. "That way, you can wake up hurting at both ends."

"You're enjoying this," Case accused before turning his head to glare at the rookie tech who was preparing a syringe. "Forget it, kid. No needles."

The raspy command in his tone had young Tamara Kelly going pale beneath her freckles. "But—"

Prudy lifted a warning hand, effectively stemming the protest she saw poised on Tamara's prettily glossed lips. At that same moment she heard the sound of sirens, signaling the arrival of more patients. Accident victims from the freeway pileup, she assumed.

"I'll see to this patient, Tam," she said, reaching for the syringe. "Do me a favor and make sure B Team is in place to receive the incoming."

Nodding, the tech handed over the syringe and hurried off. Prudy took a deep breath before leaning over Case's wide chest.

"Listen here, tough guy," she grated through a tight jaw. "None of us would presume to tell you how to run an investigation, so don't you dare try to tell us what we can or can't do here."

He narrowed his eyes, but not before she saw amusement in the dark irises. "It's my body you and your friends are so eager to slice up," he grumbled, trapping her hand with his.

Aware that four members of her triage and treatment team were hovering impatiently, she forced herself to shunt aside her personal fears and doubts, and, instead, forced the tired muscles of her face into the stern, no-nonsense look Hollis had once called "awesome to the max." In the next cubicle, she heard another patient being brought in.

"Are you officially refusing treatment, Sergeant?" she challenged, leaning closer. He smelled like rain and coffee—and the distinctive, metallic scent of blood.

"I didn't say—" His dark lashes fell against his cheeks, fluttering like the wings of an injured butterfly. Pain and blood loss was sapping even his incredible strength. She tightened her fingers around his big strong hand. His hard fingers were icy.

"Then you agree to let us do our job?"

"No 'us,' just you." He gave in to some inner signal and let his eyes remain closed. "Just you, Prue."

After cutting away his shirt, Prudy sterilized Case's upper arm with an alcohol swab, then gave him the injection. "There you go, big boy."

"Should've gone for the ass," he muttered in a gravelly voice. "Y'always were too short t'kick it."

Prudy managed a grin before saying gently, "I've sent for

Boyd, Case. Boyd MacAuley. You couldn't be in better hands."

"Damn, I feel...odd," he whispered, his lashes quivering again. She saw his face go slack and knew he'd slipped into unconsciousness.

It was well past midnight when Prudy finished dictating her end-of-shift reports. Case was still in surgery downstairs. Only the press of her responsibility in the ER had kept her from haunting the corridor outside the OR. Still, she'd kept in contact with Kit Forrest in recovery, who'd told her they'd been alerted to receive him any minute now.

As soon as she was off duty, she dialed Kit's extension, only to be told that they were still waiting.

"I'm going to grab a quick shower before I head downstairs," she told Kit with a sour glance at her blood-spattered smock. "Five minutes, max. After that, I'm heading for the waiting room. Case's niece and nephew are already there." According to Thad, a neighbor had volunteered to keep Casey for as long as necessary so that they could keep a vigil.

"No problem, Prue," Kit promised. "If I have word on your cop, I'll track you down."

It took her ten minutes to shower and change into the jeans and sweatshirt she always kept in her locker for just such emergencies. By the time the elevator door opened onto the ground floor, her heart was pounding violently.

He's going to be just fine, she told herself as she hurried along the empty corridor toward the buzz of voices spilling from the small waiting room at the end.

To her surprise, she saw that the room was nearly filled, with men mostly, many of whom had the hard, lean look of control she invariably associated with cops. A young African-American man toting a minicam was leaning against the wall by the entrance, chatting with a svelte and stunning female reporter from a local network affiliate. Prudy recognized her instantly. Giselle Francis was Portland's media darling, a go-getter, destined someday for more lucrative markets. Prudy had seen her occasionally, usually in connection with a local disaster.

"Aunt Prudy!" Molly's voice reached her first, followed by Thad's deep-toned greeting. "Nobody will tell us anything," Molly wailed, her eyes red-rimmed and her cheeks stained with fresh tears.

"SOP," Prudy said, pulling Case's distraught niece into her arms for a hug.

"Standard operating procedure," Thad translated for his wife after he and Prudy hugged.

"But—"

"He's going to be fine," Prudy said with a stiff smile and far more confidence than she actually felt. "Just fine."

"Hell, yes, he's going to be fine," a familiar bass voice boomed from behind her, causing Prudy to whirl around so fast she nearly toppled.

Case's partner, Don Petrov, was standing with his arms outstretched and a tired smile softening the harsh angles of his weather-beaten face.

"Don! I am so glad to see you," she managed before becoming enveloped in a smothering embrace that nearly cracked her ribs.

When he let her go, she realized that tears were streaming down her face and reached up to swipe them away. Case's partner had been like a big brother to her during the years she'd spent as Case's wife. After the divorce, they'd gotten together several times for dinner, but, even though Don had tried hard not to take sides, Prudy had sensed a subtle shift in his attitude toward her. She had never held that against him; Case was like a son to him.

"Hey, no tears, half pint," Don ordered with the horrified look of a man out of his depth. "Our boy is a fighter. He'll punch his way through this as easy as you please."

Before Prudy could do more than offer him a watery smile, Don had looped one grizzly-sized arm over her shoulder, offered Molly and Thad a quick apology and was leading her over to a couple of empty chairs in the far corner.

"Sit," he ordered, all but pushing her down into the hard ugly chair.

Prudy sat. For only a moment, she promised herself. Just until she was able to reassure Don that his partner was in good hands. Boyd's hands.

"Dr. MacAuley's a wonderful surgeon, Don. The best, even though he's still a resident."

"So I hear." Petrov sat heavily, his big body dwarfing the chair on which he was perching with obvious discomfort. The Naugahyde creaked in protest beneath him.

"You checked him out."

"Hell, yes. But when I found out you were in charge of the trauma unit, I figured you wouldn't have called anybody but the best."

Prudy managed a wobbly smile. "I didn't feel in charge when I saw who it was they were wheeling in on that stretcher." Before she could prevent it, a shudder shook her. Instantly, Don had her hand pressed between his.

"I had a few bad minutes myself." He hauled in about a cubic yard of air, then let it out again. "Damn, but I nearly lost it when he took that flying tumble down the stairs. Thought for sure he was going to break his neck."

"I...saw the bruise on his belly. Where the Kevlar deflected the bullet."

Don acknowledged her implied question with a nod. "He hated wearing that damned vest. Always swore it was more trouble than it was worth."

Prudy drew a shaky breath. "Yes, he always hated to be restricted."

"Tell me about it."

Don was tired. She could see the weariness in his eyes. And he was also worried, no matter how he blustered to the contrary. Deeply worried. Prudy just wished she had the reserves of strength and energy to reassure him.

But she didn't. She barely had enough to keep air moving in and out of her lungs.

Prudy realized she was wringing her hands. Unable to bear sitting there another second, she shot up from the chair to pace on legs so weak with anxiety and exhaustion and lack of food she wasn't sure they'd hold her up.

Why was it taking so long to get word? she wondered. Had something gone wrong and Kit just hadn't come down to tell anyone yet? Was Case in there dying, even now? Or already dead? Oh, God, why hadn't they come out to give news of his progress?

Visions of Case's pasty gray face kept flashing through her mind. Professionally, Prudy knew that they were probably just swamped in recovery, that Case was probably fine. And he was strong. Wonderfully strong.

Still, medical science had its glitches. In her years as a nurse, she'd seen more than one patient slip away due to unforeseen surgical complications. Or sometimes, plain bad luck.

Case had lost a lot of blood. His heart would have been under incredible stress. Add to that the shock of a bullet wound and the usual risks of administering anesthesia, and you had good odds, but no guarantees.

An awful, choking sensation grabbed Prudy by the throat, and a burning feeling washed over her eyes that she couldn't blink away. She placed a trembling hand over her waist, acutely conscious of the tiny life that was nestled deep within her. *Case's baby.*

Oh, God, what if something went wrong? What if she never got a chance to tell Case that he'd fathered a child, *their* child? What if—

Her stomach heaved, and her throat felt as though she were being strangled. She had to get out of here, she thought a little frantically. To someplace private, even if it was nothing but a laundry room. Anywhere she could fall apart without a dozen pairs of shocked, curious eyes staring at her while she did it.

"Excuse me," she mumbled in Don's direction before bolting for the door. Once out in the hall, Prudy reeled to a stop, uncertain where to run. Like a German tank racing down a decline, Petrov plowed into her back and nearly knocked her into a headlong sprawl. Only the quick reflex of his strong hands on her shoulders saved her from falling.

"Dammit, girl. Either get taillights installed, or give hand signals so a fellow knows when you're going to brake."

Prudy glanced frantically around, saw no escape route and cupped a hand over her eyes. "Go away. I need to be alone for a minute, Petrov."

He looped a beefy arm around her quaking shoulders. "Sweetheart, he's gonna be okay. He's too ornery to die."

Prudy struggled for a moment, not only against the iron strength of his hug but against the emotional maelstrom whirling inside her. She lost the battle with both. Don felt so solid—so big and safe and warm. If she closed her eyes, she could almost believe those strong arms anchoring her to his chest were Case's, that the hands massaging her back and meting out those body-jarring pats were Case's hands.

A sob tore up from Prudy's chest. An awful, tearing, dry sort of sob that felt as if it had ripped her throat out. She made fists on Don's jacket, her legs turned to water, useless things that would no longer support her weight. Dimly she heard herself talking, but she was past caring what she said or who heard her. Let them stare. Let them wonder what on earth had come over her. Other people got sympathy and understanding in this place when *their* whole world was shattered. Just because she was a nurse didn't meant she didn't need a little compassion, as well.

Somehow Don shifted his hold on her, one strong arm hooked around her back, the other over her ribs, his hip and thigh jutted against her to support her weight as he half swung and half dragged her down the hall in a clumsy imitation of two people walking. Prudy had no idea where he was taking her. Didn't care. She still had a death hold on his jacket, was still sobbing with her face embedded in the coarse wool of his lapel.

"Where the hell can I take her?" she heard him growl. "We need some privacy."

As if from far away, Prudy heard a woman's voice, then felt Don lugging her along again. Then a door opened, hinges squeaking slightly. A moment later, a lock clicked. Prudy tried to make herself turn loose of him, tried to regather her composure and tell Petrov she was all right, that she wasn't sure what had come over her. The words wouldn't come.

"Just shut up, Prudy," he said gruffly, his big hands kneading her back and shoulders. "For once in your life, let someone take care of you instead of the other way around."

That sounded so good…to let someone take care of her. She was so tired. And scared. She'd never been so scared. Eight years ago, she'd stuffed her feelings for Case into a little black box somewhere deep inside of her, and she'd turned the lock on that box with an iron key of bitterness and regret, swearing she'd never let those emotions run rampant within her again. Over, finished, kaput. No more hurting. But one night in Case's arms had dynamited the lock to that box open again, and seeing him today on that gurney, with his life's blood seeping into the sheet under him, had sprung open the lid. Love was ripping her apart again. Slicing her to ribbons. Making her bleed. And, oh, God, she couldn't stand the pain of it.

Suddenly, as if in protest of the sobs that racked her body, Prudy felt a wave of nausea hit her stomach. Not a twinge. Not a manageable ripple, but the kind of wave surfers rejoiced in. It hit her so fast, all she could say was, "Sick!" before she made an attempt to jerk away from Don.

He cursed under his breath, swept her into his arms and charged like a she bear in defense of her cubs into what Prudy thought for a minute was a closet. Only the next second, he deposited her gently on the floor, her knees pressed against something hard and cold. Then his big hand clamped over the back of her head and shoved. *A toilet bowl.*

Prudy grabbed for the porcelain rim, suffering the dry heaves for several body-draining seconds. By the time the nausea passed, she was so weak she didn't care if she drowned, which she was perilously close to doing and might indeed have done if Don hadn't cupped a hand under her chin to keep her lolling head out of the water.

The indignity of it occurred to Prudy—but only in the most detached sort of way. She was too trembly and weak to actually feel embarrassment.

"Finally," she managed to say in a shaky little voice.

"Finally what?"

"I've discovered something good about morning sickness. It takes your mind off your troubles."

Petrov, who was kneeling behind her and supporting her weight, stiffened slightly. At his reaction, Prudy also realized what she'd said.

"Morning sickness?" he echoed.

She closed her eyes and cursed her too-quick tongue. "Yeah, well, that's what some idiot male doctor decided to call it, eons ago," she admitted wearily. "With me, it seems to strike at all hours. Just my luck, huh?"

Chapter 6

Don shifted behind her. She heard the towel dispenser go *kerklunk* somewhere above her, then water running. The next second, a cold, slimy paper towel went *splat* over her face. She sputtered and grabbed, trying frantically to get some air.

"Dammit, girl, stop wiggling. I'm trying to wash your face."

Prudy captured a wrist so broad she couldn't encircle half of it with her fingers. "Petrov, for pity's sake, you're suffocating—"

The paper towel fell away, and she gasped for breath even as Don began hauling her to her feet. Her legs felt a little stronger, she thought as she teetered and then gave in to the strength of his arm. As they exited the bathroom, she saw, through eyes gone blurry with tears and violent nausea, that he'd brought her into the antichamber of the chaplain's office. A fitting place to die, she thought as she allowed him to lower her onto a soft, cushiony chair.

"You feelin' better?" he asked.

Prudy sniffed, feeling oddly abandoned without his embrace

enfolding her like a steel jacket. Cupping a hand over her eyes, she propped her elbow on the wooden armrest.

"Yeah, I guess. Bearing in mind that the word *better* is relative. Better than dead isn't saying a lot, is it? I'm sorry, Don. For losing it like that, I mean."

"You're entitled," he said gruffly.

Through her splayed fingers, Prudy saw that he'd hunkered in front of her. Harsh light from the overhead fixture picked up the steel gray of his hair and cast lines over his craggy face. The face of a friend, she thought. One of the best friends she'd ever had, in fact. Until her divorce from Case. He and Case were far more than just partners, sharing a deep and unshakable love for each other neither ever expressed.

"Does Case know?" he asked in a gravelly voice.

Prudy's heart tripped. "Know what?"

He narrowed an eye. "Don't be a twit with me, Prue. About the baby, of course. That he's gonna be a daddy."

She was too exhausted to deal with this, she thought a little wildly. Too shaken and too sick. "Wait a minute, Petrov. Let me understand this. Prudy turns up pregnant, so that automatically means Case is factored into the equation somewhere? Give me a break. I may not be drop-dead gorgeous. But I'm not so dirt ugly that Case is the only man in Portland I might—"

"Dammit, Prudy. Don't lie to me. Case is the father. What do you take me for? An idiot? There could be a million men pounding down your door, but there's only one you'd open it for. I know it, you know it. Even Case would know it if he'd get his head out of his—" He broke off and ran a hand over his hair. "Out of the sand."

Prudy closed her eyes. "Don't press me, Don. Please. Not right now. We'll talk about it later, okay?"

"Later, right. When you're less upset and can get your story straight? No way, sweet cheeks. That's Case's baby making you heave those pretty little toes of yours up. Don't tell me it isn't. And you haven't told him about it yet, have you?"

Prudy wished the soft cushion of the chair would turn to quicksand and swallow her. Just her luck that a wave of nausea would strike when Don was present to witness it. Now—before she'd even had a chance to tell Case—she was going to have to 'fess up to Don?

"I can't talk to you about this. Please, Don, just let it ride."

"When were you planning to tell him? On the kid's first birthday? Not classy, Prue. I would've expected better of you."

Anger mushroomed in Prudy—so fast and unexpectedly, it was there and going volcanic before she could contain it.

"Don't you *dare* pass judgment on me, Don Petrov. I *tried* to tell him. I called the police station just before you two left. And I do stress the word *before!* I heard him yell across the station to the woman on the phone to tell me he'd already left."

Don rubbed his nose, sniffed. "Yeah, well. That's another puzzle piece that's suddenly starting to fit, why Case looked like the wrath of hell at the sound of your name and refused to take the call."

The only puzzle Prudy could see was the flow of this conversation. "I rest my case," she said wearily. "I tried to tell him, he didn't take the call, and now—" Her throat closed off, and she had to force her words out. "Now he could die without ever knowing."

"Trust me. He isn't going to die. He's got more steel than that."

Prudy pressed her fingertips against her eyelids. Rationally, she knew he was probably right. "You know how it is with us pregnant ladies. Emotional, and all that. I guess I'm a prime example."

"You might be a little less of a basket case if you'd eat every day or so," he said grumpily. "And judging by those circles under your eyes, sleeping every once in a while might be a good idea, too."

"I eat."

"Right. I saw what came up while you were in the bathroom. Zip. When was your last meal?"

"I can't remember, and please don't talk about food. The thought makes me sick."

"You're really taking well to this motherhood business. Like a duck to a vat of oil."

"I'm doing all right."

"No offense, Prue. But you look like hell. And you're not even that far along yet."

She dropped her hand from her face and stared at him. "Excuse me? Have I mentioned my due date?"

"Don't need to. Puzzle pieces, remember? I know the date you conceived. July fourteenth."

"Thirteenth, and how do you—" Prudy broke off, heat rushing up her neck to pool like fire in her cheeks as she recalled that the pumpkin hour had already chimed when she and Case had finally made love. Petrov was right; technically, even though foreplay had occurred late the evening of the thirteenth, she'd conceived after midnight on the fourteenth. Suddenly, she was so furious she would have wrung Case's neck if he hadn't been struggling for his life in surgery.

"He told you about us? He *told* you?" She bit down hard on her back teeth. "How dare he? He walks out on me in the middle of the night, without so much as a goodbye or a thank-you. He refuses to talk to me on the phone so I can inform him he left a calling card. And come to find out, he's been talking to *you* about it?"

Don held up a hand. "Not so fast. You know Case better than that. He's not a man who kisses and tells, never has been. I'm a cop, remember? Deductive reasoning is my specialty. After he spent the night—or part of it—with you, I caught him straggling home just before dawn. He's been hell on greased wheels ever since, biting my head off and everyone else's within snapping distance. Hell, it's been two years since he stopped smoking, and now, out of the blue, he's craving cigarettes." He smiled slightly and shrugged. "Puzzle pieces. Now they're all falling into place. I suspected he had woman trouble. Haven't seen him so miserable since right after your divorce. I just didn't think—" He broke off again, looking apologetic. "Well, the truth is, Prudy, I never suspected the woman might be you. He, um, sort of swore off one particular redhead, and once Case swears off, he very seldom..."

His voice trailed away, and silence fell over the room. Prudy angled forward, resting her elbows on her knees. "Oh, Don…" She closed her eyes, the anger that had roiled so furiously within her only seconds before being replaced by sadness. "If he hated me before, he's really going to hate me now. I told him I was protected, that we didn't need to worry. He's never going to forgive me when I tell him I'm pregnant."

"You didn't lie to him again?"

She was too tired to wince. "No. I was on the pill. What I didn't stop to consider was that I'd had the flu a few days earlier and couldn't keep much down. Evidently I upchucked a couple of my pills along with the 7UP and antacid." She cast him a miserable glance. "I'm forty-one, for pity's sake. This pregnancy caught me completely by surprise. Not that Case will ever believe it. And now, to compound trouble, you know about it before he does. If he lives through this, he's going to—"

"Be the proudest daddy who ever walked," he finished for her with a grin teasing the corners of his mouth. "But only after he chews you up, spits you out and uses your bones to pick his teeth."

"Thanks. I needed to hear that. Why do you think it took me so long to get my courage up to call him?" Prudy hauled in a shaky breath. "Oh, Don, why does he hate kids so much? Why can't he just be happy for me? I won't expect him to actively participate in child rearing or to support us. If he'd just not *hate* me, that would be enough."

"Sweetheart, he isn't going to hate you. And he doesn't hate kids, either."

Prudy guessed that was true. She could still remember the tender expression on his face when he'd held little Casey at the christening. "No, he just hates the idea of *my* giving him one."

Don sighed and flexed his shoulders. "Yeah, well, as irrational as it is, can you really blame him? Having parents like his—it does something to a person, you know? I think Case is afraid he'll wind up being one of those statistics we're always dealing with if he tries his hand at parenting." At

Prudy's questioning look, he expounded. "You know, doing the same rotten things to his kids that his parents did to him. It happens, you know. And in Case's line of work, he sees it all the time, abused kids becoming abusive parents..."

Prudy's heart had started to race. She knew it was wrong. Oh, God, she knew it was *terribly* wrong. Case had never told her about his childhood, and she'd long since despaired of ever learning anything about it. Now, here was Don, assuming she knew.

"Did you ever meet them? His parents, I mean?"

Don nodded. "At the lockup, right after I tossed Case into a cell."

Stunned, Prudy stopped breathing. Into a *cell?* Case had been in jail? Dear God, he'd never once said a word about being arrested. And by Don?

For an awful moment, Prudy thought Don would say no more. Then he sighed and added grimly, "I don't know why I believed what Case told me instead of that bitch who called herself his mother, but I did. I tried every way I could think of to make her tell the judge the truth, but protecting his sister's reputation was more important to her than Case's freedom."

Prudy licked her lips. "She, um... Do you think what she did is the reason why Case never wanted children?"

He pushed to his feet and sank onto a chair beside her. "I'm not sure, Prudy. I know she was the reason he swore he'd never get married." He grinned. "Course that was before he met you and found out the only way he could keep you was to put a ring on your finger."

"I didn't know he'd sworn never to marry," she said quietly.

Don cast her a sympathetic look. "It took him a while to sort it out in his mind. I think in the end he convinced himself that not all women were like his mother."

Prudy took a careful breath. "Like her how?"

A heavy silence fell. When she glanced up, she found Don glaring at her with one eyebrow raised. "Case never told you about his past, did he?"

She shook her head.

"Hell, I walked right into this one, slick as you please."
He narrowed his gaze. "Damn, but you're good, half pint. You
woulda made a great cop. Or a con woman."

Prudy managed a small smile. "Please don't be angry at
me because I want to understand the man I love."

He squeezed his eyes closed for a second. "Prudy, I'd like
to help you, but—"

She stopped him with a hand on his arm. "He's the father
of my child, Don. I have a right to know what happened to
make him so…unforgiving." She hesitated, then pleaded
softly, "I *need* to know why I hurt him so much."

He averted his face for a second, then cleared his throat.
"I'll tell you what I know, which isn't all that much. And
some of it I put together from bits and pieces, okay?"

She nodded. "Whatever you know is more than I do."

He exhaled heavily, then drew in fresh breath. "Case was
the middle child, a second son, and, from what I could find
out, a real hell-raiser. Had him a chip on his shoulder and a
real aversion to authority figures and rules."

"That hasn't changed," she murmured softly.

Don chuckled. "His old man sold real estate in Hillsbor-
ough, which is damn near drippin' with old money. His mother
was one of those skinny, lacquered society bitches. You've
seen 'em, all flash and no heart. Geoffrey, his brother, was
what you'd call the family hero. Smart, good-looking. I only
saw him once, but that was enough. Had rabbity eyes, never
looked you square in the face."

"I know the type," Prudy murmured. "And I can't imagine
Case growing up in a family like that."

"It wasn't easy. The more they nagged him to fit in, the
more trouble he made for them. They found out he had a high
IQ, higher than his damn brother's even, and demanded
straight *A*s and the leadership of a Rhodes scholar from him.
Case gave 'em *D*s and ran with a bad crowd. Same with sports.
They wanted him to be an all-American at somethin', football
preferably, but soccer or tennis was acceptable."

Don grinned. "Instead, Case was smoking two packs of

unfiltereds a day and downing a quart of Scotch in one sitting without turning a hair before he was old enough to drive.''

He sighed. ''Funny thing, though. He was crazy about his kid sister. Cilla, that was her name, a snotty, spoiled little princess who played her parents like a damned violin. Oh, she had a way about her, no doubt about it. Otherwise, Case never woulda figured she needed protecting.''

A phone in the adjacent office rang twice, then stopped. The fluorescent bulb overhead flickered. Prudy realized she was holding her breath again and made herself release the trapped air.

''What happened?'' she prodded when she realized Don was lost in thought.

''Cilla had just turned fourteen when she got mixed up with a fast crowd. Kids like her with too much money and too much time to spend it. In short, she ended up with a messy habit.''

''Drugs?''

Don nodded. ''Coke, mostly. High grade. She and her so-called friends had a connection in Chinatown.''

''Case hates drug dealers,'' Prudy said softly.

''So do I, but my reason isn't quite as personal as his.''

''His sister ODed?''

''Hell, no.'' Don shifted in his chair, too big to fit properly. ''Thing of it was, her mother found out what was goin' on and freaked. Slapped the girl up one side and down the other, threatened to throw her out of the house, cut off her funds.'' Don snorted. ''Cilla just laughed at her, then tripped off on a date with this guy who was a hell-raising friend of Case's. To a party in Chinatown.''

Prudy realized she was hanging on every word, desperate to know what happened next. ''And?'' she said when Don paused again.

''Case had just gotten home when his sister roared off with the guy. His mother begged him to go after her. To stop her. Case told me later he'd never seen such naked fear in his mother's eyes.''

''He did what she asked?''

Don nodded. ''Took his mom's Mercedes, even though he

was still a few months shy of his sixteenth birthday. He had a hunch where the guy was going."

"He found them?"

"Yeah, he found them. His sister was already stoned when he hauled her out of this basement dive and shoved her into the Mercedes. He drove her home, then went back to the place and ripped into the guy who'd brought her there. The two of them were still goin' at it when my partner and I happened by. The spectators split as soon as they saw the black-and-white. Case's so-called buddy, too. Case moved a step too slow."

"You arrested him?"

"Had to. He had a dime bag of coke in his pocket."

Prudy rubbed her temple. "But you eventually let him go, right? Once you found out what happened?"

"Couldn't. Not without corroboration from his mother and sister."

Something in the look in his eyes had her blood icing. "They refused to back up his story?"

"Denied the whole thing happened."

Her gasp slipped between them. "How awful for him."

"It was worse than that. His bitch of a mother claimed she'd never given him permission to take her Mercedes, so the DA added a charge of car theft to possession."

"In other words she…lied," Prudy said very softly.

"Yes, she lied. And because of that lie, Case spent the next two and a half years at Chino."

"Chino?"

"California's version of a vocational training school for criminals. In other words, a regular prison with a section for offenders under the age of twenty-five. Supposed to keep the young guys away from the hardened cons, but—" He shrugged. "Like most things these days, it didn't always work the way it should. I have me a hunch Case had a pretty rough time of it, although he's never once talked about it. Not one word. Ever."

Prudy gasped. She'd had no idea. "What about his father? Didn't he stand up for his son?"

"No, the spineless bastard," Don said venomously. "He sacrificed his son to preserve his daughter's reputation. Did a good job of it, too. The summer Case was released from Chino, she was named San Francisco's Debutante of the Year. Right before I took the job up here, I heard she'd gotten herself married to some rich guy who worked with her old man."

Prudy could only shake her head, her throat so tight with sadness for the boy Case had once been that she couldn't speak.

"Oh, Don. This explains so much." She gnawed her bottom lip. "Tell me. After he was released, did he ever go back to see them?"

Don shook his head. "When he got out, he put himself through college by working in the woods, and became a cop, just like his mentor—after a friendly judge sealed his juvenile record."

Prudy guessed exactly who that mentor had been. She also knew Don would never admit to it.

"You kept track of him?"

He nodded. "Visited him a time or two when he was inside, lent him a few bucks when he got out. By that time I'd taken a job in Portland and heard about this work-study program for ex-offenders at Bradenton College up here in Oregon. Proudest day of my life was when he told me he wanted to be a cop, and now, dammit, I wish he'd become an insurance salesman."

So do I, Prudy wanted to shout. Or a carpenter. Anything but a man who put his life on the line every day. "He's in good hands," she promised softly. That, at least, she knew for certain. Boyd was an exceptionally skilled surgeon. "The last report was he was doing fair. He'll make it."

She smiled slightly and placed a hand on his knee. He lay a rough palm over her cold fingers. "He promised me once that he would never go down in the line of duty."

As Prudy said that, she couldn't help but think that Case

had emerged into adulthood a far finer man than his parents had raised him to be. For all his faults, and she could make a long list of them, he'd never broken a promise to her yet.

She would never forgive him if he broke this one.

Chapter 7

It was past two when she and Don returned to the waiting room. Molly and Thad sprung up from their chairs as soon as she entered, but she shook her head.

"No news yet," she said as she and Don took seats on one of the vacant couches. Time crawled past. People came and went. Brought back coffee and drank it. Went to get more.

No one said much. Nor did they look at one another.

Prudy had seen a death watch before. *He's fine!* she wanted to shout. But she made herself sit quietly, conserving her energy. For the baby's sake.

It was nearly two forty-five when Prudy saw Giselle Francis glance toward the door, then straighten and pat her hair. An instant later Boyd stepped into the waiting room. He was still dressed in faded blue scrubs, his disposable mask dangling under his chin, his broad, muscular forearms ringed where the tight cuffs of rubber gloves had cut into his skin for the duration of the surgery. Weariness etched even deeper than usual on his seamed features.

"Doctor, how is Sergeant Randolph?" Giselle Francis called over the sudden murmur of speculation. Microphone extended, she advanced on Boyd like a knight at full tilt. Next to her, the cameraman was hastily hefting his minicam to his shoulder.

Molly was once again on her feet in a flash, her hand groping for Thad's and her expression hopeful. With no memory of leaving her seat, Prudy found herself standing, as well. Next to her Don surged to his feet, his hand heavy and warm on her shoulder.

"Boyd?" she called, drawing his gaze. He nodded, then moved toward her.

"Doctor, wait!" Giselle called, frowning. "A word, please."

"In a minute," Boyd told her as he reached Prudy's side. Though his handsome face was lined with fatigue, his gray eyes twinkled with a smile, and Prudy felt relief run like a shot of adrenaline through her body.

"Aunt Prudy?" Molly nearly collided with the cameraman in her haste to get closer.

"Boyd, this is Case's niece, Molly, and her husband, Thad," Prudy explained with hasty courtesy. "And we're all waiting—"

"He's pretty beat up, but, barring complications, he should make a full recovery."

Molly sagged against her husband and burst into tears. Prudy felt Don's burly arms encircle her waist. She laughed as he lifted her off her feet and into a huge bear hug.

"I told you he was tough," he rumbled in her ear.

"You also said 'ornery,' as I recall."

"Yeah," he whispered. "I'm recalling us both sayin' a lot of things we might be smart never to repeat."

Prudy glanced up. "You're a good friend, Don. To Case and to me."

Don managed a tired smile. "Whatever happens, I wish you well. Sincerely."

"Thank you. That means a lot to me."

He leaned down to give her a hug before a man with a pug nose and exhausted eyes drew him away for a bout of back-slapping and an exchange of grins while the man with the minicam recorded every macho comment.

Prudy couldn't blame Case's fellow policemen for celebrating the good news. Case was going to be all right. He really was going to be all right.

"Can we see him?" Molly asked, still clutching her husband's hand.

"Better wait until tomorrow," Boyd replied. "He'll be in recovery for another few hours yet." He redirected his attention to Prudy once again. "Kit Forrest said to tell you they're giving him VIP treatment."

It took all of Prudy's remaining energy to summon a smile. "Bless her."

Molly turned a worried gaze on Prudy. "Aunt Prudy? Can't you pull strings or something? So Thad and I can see him. Just long enough to tell him we love him?"

"Boyd's right, honey. Most likely Uncle Case wouldn't even know you're there. Besides, no one's allowed in recovery except staff."

Molly looked close to tears again, and Prudy's heart went out to her. "You'll stay with him?"

Prudy nodded. "Until he wakes up. I promise."

"Thank you," Molly said as Prudy hugged her. "And thank you, too, Dr. MacAuley," she added, leaning up to kiss Boyd on the cheek. A dark flush replaced the pall of weariness on his chiseled features as he exchanged embarrassed male shrugs with Thad.

"I'll call you first thing in the morning," Prudy promised Molly, and they hugged again.

"Give the big guy our best," Thad said hoarsely before stretching a protective arm around his wife's waist. Prudy felt tears fill her eyes as she watched the young couple hurry from the crowded room.

It took her a moment to realize that Boyd had shifted his attention her way. "Son of a gun still looks as mean as ever," he said with a weary grin. Boyd had told her once that Case had called him several times after his first wife and child had died. The first call had been to offer his sympathy. The second had been an invitation for the two former neighbors to get good and drunk together.

"Case isn't mean, and you know it," Prudy chided, her throat tight.

"Hell, yes, he's mean," Petrov interjected as he returned to stand by Prudy's side.

"What about his thigh?" Prudy asked so quietly Boyd had to lean forward to catch her words.

"The bullet missed the femoral artery, but managed to do a job on the femur. Took me and the orthopedic resident a couple of extra hours to fish out the bone slivers and put him back together again. I've slapped him in traction until the bones begin to knit, then we'll cast his leg."

"And his wrist?"

"A clean break. Four or five weeks in a cast should do it." His expression grew somber. "His blood pressure is still elevated more than I'd like."

Prudy felt a jolt of alarm. "I noticed that when we took the initial readings, but I put it down to the sudden shock."

"Which isn't at all uncommon," Boyd agreed, moving his shoulders as though easing a painful tightness. "In any event, we'll be keeping a close watch to see if the high numbers were caused by the trauma, or are reflective of a preexisting condition."

"He told me he wouldn't die on duty," she repeated, pressing her hands together. "He promised, and Case always keeps his promises, you know." She was suddenly very cold and her breath was coming in odd little gasps.

"Prudy? Are you okay?"

"Hmm?"

"Watch out, she's going to faint!" Petrov boomed, making her wince. Turning her head in his direction, she licked her lips and started to reassure her big, shambling friend, when all of a sudden she felt dizzy. Very, very dizzy.

Prudy opened her eyes to find herself lying on one of the waiting room couches with two grim-faced men leaning over her. She didn't know which one looked more worried, Boyd or Don.

"I guess I was more tired than I thought," she murmured before licking her dry lips.

"You should be taking better care of yourself, half pint," Don declared gruffly. "Case wouldn't want you to get yourself in a state over him."

A dozen male voices chorused agreement, drawing her attention to the clutch of men standing in a ragged half circle behind Don and Boyd. The TV contingent was also there, standing to one side. As soon as she made eye contact with the reporter, the lady surged forward, microphone in hand, and a blinding light hit Prudy squarely in the face.

"How do you feel?" Ms. Francis shrilled eagerly.

"Later," Petrov ordered, putting his considerable bulk between Prudy and the media. "Bloodsuckers," he muttered, grinning.

"Tell me my swan dive wasn't captured on camera," Prudy pleaded, trying to sit up.

"In living color," Boyd admitted, offering a hand to pull her upright.

As soon as she sat up, her head began swimming and her stomach clenched. "Whoa," she muttered, dropping her head to her chest.

"Deep and slow," Boyd ordered, watching her closely.

"I'm fine," she said when the giddiness finally eased and it was safe to lift her head again. To her surprise, everyone was still staring at her, as though afraid to move.

"How about some water?" Don offered. "Or, uh, whatever?"

Prudy laid a hand on his arm and smiled. "Stop fussing, Don. I was just overtired, that's all."

"You're sure?" He dropped his gaze to the vicinity of her tummy before jerking it back an instant later to her face. A wash of red bloomed under his deep tan, and he bit his lip.

"I'm sure," she said as she patted his arm. In an attempt to show him just how fine she was, she got up and straightened her shoulders. "I'm going to see Case, now," she announced when Don would have reached out a hand to stop her. "And then I'm going home to sleep for two days straight."

"Good plan," Boyd said, stepping back to let her move past him.

"Mrs. Randolph, did you know it was your ex-husband the ambulance was bringing to the emergency room?" Apparently seeing a golden opportunity for a scoop, Giselle Francis had leapt right in.

"Excuse me," Prudy said, increasing her pace.

"Did he tell you who fired the first shot?" the woman persisted. "Did you see Felix Cardoza when he was brought in? Have they done an autopsy on his body? Whose bullet—"

Prudy brushed aside the microphone and escaped into the hall just as she heard Don's gravelly voice giving a concise— and decidedly unflattering—appraisal of Giselle's manners.

Recovery was located at the far end of the corridor, behind double doors plastered with signs warning unauthorized persons to stay out.

"Not a chance," Prudy muttered as they swooshed open at her advance. Her heart was hammering in her head, and her throat was achingly dry as she stepped into the room.

Though it was the middle of the night, five of the eight beds were occupied. Case was lying in the bed closest to the doors, his heavily bandaged left leg affixed at a forty-five-degree angle to a traction pulley above. He was wearing a regulation hospital gown, which did little to soften the powerful lines of his chest, and his face was turned slightly toward the door, allowing her to look her fill at the hard, angular features that haunted her dreams.

Kit Forrest looked up and waved from the desk at the far end of the room. Prudy waved back before turning her attention to Case. Prudy recognized the nurse standing by his side by sight, but not by name. Forcing a smile, Prudy quickly introduced herself in hushed tones, adding that the big man lying so still was her ex-husband.

"He's still zonked, although he's been doing a lot of frowning for the past ten minutes or so."

"That sounds like Case."

The nurse offered an understanding nod before returning her gaze to the woman in the next bed.

Even though Prudy knew what to expect, she wasn't as prepared as she'd thought to see him lying so still and white and, at the moment, helpless. Because she knew Case was still unconscious and unaware, she allowed herself to stroke the thick tangle of black hair away from his forehead. Not even the post-surgery pallor completely eclipsed the burnished darkness of his skin. Her gaze fell to his lax mouth, the firm yet sensual lips softened in sleep, his usually bunched jaw still defined with muscle, lending his harsh masculinity a boyish appeal. Her heart twisted, and bled a little, at the thought of how close she'd come to losing him.

Prudy couldn't imagine the world without Case in it. In the eight years since their divorce, she'd thought of him at least once every day—if not dozens of times. Case with the fluid, muscular stride. Case with the harsh, don't-mess-with-me scowl that could alter into a heart-melting grin when he saw her. Case with the big, hard, incredibly warm hands that had always made her knees turn to water when they touched her. In her mind, she'd known and accepted that their marriage was over. But in her heart, there had always been a granule of hope that one day—when she least expected it—she'd look up and he'd be standing there.

How could she have continued to live if he'd died and she'd no longer had that foolish hope to get her through the days? And the nights. The incredibly long and lonely nights.

"Nurse?"

Prudy leapt with a start, then realized the plaintive voice belonged to the new mother in the next bed who'd spoken, and that she was addressing the on-duty nurse, not her. "Is my baby all right?"

"A perfect little girl," the recovery nurse hastened to assure the anxious patient while checking her blood pressure.

Smiling wearily, Prudy turned back to Case. To her surprise, his eyes were now open, and she could see he was trying to focus on her.

"Welcome back," she whispered.

When she tried to withdraw her hand from where it rested on his dark hair, he reached up with his good hand, his fingers clamping down hard over her wrist, his grip amazingly strong for a man who still wasn't quite awake.

"Prue?" he grated, his voice hoarse.

"Yeah, it's me."

He licked his lips, blinked, then tightened his grip on her wrist even more. "Guess MacAuley didn't kill me, after all."

"I'll pass on your appreciation."

He blinked again, then shifted his gaze to his leg. "What's all the hardware?"

"Traction." Seeing him scowl, she hastened to add, "Trust me, it's necessary."

He expressed his opinion in a pithy obscenity that had Prudy choking back a laugh. "Behave yourself, Case," she ordered in a low voice. "You're not the only patient in recovery."

He glanced past her hip to the new mommy in the next bed and winced. "Sorry," he muttered, closing his eyes. If not for his death grip on her wrist, Prudy might have believed he'd gone back to sleep.

She cast an apologetic glance at the young mother. "He's just coming around."

"It's okay," the younger woman replied. "I said the same thing when I was in labor."

Prudy managed another brief smile, then, returning her gaze to Case, tried to ease her imprisoned wrist from his grip. His eyes fluttered open, and he tugged her closer, relaxing his hold slightly to entwine his fingers with hers. Prudy's heart twisted, skipping a beat, then skittering. How was it that this man, by just a touch, had the power to devastate her like this? He'd made love to her, and then walked out. Just before the shooting, he'd refused to take her phone call at the station. Had she no pride at all?

None, she admitted in her heart of hearts. Where Case was concerned, pride was a commodity in terribly short supply.

"Petrov? Is he...okay?"

Struggling to inject a note of joviality into her voice, she said, "Don's fine and dealing with the press, so you know what kind of mood he's in right about now."

His hard mouth slanted. "And that b—" He stopped suddenly, as though remembering her earlier admonition. "And Cardoza?"

"DOA."

He grunted, his eyelashes drooping to hide his eyes. "I'm sorry," he said, his tone brusque, his voice strained.

"For what?" she asked softly, thinking he was apologizing for shooting Cardoza.

He forced his eyes open. "For leaving the way I did."

Prudy could tell he was still fighting to stay awake, as if a growing weakness was draining away the little remaining strength left to him. "The night of the christening. No rose. It was...lousy of me."

A burning sensation washed over the backs of Prudy's eyes. She knew the apology didn't come lightly, not when it was all he could do to talk. And, God help her, that meant the world to her—knowing that he'd had to struggle to say each word.

"Don't worry about it," she said tightly. "I'm not."

Liar, her heart accused. Prudy ignored the tormenting little taunt. She might not have any pride where this man was concerned, but knowing that and letting him know it were two different things.

"I—" He licked his lips again and swallowed. "Meant to call you, or stop by. Kept puttin' it off. Work and stuff."

"I never gave it a second thought," she whispered. She'd just wept until her eyes swelled closed. No big deal.

His mouth twisted. "Didn't know what the hell to say to you." His dark brows drew together in a little frown. His gaze became slightly unfocused again. "You phoned the station. What'd you want?"

Prudy nearly told him about the baby then—longed to tell him—but instinct warned her that now wasn't the time. No, he needed to be stronger when he learned he was to be a father. Surely a few more days wouldn't matter.

"Nothing that can't wait. You're tired now. You need to get some rest." She lifted his hand to her cheek.

His fingers tightened even as his eyes drifted closed again. "Come see me tomorrow."

"Is that an order?" she teased gently, loving the feeling of his hard fingers laced with hers.

"Damn straight," he muttered, one side of his mouth moving. It wasn't much of a smile, but Prudy thought it was beautiful.

Prudy cried all the way home. She knew the tears stemmed from relief and fatigue, with a hefty dollop of hormones thrown in. Still, she was getting very tired of this uncharacteristic loss of control. As soon as she caught up on her sleep, she intended to take herself—and her roller-coaster emotions—in hand.

If Case could discipline his emotions, so could she. It was simply a matter of practice and determination. Yes, she would definitely make changes. For the baby's sake, as well as her own.

The sun was nudging over the eastern horizon as she parked her Volvo under the carport and stumbled from the driver's seat. She was halfway up the walk leading to her back door when she heard Stacy's screen door squeak open.

"Come in for some tea and breakfast," Stacy called softly as she hurried in Prudy's direction.

"Thanks, but I don't think I could swallow."

"Try," Stacy urged, putting her arm around Prudy's shoulder to lead her across the grass. "Doctor's orders. I got a call from Boyd. Don Petrov told him you had the dry heaves at the hospital and that he didn't think you'd eaten in far too long. Boyd told me to have something waiting for you, and being the dutiful wife I am, I do. And you, my dear friend, are going to eat every bite."

"Boyd called?" Prudy asked when they reached Stacy's door.

"Oh, honey, you really are dead on your feet, aren't you?

Yes, he called. About a half hour ago. He knew Tory would be up and raring to go.''

Prudy managed a tired smile. "And is she?"

"Of course," Stacy said as she opened the door to the MacAuleys' yellow-and-white kitchen. The smell of freshly perked coffee made Prudy's mouth water, and she longed to down an entire pot instead of the one measly cup a day Luke was allowing her.

"Prepare yourself," Stacy said, laughing over her shoulder as music blared from the small TV on the counter. "Tory will only eat oatmeal if I allow her to watch cartoons. Not that I can blame her, you understand. I won't eat the stuff under any circumstances."

Through bleary eyes, Prudy glimpsed a cartoon rabbit flying across the kitchen television screen before her attention was snagged by a pint-sized doll in pj's and fuzzy slippers laughing wildly at the antics.

"Aunt Pwudy!" Victoria Patterson MacAuley called from the high chair by the table as Prudy entered. A few months shy of her second birthday, Stacy's little girl was as charming as a fat little cherub when she was asleep. At all other times she was an energetic imp, with an insatiable curiosity that frequently led her into mischief. From the moment she learned to walk, she'd been her father's darling and her mother's nightmare. Prudy adored the tiny hellion nearly as much as her parents.

"Good morning, punkin." Leaning down, Prudy planted a kiss atop Tory's thick dark curls. It was all her tired body could manage to stand erect again. "How's my little love this morning?"

"Hungwy," Tory declared, pouting.

Prudy took in the empty cereal bowl and smear of banana on Tory's rosy cheek and nodded. "I see she has her father's appetite," she told Stacy, who sighed.

"I'm thinking of planting a kitchen garden this spring to help with the grocery bills." She poured tea into a mug and set it on the table. "You don't happen to know anything about canning, do you?"

Prudy collapsed onto a chair and pulled the tea closer with the single-minded intensity of a starving person.

"Are you kidding? I spent one entire winter in the library, reading up on food preservation. Drying, canning, freezing, all that stuff. I even made my own pyramid to put over the drying trays. Case called it my 'back to nature' phase." She managed a hollow laugh. "I almost blew up the kitchen canning tomatoes that summer. Case came home to find me sitting on the kitchen floor covered in tomato sauce, crying my eyes out." She shook her head. "Boy, did he ever lose his temper."

Stacy offered a sympathetic nod. "Because you'd made a mess?"

"No, because for an instant he thought the red stuff dripping from my clothes and my hair and everything else was blood. He froze in his tracks and turned as white as death."

She bit her lip, her mind lost in the past. Case had been shaking violently when he'd reached her, too upset to do more than scoop her into his arms and hold her tight until his huge body had stopped shuddering. "But of course, he made it up to me later," she remembered aloud. "In bed."

Laughing softly, Stacy handed her daughter a peeled banana and sat down.

"He sounds like my kind of man."

Prudy watched Tory squish banana between her fingers. She was too exhausted to smile when the little girl slanted her a peek from beneath her curly bangs. She took a tentative sip of the tea, then sighed.

"Yes, Case is—"

"Oh, my goodness, look!" Stacy cried, cutting Prudy off.

Brain dead from lack of sleep, Prudy glanced stupidly around the room.

"The television!" Stacy elaborated, waving a hand before Prudy's nose. "On the morning news."

Prudy blinked, trying to bring the picture into clear focus. Evidently, while they'd been talking, the cartoon show had given way to "Wake Up, Portland" on KORP, and the perky morning anchor was talking in solemn tones about the shooting. Behind the woman's artfully streaked and moussed blond shag, they were showing a picture of Case in uniform. It was his official department photo, taken when he was a rookie, and Prudy's heart took a little hop.

"Mama—"

"Shh, baby," Stacy whispered, leaning forward to kiss her daughter on the forehead. "Aunt Prudy and I want to listen to the lady on the TV telling us something important."

"...and according to PortGen's chief surgical resident, Dr. Boyd MacAuley, who performed the surgery in the wee hours of this morning, Sergeant Randolph is expected to make a full recovery. In the meantime, questions still remain about the exchange of shots that left Felix Cardoza dead at the scene from an abdominal wound. Only minutes before we went on the air this morning, KORP reporter Giselle Francis interviewed the slain man's younger brother, Arturo."

Prudy bit her lip as a man's skeletal face filled the screen. His Latin features held the promise of good looks, but his skin was the color of putty and dotted with sores. His eyes were dull, with half-closed lids, and his black hair hung in long oily ropes to his shoulders, which were stooped and thin. Years of experience prompted Prudy to peg him as a heavy-duty cocaine addict. Mixed feelings stirred her. She felt sorry for anyone who was enslaved in mind and body, but she also knew that it was possible for anyone, even an addict, to make a decision to change.

"He looks like a real solid citizen if I ever saw one," Stacy muttered as the man began to speak in answer to Giselle's first question. In spite of his Latin looks, Cardoza spoke without an accent, his voice surprisingly reedy, almost feminine.

"Ain't no excuse for what happened, no, ma'am! My brother, he wasn't doin' nothing wrong when them cops came bustin' through his door. Felix musta figured they'd come to rob him or somethin', which is why he went for his gun. To protect hisself."

Giselle interrupted to ask with what Prudy thought was a sickening eagerness, "You're saying then that Sergeant Randolph fired first?"

Cardoza's eyes flashed. Even as numb with exhaustion as

Prudy was, she gasped at the raw fury she glimpsed burning in those drug-dull eyes. "Don't make no never mind what anyone says. Randolph killed my brother in cold blood. Gut-shot him like an animal and left him to bleed to death."

"Oh, for heaven's sakes!" Stacy cried over the sound of the anchor's voice explaining that the Portland Police Department had refused to comment on Arturo Cardoza's accusations, "pending an Internal Affairs investigation, which, according to Captain Bill Walters, is standard procedure whenever a policeman is involved in a shooting."

"Don't worry about it, Stace," Prudy soothed, while trying to level her own anger. "The media loves to criticize the police. Case used to say—"

"Oh, my God, Prue, that's you!"

Prudy jerked her gaze back to the television set and groaned at the image of herself crumpled on the floor. "...is perhaps the oddest irony of all that Sergeant Randolph's ex-wife, Prudence Randolph, an RN, was the one in charge of the emergency room at Portland General where he was taken after the shooting. Seen here immediately after she fainted in the waiting room outside the operating room where Sergeant Randolph was being treated, Ms. Randolph was revived by Randolph's partner, Sergeant Don Petrov, and Dr. Boyd MacAuley."

"Poor Boyd looks so exhausted," Stacy murmured, staring intently at the screen where the picture of Prudy's embarrassing performance was dissolving into a commercial.

"And I looked like a wimp," Prudy muttered, disgusted with herself and that snip of a reporter and, most of all, the cameraman who'd also made her look dumpy and old.

"You looked like a woman who'd finally reached the limits of her endurance. A pregnant woman at that."

Prudy felt her eyes widen. "It shows?" she asked in horror. "What if Case sees the news? What if—"

"It doesn't show, I promise," Stacy interrupted with a reassuring smile. "In fact, I think, if anything, you've lost weight instead of gained."

"Five pounds," Prudy admitted absently, her mind rerunning the short snippet she'd just glimpsed. She'd looked like a limp rag doll, with her wild red hair and freckles, but she hadn't looked pregnant.

"I have to tell him soon. I can't stand feeling guilty all the time." Prudy dutifully filled her mouth with scrambled eggs, chewed and swallowed. "I'm sorry, Stace. I'm just too tired to eat. I think I'll just head home."

Stacy directed a pointed glance at the nearly untouched meal she'd fixed. "Three more bites of egg, and one piece of toast. It won't take you three minutes." She softened the directive with a smile. "For the baby, Prue."

That was an argument for which there was no defense. Prudy stuffed toast into her mouth, thinking, as she chewed, that it tasted like cardboard.

"Come on," Stacy encouraged. "Just a few more bites."

Somehow Prudy managed to ingest enough of the meal to satisfy her friend.

Then, draining the last of the tea from her cup, she stood. "Now can I go home, turn off the phone and sleep?"

"Stowy?" Tory asked with wide-eyed eagerness.

Prudy stared at the child, too exhausted to comply, but reluctant to tell her no.

Stacy saved the day. "Not right now, punkin. Aunt Prudy's going to take a nap."

Tory shook her head so vigorously her dark curls danced. "No nap," she declared firmly.

"Not for you, darling," her mother soothed. "Aunt Prudy's going to take a nice long nap, and when she wakes up, she's going to feel much better about everything."

Chapter 8

The afternoon sun hadn't yet started its slide toward the horizon, and Case was already furious. Twice, since they'd dumped him into a room of his own around 5:00 a.m., a bossy nurse with the face of a prune had barged into his room to jerk him out of a sound sleep. To take his blood pressure and temperature, she'd had the nerve to chirp brightly when he'd mumbled an order for her to get lost and stay there.

The second time she'd startled him awake, he'd nearly come up swinging—and then when she'd squeaked in surprise, he'd told her exactly what she could do with her blood pressure cuff. The witch had shouted right back at him, adding a razored edge to his already lousy mood.

Though he hadn't intended to, he'd slept most of the day, then snapped awake when the kitchen help started rattling trays outside his room. His stomach had growled in anticipation. Getting shot was damned hungry work.

He'd been expecting a steak, or maybe a slab of rare roast beef. They'd brought him baby food, all of it white and runny.

Damn it, he wasn't about to put up with any more guff. Not

in this lifetime, which was exactly what he'd told Boyd MacAuley the instant Boyd showed his face about five-thirty.

By five-forty they'd been engaged in a hell of a shouting match, one that Case had been doomed to lose, no matter how creative he waxed in his description of Boyd's bedside manner. Case's spirit was willing, but he'd soon discovered that his body was severely lacking in strength.

Still, he wasn't quite finished, he told himself as he leaned back against the pillow and crossed his arms over his chest. He'd forgotten what a stubborn jackass MacAuley could be.

"Ten days, max," Case declared, glaring at the big man in scrubs who had just finished laying down the law to him about how long he'd have to remain in the hospital.

After checking to make sure the pulley tension on the traction device was adjusted properly, MacAuley flashed a pleasant grin at his grumpy patient. Case thought the smile looked exactly like that of a shark he'd seen once near the Golden Gate Bridge where he and some buddies used to hang out.

"Two weeks, Case," MacAuley said with the smug tone of a man who knew damned well he had the upper hand. "Not a day less."

"Forget that. I'll leave on my own."

MacAuley glanced at the steel cables attached to a pin stuck through his leg and looped over the pulley, pulled taught by weights. "How?"

Case ground his teeth at the amusement lurking in the other man's gray eyes. It was bad enough waking up with a hot poker stabbing his thigh and a drug-induced sluggishness in his head. Boyd had just made it worse by sentencing him to fourteen days of imprisonment in a bed as hard as the slabs downstairs in the morgue and a room with about as much privacy as a zoo cage.

"I hate hospitals," Case muttered, feeling the stark white walls already squeezing the air out of the room. He'd long ago shucked the nightmares that had plagued him for a lot of years after his release from Chino, but he was still uncomfortable in confined spaces.

"Think of it as a paid vacation," Boyd offered with a shrug. "A time for reflection and contemplation."

"Of what? The view?"

Boyd glanced at the window overlooking the brightly lit parking lot. Stacy had been on the floor above in a room with a similar view when he'd started falling in love with her. Now, after a year of marriage to a woman he adored more with each passing day, he was hard-pressed to remember why he'd fought the attraction for so long.

"I'll bring you a couple of books tomorrow. Got a couple of good police procedurals you might enjoy."

Case groaned, not from pain, but from sheer frustration. "Got any *Playboys*?"

Boyd laughed. "No, but I think I can scare up a few for you—as long as you promise not to tell my wife. She's ordered me to keep my sexual energies strictly focused in her direction."

Case cocked his head and studied his old friend. Boyd had beefed up considerably in the eight years since he'd seen him. Newly married in those days and new to Portland General, Boyd had seemed impossibly young, an idealist who'd really thought he'd had a lock on happiness.

With his own marriage in lousy shape, Case had been tempted to issue a blunt warning, but finally figured that the kid had to make his own mistakes and learn his own lessons. But damn, he hadn't figured on Boyd slamming up against life so damned hard. Still, it looked as if he'd survived with only a few more lines of cynicism on his handsome puss.

"Sounds like you got lucky two times in your life, old son," he found himself saying gruffly. "Hope you realize how lucky you really are."

"Oh, yeah," Boyd said with an unabashed grin Case envied. As though suddenly embarrassed, Boyd cleared his throat and glanced toward the door. "Guess I'd better get moving. I'll stop in tomorrow morning to check on you."

"Bring me some steak and eggs while you're at it."

"In your dreams," Boyd called over his shoulder before disappearing into the corridor.

Hell, Case thought. Now what? He couldn't remember the last time he hadn't organized his life around his job.

Scowling, he twisted around—God, a man had to be a contortion expert to move when trussed up in this contraption—to jab at the TV remote buttons on his bed rail. He didn't care what was on. Noise was what he wanted. Something to take the edge off the hot throbbing in his thigh.

Clumsy with his left hand, it took him a moment to work the buttons. The six o'clock news was just coming on. The image that greeted him had him hissing a foul obscenity. Arturo Cardoza, spouting garbage.

He wasn't surprised. With the death of his brother, Arturo had lost his source of free dope. Hell, he couldn't even blame the poor bastard.

No, he blamed the bimbo with the mike. He'd crossed paths with that lady before. Now *she* was a shark, he thought grimly. The kind who made MacAuley look like the fish-tank variety in comparison. As news sharks went, she was about as ambitious as they came, completely unethical in how she circled for a story and merciless when she went in for the kill, relying on her sex appeal to get the first bite.

He was about to punch the off button when the picture changed. As fast as he could blink, the image of the anchor changed to a shot of his partner and a half dozen of the other guys from his precinct. He started to grin, only to suck in hard when the shot again changed to a close-up of Prudy lying on a blue couch.

God, she looked fragile, he thought as the camera caught the fluttering of her thick coppery lashes against too-pale skin. And only about as big as a minute in those butt-hugging jeans and a soft pink sweatshirt.

He was about to stab his thumb against the call button with an order for the nurse when the smarmy anchorwoman went on to add that "Ms. Randolph regained consciousness quickly and has apparently suffered no ill effects from her fainting spell."

Case drew a long breath before reaching for the phone on the stand by the bed. It took him a moment to dredge Prudy's number from some dark place in the back of his mind. The cast on his right hand prevented him from using all but the tips of his fingers, but he managed to brace the phone against his forearm long enough to punch out the number.

"Prudy, you need to wake up. Prudy, it's Stacy. Open your eyes, okay?"

Prudy burrowed her face deeper into the pillow and tried to ignore the low, feminine voice whispering nonsense in her ear.

"Don't hate me, Prue, but you have to wake up. Now."

Prudy tried to scoot away from the hand shaking her by the shoulder, but only succeeded in nearly tumbling off the edge of the mattress.

"Mmm?" she mumbled, trying to pry her eyes open.

"Prudy, you have to call Case at the hospital. Now, before he tears the place apart."

That got her attention. "What's wrong?" she managed to say, her eyes popping open. Though she was still groggy, she was awake enough to feel a sudden stab of fear.

"Boyd just called," Stacy said as she pushed open the lacy curtains, flooding the room with sunshine. Prudy winced even as she urged Stacy to continue.

"Apparently Case saw a replay of the story on you on the evening news—"

"Oh, rats!" Prudy struggled to sit up, only to feel a wave of weakness run through her like a long, slow shiver.

"Naturally he tried to call to make sure you were okay, but—"

"I have the phone turned off—"

"So he got worried and started bellowing for Boyd. Which Boyd says is not good for Case's blood pressure."

Prudy gaped at her. She could count on one hand the number of times she'd heard Case raise his voice. "He was worried?" she repeated, her voice still thick with sleep.

"According to my darling husband, he was threatening everyone in earshot with, uh, dire consequences if they didn't help him get out of bed."

"It's not funny, Stace," Prudy chided when she saw her friend fighting to contain her grin.

"No, it's actually very endearing, although, from the exasperation in Boyd's voice, I doubt he would agree with me."

Prudy blinked, then cleared her throat. "I, um, suppose I should call Case and reassure him."

Laughing, Stacy picked up the phone and set it in Prudy's lap. "Please, for my sake. Otherwise, Boyd will have my head."

"We can't let that happen," Prudy muttered as she poked out the hospital's main number. "Did Boyd tell you what room Case is in now?"

"Six-twelve."

"Six-twelve, please," Prudy repeated an instant later when the switchboard operator came on the line.

"Randolph," Case answered on the first ring. The harsh bite to his voice had her sucking in air.

"Case, it's—"

"Damn it, Prue, what's the matter with you? Are you sick?"

"No, I—"

"Don't lie to me again, dammit. I saw how you folded up."

Don't lie to me again. Prudy tightened her suddenly bloodless fingers around the phone and willed her stomach to settle. The faint hope she'd allowed herself to nourish in some fragile place in her heart shriveled, leaving her with the stinging taste of disappointment in her throat.

"I'm not lying," she said very quietly. "*And* I'm not sick. I was simply worn out after ten hours on my feet and then putting in another *long* shift waiting until you got out of surgery and into recovery."

She paused to take a breath and realized she was behaving like the wimp she'd resembled on the tube. No, she thought. I won't apologize again. I *won't!* She took another breath, letting her anger build.

Don't lie to me again, don't lie to me again.

He would never forget, never forgive, and she was finally tired of thinking he would. Still, losing her temper would be unproductive. Better to handle this particular situation in a calm, rational manner. Far better, she reiterated as she took a breath.

"But now that I think about it," she continued in a voice that vibrated with frustration and hurt, "I *am* embarrassed to think how worried I was about a rigid, unforgiving, bullheaded jerk I thought I cared about. Silly me, I should have known better. Don't worry about me ever lying to you again, Mr. Randolph! If I never even *speak* to you again, I'll be happy."

She slammed the receiver down so hard her fingers stung. And promptly burst into tears.

"Damn, damn, damn," she muttered, clutching fistfuls of sheet. "I hate that man. I really h-hate him."

"Because he's rigid and unforgiving," Stacy affirmed in a solemn tone as she returned the phone to the nightstand, then sat down on the edge of the bed.

"And bullheaded," Prudy added, choking on a sob. "I was so sure I was over him."

Stacy nodded, her green eyes warm with understanding.

"I was content. Happy." Prudy uncurled her fists long enough to swipe most of the tears from her cheeks. "I was even thinking of taking a t-trip to Ireland. To look up my O'Grady relatives in Cork." She glanced up and caught Stacy's nod.

"That sounds like a wonderful idea."

Prudy nodded again, her hands once more clutching wads of sheet. "Case had no business looking so…handsome and sexy when he walked into that church. No, Case never just walks," she corrected. "He swaggers, like some arrogant warlord."

"Ah, that's why you hate him. Because he has a sexy walk."

Prudy frowned at the amusement in her friend's voice, then felt a laugh bubbling in her throat. "No, I don't hate him, but I just realized something I should have figured out long before this."

"Which is?"

"That I don't dare love him. And somehow, I've got to make myself stop. Because if I don't, he'll break my heart. Again."

Chapter 9

"Prue, telephone!" Hollis bellowed from the desk.

Prudy nodded as she finished giving instructions to her young patient's plump, pleasant-faced mother. "And whatever you do, Mrs. Yarnell, don't let Teddy get that cast wet. It's made of plaster, not concrete."

"Hey, cool," nine-year-old Teddy Yarnell piped up, his blue eyes sparkling in his too-pale face. "Guess that means I don't have to take a bath till I get rid of this sucker."

"Forget it, Ted," his mom declared, ruffling his shaggy brown hair with a work-worn, capable-looking hand. "We'll figure out something."

"Try wrapping the cast with plastic bags," Prudy suggested before reaching for the phone on the cubical wall.

"Prudy Randolph," she said after punching the blinking light.

"Prue, don't hang up—"

Very carefully, Prudy replaced the receiver in its cradle. With one broken phone to her credit already, she figured a little restraint was in order. Too bad hanging up softly wasn't as satisfying as slamming it down in Case's ear. As she turned back to Mrs. Yarnell, she forced a smile she hoped was brilliantly sweet but felt more like a snarl.

"Now...where was I?"

"Plastic bags," Mrs. Yarnell supplied helpfully. "How do I keep them from leaking at the top?"

"One of those large, wide rubber bands works nicely," Prudy told her. "Just make sure it isn't too tight. If you don't have a rubber band, you can fashion a tie from a strip of cloth." She slanted a glance at Ted, giving him a fond pat atop his head in farewell. "You're old enough to follow orders, right?"

Ted's response, an unenthusiastic "right," trailed after Prudy as she returned to her workstation.

"You're very popular this morning," Marge teased as Prudy circled her desk. Since seven that morning, when Prudy had come on duty, Case had been dialing the ER incessantly, and Marge had answered his calls three times.

"Hardly." Prudy grabbed her coffee mug from its place on the bottom shelf and filled it to the brim from the nearby pot that was rarely empty. Her first and *only* cup of the day. As the rich aroma of caffeine trailed to her nostrils, she half closed her eyes in blissful appreciation.

"Mmm, you haven't lost your touch, Margie girl. You still make the best cup of French roast this side of the continental divide."

"Whoever your caller is, he sure has a luscious voice," Marge commented.

"Gosh, this tastes *so-o-o* good!"

"Are we talkin' about the guy or the coffee?"

Prudy narrowed an eye. "Fish all you like. I'm not biting."

"I mean it, Prue. He's got a great voice. Like rich dark chocolate. *Melted* dark chocolate. The kind that makes love to your tongue."

"Chocolate makes me nauseated."

"Since when?" Marge's gaze dropped to Prudy's waist. "Oh," she said, then waved a hand. "Don't worry, honey. It passes."

Wishing she hadn't had to explain the drastic changes in

her life-style so quickly, Prudy blew the steam from the coffee's black surface before taking another cautious sip. At least no one had pressured her to reveal the name of her baby's father. Only Luke, the MacAuleys and Don Petrov knew that Case had fathered the child she was carrying—and they'd been sworn to secrecy. Everyone else could waste time on guessing and speculation. At the moment, Prudy didn't care. Unlike the dark ages before women's liberation when an unmarried woman expecting a baby was stigmatized, these days a woman was entitled to her privacy.

Still, no amount of social change could make *her* forget the name of the baby's daddy. Or ignore the turmoil he'd caused her. Was still causing.

Otherwise, things were going surprisingly well for a Monday morning. It was nearly eight, and so far, the shift had been surprisingly quiet. Since she'd taken over the watch, Teddy Yarnell had been their only patient.

Thank heavens for small favors, she thought as she managed another sip. Like just about everyone else she knew, she hated the rotation from night shift to day. It usually took a good four or five days for her system to adjust. So far, it hadn't even tried.

Marge completed the patient dismissal form on Teddy Yarnell and signed her name with her usual flourish. "So who is this mysterious hunk who's pursuing you with such stubborn dedication?" she asked as she slipped the form into the proper folder.

"That's no hunk." Prudy declared wearily. "That's my ex."

Marge glanced up and grinned. "Ah, the cop. That explains a lot."

"It does?"

"Absolutely." Marge's grin widened. "According to the nurses on six, he's got every one of them ready to brain him with the nearest bedpan, the old-fashioned, metal kind that would really make a dent."

Prudy felt a muscle at the corner of one eye twitch. "That sounds like Case."

"Of course, they also said he's just about the best-looking guy they've had on the floor in recent memory." Marge smacked her lips. "According to Amy Swenson—remember her, Miss Teen Portland a few years back?—he has a great body. Very *impressive,* if you get my drift. Even...intimidating."

"The former Miss Teen Portland needs to learn some professional discretion," Prudy retorted before she remembered she'd resolved to quash this disastrous "thing" she had for Case Randolph. "It's not acceptable to gossip about a patient," she added primly.

"Hmm."

"Don't 'hmm' me, Marge Malcolm. I'm just thinking about the integrity of our profession."

"Amy also said—"

"I'm not in the least interested in what Amy had to say."

"—that he has these magnificent shoulders. About as wide as the bed, and packed with hard muscle. You know, the kind that feels like warm steel when you run your hands over—"

"You've been reading romance novels again, haven't you?"

"Like you haven't?" Marge challenged, arching one sandy eyebrow.

"I'm too busy to—"

"Prudy!"

She whirled at the sound of Boyd's furious cry. "Lord, MacAuley, you don't have to shout!"

"You have to do something before I kill that crazy SOB," he grated, his hand plowing a set of furrows in his dusty blond hair.

Prudy didn't pretend to misunderstand. "Me? What can *I* do?"

Still scowling, he plucked the mug from her hands and drained it.

Prudy snatched the cup back. "Boyd!" she cried, gazing down at the dregs. "I can't believe you did that!"

"What?"

"You drank it!" She fixed an accusing gaze on him. "Approximately how many swallows did you take? It's important, Boyd. How many?''

An odd look came across his face. "Five, I think." He began to look a little green. "Why, what was in it?"

Prudy glanced at Marge. "What'd you think, Marge? About an ounce per swallow?"

"That's probably close," Marge agreed.

Prudy returned to the coffeepot, Boyd on her heels. She carefully poured herself what she estimated to be five ounces of coffee. Glancing up at Boyd, she said, "Lay a lip on this cup, MacAuley, and you're dead."

Sudden understanding came into his eyes. "For God's sake, Prue. How can you be worrying about a thing like your daily ration of coffee when—"

Prudy elbowed her way past him. "Easy for you to say. You're not on a one-cup-a-day limit."

"He's got the entire sixth floor in an uproar, Prue," Boyd said from behind her. "Are you listening to me?"

"Don't bother me right now. I'm on coffee break."

"Prudy, this is—"

"My only coffee break of the day," she finished for him, bending down to fish around on the bottom shelf of her desk again. "Marge, did you take my koshers?"

Just as she spoke, Prudy located the fat jar she'd been seeking. She plopped it on top of her desk and strained to unscrew the lid.

"Here, let me." Boyd gave the yellow cap an easy twist, then stepped back.

Prudy dove a forefinger into the juice, hooked a gigantic pickle and dragged it to the mouth of the jar. She sighed with contentment as she sank her teeth into brine-soaked cucumber. Boyd watched her chew with equal parts abhorrence and male fascination, his eyes widening slightly when she chased the vinegar with a big swallow of coffee and said, "Sheer ambrosia."

Her craving slightly appeased, Prudy managed to smile. "Now...where were we?"

"We were talking about the total havoc a certain Case Randolph is causing on the sixth floor," Boyd reminded her.

"Oh, that." Prudy stuck the remaining half of the pickle into her mouth, then went fishing in the still-uncapped jar for another. "Care for one?" she managed to say with some semblance of clarity as she munched. "I have another jar of them in my locker. Help yourself."

"No, thanks." Boyd raked a hand through his hair again, his expression vague. "Prudy, help me out here, okay? The guy's being impossible."

She swallowed, sipped, took another bite and, between crunches, said, "What can I do?"

"You might take his damned phone calls instead of hanging up, that's what you can do."

"No."

"Why the hell not?"

Prudy shifted her gaze from the deep-set gray eyes probing hers and concentrated instead on the jagged frown lines permanently etched between his thick, tawny eyebrows.

"None of your business."

"Okay, I admit it. I'm desperate. Name your price. Anything within reason, of course. How about a case of kosher dill pickles?"

She set her mug on the desk with a decisive thump. "I can afford to buy my own, thanks."

"Come on, Prue."

"Boyd—"

"I'll shovel your snow and cut your grass for a solid year, plus I'll even prune the hedge between us."

"You keep your hands off my hedge," she muttered around a mouthful of pickle, horrified at the very idea. Boyd's idea of pruning was to shave her poor bushes to within a paltry few feet of the ground.

He narrowed his gaze, but not fast enough to hide the sudden calculating glint. "It's a deal. I'll stay away from your precious hedge and you'll come with me to the sixth floor."

Prudy heard Marge choke on a laugh and shot her a warning scowl before returning her attention to Boyd's face.

"It's not a deal. Besides," she said, gesturing with her pickle, "I'm busy."

Boyd lifted one eyebrow before taking a long, slow look around. The hall was empty, eight curtains pulled back to reveal eight empty treatment cubicles. The radio was deathly silent. Prudy decided she would give a major chunk of her savings to hear a siren right about now.

"He's got you there, Prue," Marge chortled.

"I give up." Prudy muttered, stalking toward the elevator. Behind her, she heard Boyd chuckle. But when she whirled around, his expression was stone-cold sober.

"I'm giving you fair warning, MacAuley," Prudy said firmly as they stepped off the elevator onto the sixth floor. "I expect you to wash my car once a month in addition to all the other things you've promised."

Boyd gave her a startled look as he sidestepped a stray wheelchair. "No way. My part of the deal consists of promising to stay away from your hedge."

Prudy stopped dead in the middle of the wide corridor and would have turned back to the elevator if Boyd hadn't grabbed her arm.

"All those years living next door to you and I never realized how cold and calculating you really are," he groused.

"That's me, cold and calculating Prue, and don't you forget it."

Boyd's sigh was heavy and shaded toward long-suffering. Prudy refused to soften. The last thing she wanted to do was walk into Case's room, but since she was committed, she wanted to milk as much out of the ordeal as she could.

"Gray Lady really could use a bath," she wheedled.

Before Boyd could reply, a woman's shrill shriek drifted along the hall to them. Both Prudy and Boyd froze as a tall, willowy blonde bolted from room six-twelve, a digital thermometer in her hand and a look of fury on her pretty face.

"That's the last straw, Doctor!" she exclaimed when she spied Boyd and Prudy staring at her. "That man's impossible.

He can burn to a crisp with fever before I'll go back in that room again.''

Boyd shut his eyes on a self-pitying groan. "What's he done this time?"

Clearly shaken, the nurse drew a harsh breath, her turquoise eyes wide with alarm. "He almost slugged me!"

"He did what?" Prudy and Boyd burst out simultaneously.

Amy looked from one to the other. "All I did was walk into the room to take his temperature, and he practically came off the bed. I thought sure he was going to hit me."

"Did you wake him up?" Prudy asked.

The nurse shrugged. "Maybe." She considered for a moment. "Yeah, I guess maybe I did. But, so? He shouldn't have reacted like that."

Prudy and Boyd exchanged looks.

"Amy, Sergeant Randolph's been a policeman for a long time," Boyd said gently. "In that line of work, men learn to sleep with one eye open, so to speak, and come up swinging at anything they perceive as a threat. The sergeant lives alone. He's not accustomed to strangers slipping into his room."

Amy blinked her long, perfectly mascaraed eyelashes. "All I wanted to do was take his temp." She held up the thermometer as though to prove her point. "Geez, give me a break."

"You probably just startled him," Prudy told her with a smile. "When we were first married, I used to wake him up by poking the bottom of his foot with a broomstick." She rested a hand on the young nurse's arm. "I'll bet you touched him, didn't you?"

"Well, yes. Just on the shoulder to wake him up, though."

Prudy chuckled, imagining how Case must have reacted. She gave Amy a comforting pat. "Trust me, he wouldn't have actually hit you. Another commonality with veteran cops is that they come instantly awake. He would have drawn back before he connected."

Amy rolled her lovely eyes. "Easy for you to say. It wasn't your face that nearly got cozy with that fist of his." Despite the sarcasm, she finally smiled, looking somewhat mollified. "I guess next time I could call out from the door."

"And try not to touch him," Prudy advised. Case didn't like to be touched, awake or asleep—unless, of course, he happened to be making love. And then he tended to purr like a pampered jungle cat.

"Why don't I take his temp for you this time?" Boyd suggested with a lopsided grin that Prudy suspected few women knew how to resist. Judging by the dazed look on Amy's face, his status as PortGen's sexiest resident was still intact—in spite of his well-known devotion to his bride.

After taking the thermometer, Boyd watched Amy walk away, then turned to Prudy. "Here," he said, thrusting the digital instrument into her hand.

"Coward."

"You got that right."

Case seemed to be asleep when they reached the open doorway of his room. His black hair was unbound and mussed, the hard angles of his face taut and pale beneath the bronze. Under the crisp sheet, his broad chest rose and fell in a steady rhythm.

Prudy couldn't help but notice that his shoulders were bare. In contrast to his bronzed skin, the cast stretching from his knuckles to his elbow was startlingly white. A fast scan of the room revealed a faded blue hospital gown lying in a heap on the floor near the far wall.

Finding his determinedly rebellious patient looking so tranquil had Boyd raising both eyebrows in disbelief. Prudy sighed. Instantly, Case opened his eyes and glared at them. As soon as his gaze meshed with Prudy's, his face went from a pasty white to a dusky red.

"If you're going to shout at me, I'm leaving," she warned before he could speak.

His mouth relaxed into that beguilingly crooked grin she used to adore. "Okay."

Prudy eyed him warily. Even with one leg and one arm out of commission, he was far from helpless, which only increased the feeling of vulnerability that inevitably came over her whenever he was near.

"I mean it, Case," she warned.

"I believe you." His voice was husky and disarmingly calm. Prudy refused to be reassured. Like the big cat he resembled, Case was always more dangerous when he was silently stalking his prey.

From the corner of her eye, she caught Boyd's slow grin a split second before he leaned close to whisper into her ear, "Why didn't you tell me you were a lion tamer in a former life?"

In answer, she jabbed him in the ribs with her elbow, and he laughed. "No low blows, you two," he said before beating a hasty retreat.

Prudy drew in a bracing breath before advancing toward the bed. With each step she was conscious of the brooding intensity smoldering in Case's disarmingly blue eyes. She stopped a few steps beyond the reach of those long, muscular arms and schooled her features to calm.

"You're pissed," he said in that same soft tone.

She gave a most unladylike snort. "What was your first clue, Sherlock?"

His expression turned sheepish, and she felt a fast little tug on her heart. "I didn't mean to come on so strong the other morning, but I was worried about you."

But not too worried to resist a dig about her past sins, she reminded herself firmly. "As you can see, I'm perfectly fit."

"I'll say." His eyes took on a teasing glint as his gaze ambled lazily up one side of her body and down the other, lingering a beat too long on her breasts. "Although I'd be happier if you'd lose the smock. You have the prettiest breasts in the whole damn place."

She should have figured he hadn't been too sick to check out the other nurses. "Don't bother to flirt with me, Case. I'm not here on a social call."

Using his good hand, he pushed himself a little higher on the pillow. Though the strain that whisked across his face was fleeting, Prudy knew that his injured leg had to be hurting very badly in spite of the megadoses of painkiller she was sure Boyd had prescribed.

"Come over here where I can see you better," he urged, suddenly looking as innocent as a boy in Sunday school.

"You can see me just fine."

"C'mon, Prue. I won't bite."

She heard the challenge in his voice and knew she'd been boxed in by a master. If she stayed put now, she'd be admitting she was afraid of getting closer. Cool and distant, she counseled herself silently. Completely detached.

"I've been delegated by a goodly number of my fellow staff members to have a serious talk with you about your outrageous behavior," she said as she moved to the side of the bed. Unfortunately, she was on his left side, which meant that his hand was free to capture hers.

She tried to jerk free, only to have his strong fingers tighten just enough to show her the futility of struggling.

"Outrageous?" he asked with an appalling innocence so transparent she wanted to laugh. Determined not to be charmed, she frowned instead.

"I know you're uncomfortable, but—"

"Uncomfortable, hell! My thigh hurts like a son of a bitch, and I can't even get out of bed to relieve myself in private."

He sounded so disgusted she nearly laughed, so she was surprised to feel the sting of tears in her eyes.

"Case, it's only for a few weeks, and then they'll put that leg in a cast and send you home on crutches."

"Twelve days," he corrected.

"Okay, twelve days, which will pass much faster if you remain calm."

"I'm calm, dammit! Or I would be, if everyone would just leave me the hell alone. Every time I open my eyes someone's poking a thermometer in my ear or slapping a blood pressure cuff on my arm. Not to mention coming in every few hours to dump that...thing." He jerked his head toward the plastic urine bottle that had replaced bedpans for men some years back. "I might as well sell tickets."

Prudy felt her lips twitch and reminded herself to remain detached and professional. After all, she was still on duty. And although Marge was fully capable of handling things in her absence, she felt guilty about leaving the floor, even for a short time.

"Okay, I'll make you a deal," she proposed in her best nurse-to-troublesome-patient voice. "You promise not to behave like a half-tamed savage every time someone comes near you, and I'll get the people on the floor to promise not to bother you unless absolutely necessary. How's that?"

He shook his head. "I have a better idea."

Prudy stifled a sigh. The man could make a fortune in Vegas at the high-stakes poker tables. "Why do I think I don't want to hear this?" she said to the ceiling.

Case tugged her closer, until her hip was jammed against the mattress. "You're a great nurse. The best."

Prudy refused to be pleased by the throb of sincerity in his tone. Case was up to something. She decided to hurry him along before the hard fingers sliding up her arm reached a more sensitive spot.

"I don't have a lot of time here, Case, so I'd appreciate it if you'd skip the flattery and lay out the bottom line." Once again, she tried to pull away, only to have his fingers squeeze gently into her upper arm. In spite of the cotton sleeve separating skin from skin, her flesh tingled at his touch.

"You could take care of me, like you did when we first met, remember? When I ripped open my shoulder?" His grin flashed, slicing a shallow dimple in one cheek. She'd licked that dimple once, with her tongue. Like Case, the taste of his skin was spicy, sending heat into her blood.

The sensuous look in his eyes urged her to surrender. She didn't dare. Her emotions were already in a mess. "I can't, Case," she said briskly. "We're short-staffed in the ER as it is."

His mouth firmed. Case had never been one to accept "no" without a fight. "What happens if you get sick? Or go on vacation?"

Prudy felt the jaws of a trap poised to close. On her. "Someone covers for me, but—"

"Boyd could arrange it."

That's it! she thought, dropping her gaze to hide her eyes from that too-sharp gaze. Her way out. All Boyd had to do was to tell Case it wasn't possible to juggle an already complicated staffing schedule. And Boyd did owe her.

"Oh, all right, I'll ask him," she conceded with a feigned reluctance, "but if he can't arrange it, promise me you'll be a good boy, anyway."

His fingers slipped to the nape of her neck, drawing her closer. She told herself to resist, then realized she'd lost the edge she needed to remove herself to safety.

"On one condition." His voice was still soft, but the calm had been replaced by a steely throb of command.

"No conditions."

"Kiss me goodbye."

Prudy sighed, pretending boredom while her pulse rocketed. "If I must," she muttered before bending quickly to plant a dry peck on his forehead.

"Very funny, honey," he grated before arching upward. At the same moment, he drew her head closer until his mouth smothered hers. His lips were hard, demanding, his hand iron, holding her still.

In spite of his awkward position and the trauma of the past few days, his eagerness was all but palpable, his hunger alive, his kiss wielding a power she was helpless to resist.

She felt the breath dam in her throat as she braced both hands on his rock-hard shoulders. He answered with a low growl, his body shuddering. His tongue was insistent, urging her lips to part.

She sighed and opened for him. His tongue slipped into her mouth, and swirled, tasting and tempting. She felt her knees wobbling and her head swimming.

He ended the kiss too soon. Yet both were breathing hard. A dark flush rode on the high hard rise of his cheekbones, and his eyes sizzled with sexual heat.

"See you later, love," he said, his voice thick and strained.

Prudy drew back, her lips still tingling and her blood pumping. "Don't hold your breath," she muttered, her voice far too faint. She felt dazed. She turned and all but ran from the room.

Chapter 10

"**D**on't even think about gloating!" Prudy ordered when she swept into Case's room at seven the next morning. She'd been up since five, fuming. Though the morning sickness was easing its vicious hold, her stomach was still iffy and not yet ready to handle her one cup of coffee. Consequently, she was grouchy and hungry and more than ready to do battle.

Case was lying with his good arm crooked behind his head and his casted arm resting on his chest. Eyes closed, his ruggedly planed face in repose, he looked deceptively like a well-behaved archangel, albeit a particularly masculine, seasoned one, but Prudy wasn't fooled. Even at rest, Case was more devil than saint.

Though his eyes were closed, some inner sense, developed during their marriage, told her he wasn't sleeping. She was proved right the instant his thick black lashes lifted and his straight white teeth flashed in a mischievous smile. Not a trace of drowsiness clouded those piercing dark blue eyes.

It didn't take much for her to read his thoughts.

He'd won, the rat. For the next eleven days, she was to be Case's "special," a slang term amongst the hospital staff for a nurse assigned solely to the care of one patient. VIP treatment. Usually such specialized care was reserved for only the extremely wealthy, people who could afford the exorbitant cost, or for political figures whose importance in the community demanded security safeguards. Begrudgingly, Prudy supposed Case fit nicely into the latter category.

Regardless, it had all been arranged. And far too easily, to her way of thinking. There were a number of qualified nurses who could have been assigned the "spec" duty. But, oh, no, Case had specifically requested Prudence Randolph, and Nursing Supervisor Gloria Fister had fallen all over herself granting his request.

Nor had Boyd helped. No, he'd gone on and on about Case's need for tranquility and peace of mind. The last thing they needed was for Portland's latest media hero to suffer a stroke because his blood pressure shot into the red zone.

Not that Prudy held the nursing supervisor or Boyd completely responsible for the impossible position she found herself in. Oh, no, she blamed the real culprit—the impossible man who was now watching her stalk toward him. Though she kept her glaring gaze trained directly on his face, she was acutely aware he still wore no hospital gown—which meant he was completely nude under that sheet. Broad, darkly bronzed shoulders eclipsed the pillow upon which they rested. Darkly tanned arms rippled with strength every time he moved.

"Good morning, sweets," he said in that slow, purring voice that always sent a thrill running through her. "You're looking particularly saucy this morning."

Prudy felt a blush spreading over her already warm cheeks, a hot, searing sensation that made her want to accidentally knock over his pitcher of ice water directly onto his lap.

"I hope you're proud of yourself, Casey Grant Randolph."

His cheek dimpled at her use of his full name. He looked so roguishly sexy, damn him. Even though she was determined to resist that rough masculine charm he wielded like a particularly lethal weapon, she felt herself weakening.

"Ah, honey, don't be mad at me. I'm in pain, remember. And a man in pain can't be held accountable for his actions."

"Bull!" she scoffed, stalking to the chart affixed to the wall.

"True story. My leg hurts like the very devil whenever I move."

"Then don't move, you idiot," she ordered over her shoulder.

He'd had a restless night, she discovered after a frustrating few seconds deciphering the night nurse's handwriting. His BP was still hovering at one fifty over a hundred, far too high. His temp was also holding at two degrees above normal. Boyd had prescribed a course of antibiotics. He'd also asked Anderson in physical therapy to come up with an isometrics routine to keep Case's body in good shape. But first came the daily routine.

Oh, yes, like all hospitals, PortGen was fanatical about routine—and meticulous patient hygiene. Prudy felt a stab of delicious anticipation. No one could fault her for following that routine to the letter.

"Well, now," she said, turning in Case's direction. "Let's get started."

The lazy glint of amusement in his eyes disappeared, replaced by a wary curiosity. At the same time he went still, like a predator catching the scent of approaching danger.

"What are you proposing we get started with, love?"

Even as she allowed her lips to curve into an evil grin, she couldn't help wishing he meant the endearment that came so easily to his hard lips.

"At the moment I intend to shave you, Sergeant. With a safety razor. So I suggest you keep very, very still."

Two hours later Case was in acute pain. A man neatly netted by his own trap. He'd wanted Prudy within touching distance—and she was. Only she was the one doing all the touching. His face and neck when she'd shaved him, his uninjured hand and leg when she'd put him through an entire series of resistance exercises. And now his chest and shoulders as she bathed him. With each slow, sensuous brush of her hand, each graceful movement of her body as she bent and turned, she was slowly, deliberately turning him into a frustrated collection of tortured nerve endings.

It infuriated him to realize how vulnerable he was to a scatterbrained, willfully obstinate, completely unpredictable slip of a woman who was a head shorter than him and tipped the scales at barely half his weight.

Until a few short weeks ago, he'd been damn proud of the way he'd been handling their divorce. Sure, it'd taken him a couple of years to talk himself out of missing the chaos and confusion she'd created in his life. No more bruised shins from tripping over furniture she'd moved without telling him. No more walls painted in blinding psychedelic colors that clashed with everything else in a room. No more spur of the moment activities. No more half-finished hobby projects strung from here to Christmas throughout the house. No more evenings spent helping her work on said hobbies. No more ''gourmet'' dinners that looked like part of her wild decorating schemes and settled on his stomach like clinically concocted acid. Living a normal life had seemed a little tame at first, he had to admit, and it had taken some readjustments in his thinking to be satisfied with day-in and day-out sanity. But he'd done it.

After that, it had only taken him a few more years to convince himself he'd stopped loving her. But he'd managed that, as well.

He'd even had a couple of long-term relationships with other women. Cool, elegant blondes, both of them. Nice ladies who never challenged him, never sent him into a fury with convoluted logic or wore him out with emotional fire storms, and never thumbed their noses at normality. His life was exactly the way he liked it—predictable, controlled and blandly color coordinated. He hadn't come home to a newly painted purple or red front door in eight years, and he *liked* it that way, dammit.

So why the hell couldn't he learn to control the raw need that burst inside him whenever Prudy was around? Was he out of his mind? He was a changed man—permanently cured of his addiction to her brand of wonderfully sweet insanity.

Why, he'd even taken some self-improvement courses. Hadn't he managed to get a firm hold on his explosive temper? The worst of it, anyway. Hadn't he purged himself of his stupidly adolescent craving for parental approval? Damn straight.

He was nearing middle-age, for Pete's sake. He was a seasoned veteran cop who'd been known to bring down perps with a threatening glare. He'd managed to wrestle his life into a rigid, well-ordered structure that might strike some people as dead boring, but he *preferred* it that way. He wasn't going to jeopardize everything he'd sweated blood and spent a thousand sleepless nights to attain by responding to the irresistible pleasure of feeling her hands brushing over his skin. Damn him for a fool if he did.

"Stop complaining, Case," she chided when a low groan slipped past his tight throat. "I'm not hurting you."

No, she was only *killing* him, he thought with a scowl. If he got any harder, he was going to burst. And Prudy, the vindictive little vixen, knew exactly what she was doing to him with each slow, sinuous brush of those clever little hands.

"Enough," he grated when she reached for the sheet bunched just below his navel.

"Now, Case, the hygiene handbook states that patients confined to bed be given a daily sponge bath. A *complete* sponge bath, which means head to toe—and everything in the middle. I'm only half-done."

He saw the laughter in her lively brown eyes and wanted to throttle her.

Almost as much as he wanted to strip her out of those baggy white slacks and haul her on top of him.

Another groan slipped past his control as he thought about her taking him deep into the hot, moist sheath nestled in the wild red curls between her silky legs.

On an oath he'd meant to be silent, he clamped his hand around her wrist and jerked her toward him. Taken by surprise, she landed on top of him, her breasts crushed against his chest and her chin digging into his sternum. She gave a muffled squeak of protest before trying to scramble backward.

"Oh, no, you don't," he grated, his voice thick, the needs of his body driving him perilously close to the edge of his control. "When you play, you pay."

Prudy heard the silken threat in Case's voice and realized she'd teased the tiger long enough.

"You set the rules of this game," she said as she braced the palm of her right hand against the mattress and pushed.

"No holds barred," he countered before somehow managing to ease her upward until his mouth was only a tiny dip of her head away from his. So close, close enough to feel the warmth of his breath on her face.

"Case, no," she whispered, her pulse leaping in her throat.

His mouth edged slowly upward at the corners, erasing a fair number of hard years from his face. "You wanted to seduce me. I've decided to let you."

She was so busy reacting with a flurry of wildly conflicting emotions she lost whatever small chance to protest he might have given her. His mouth found hers, his lips coaxing as they brushed back and forth over hers. At the precise instant when she felt herself yielding to a blissful sigh, his mouth moved on, trailing tiny kisses along the curve of her neck.

The pleasure was so sweet she wanted to melt into him, yet she knew she had to resist. Case was a marvelously giving lover, his kisses as sweetly adoring as they were arousing. But when the pleasure was spent and he was sated, he would still consider her a liar. A woman who'd deceived him. A woman he'd divorced. And forgotten.

"No," she said again, wedging her hands between them in order to push herself away. Yet somehow, surprisingly, she found herself sliding her hands over those firm, rippling shoulders to link her fingers behind his neck. His skin was warm and vibrant against her palms while the soft silk of his hair caressed the backs of her knuckles.

"Case, we have to stop," she managed to get out between clinging kisses.

Case struggled to control the wild flare of need arcing deep inside him as he lifted his mouth from hers long enough to demand, "Why?"

Between teasing kisses, Prudy struggled to remember why she had to resist him. Why she needed so desperately to guard her heart from him.

"Because you hate me," she whispered, too bemused to hold back.

"Once, maybe. A long time ago," he admitted before his tongue slipped between her parted lips to torment her for a long, sweet moment. Submerged in a sudden flood of pleasure, she struggled to resist, even as his left hand was smoothing down her back with long, caressing strokes. The longing to love him was building too swiftly, pulling her closer to a dangerous precipice. Loving wasn't supposed to hurt so terribly or cause such an agonizing fall.

A sudden panic broke through the lovely haze, as real as the sharp, medicinal smell clinging to the pillowcase beneath his head. With a choked protest, she jerked backward, only to have him tighten his hold. At the same time, he bit off a harsh cry, then followed that with a colorful obscenity.

This time, when Prudy jerked away, he didn't try to stop her. His eyes were closed, his lips compressed in a harsh, bloodless line. The hand that had been stroking her back was now clutching his thigh. Sweat dampened his face from his ragged hairline to his freshly shaved jaw.

"Take deep breaths," she urged softly, but firmly. "Don't fight the pain. Let it wash over you."

Silently berating herself for her unprofessional behavior, she lifted a hand and gently stroked his hair away from his face. Beneath the slick layer of sweat, the bronzed skin stretched taut over his strong, angular bones was hot to the touch.

"Damn, I hate this," he grated through a tight jaw. "I finally have you where I want you and my leg starts giving me fits."

"You need time to heal," she soothed, her voice still slightly strained from the passion only now ebbing. "And you need to rest, a four-letter word meaning you should stop scowling and behave yourself, in case you don't recognize it."

He glared at her through half-closed lids, but his mouth relaxed slightly. "Didn't your mother ever tell you what happens to little girls who sass their elders?" he grumbled, his voice tight.

"Shh," she murmured, stroking his face with the back of her hand.

"Feels nice," he mumbled, his thick blunt lashes quivering with the attempt he was making to fight off his body's need for healing sleep. Gradually, however, he gave in, and his eyes closed.

His breathing slowed, becoming quieter. Deeper.

Prudy let out a breath and flexed her shoulders in an attempt to work out the stinging tightness in her neck. Lord, but she was tired, and the day wasn't even half-gone. How was she ever going to manage ten more days with Case without losing the hard-won emotional distance she needed to protect herself from the man?

How could she resist him when all of her deepest yearnings and long-buried dreams were urging her toward him?

Shifting, she let her gaze trail over the sharply defined profile she loved to the massive proportions of his bronzed chest. Even at rest, his muscles bespoke the awesome power of the man, while the softly curling black hair furring his pecs hinted at a bewitching vulnerability.

Though she knew the risk she was taking emotionally, she let her gaze follow the virile thatch of hair to the spot on his flat midriff where the inky thickness narrowed to a wavering line before flaring at his taut navel.

His body was still partially aroused, forming a provocative bulge beneath the sheet. His body's way of calling to hers. It had always been that way with them. Sexually, they had been flint and spark.

Another few moments, a few more drugging kisses from his hard, clever mouth and she would have willingly surrendered to the pleasure he could give her.

Her face softened into a smile as she thought about the precious life growing within her, created by that special magic she and Case had made the last time they'd made love. Out of a rare and wonderful burst of mutual pleasure, they'd made a miracle.

A baby.

A mysterious blend of the two of them. A connection that could never be severed.

Their child.

Tears flooded her eyes, and her smile faded. She had to tell him. And soon. But dear God, where was she ever going to find the courage?

Case was a desperately sick man for the next forty-eight hours. The low-grade fever he'd been running since his surgery spiked to a dangerous high, making him acutely uncomfortable at first, and then spiraling him in and out of a restless sleep.

His wound had become infected, a not-unusual complication of gunshot trauma. Eventually the antibiotics Boyd had prescribed would kill off the infection. While the drugs were doing their job, however, Case was subjected to bouts of chills so severe his teeth chattered uncontrollably. When he wasn't shivering, he was burning up, his skin scorchingly hot, his body sweating so profusely Prudy was kept busy changing his bed linen.

She was just smoothing another fresh sheet over his chest when he opened his eyes and stared at her, his expression drowsy.

"Prue?" His voice was no more than a harsh whisper, tearing at her. Even flat on his back, unable to move more than a few inches without flaring pain, Case projected an aura of invincibility and power. Prudy knew better. At the moment, he wasn't strong enough to lift anything heavier than air.

"I'm here, Case," she said quietly, easing the sheet to his stubborn chin.

He'd always been an intensely private man. Finding himself totally vulnerable with damn near everything—including each breath he took—being monitored by strangers had him in a state of black fury. Only when Prudy was near did he submit to the poking and prodding of the other nurses and techs.

"Stay with me." His gaze was fever-bright, a flash of brilliant light in the blackest night.

"I'll stay." His hand groped for hers, his fingers lean and strong as they laced with hers. She waited until his lashes settled like stark black shadows on his cheeks before she dropped into the chair next to his bed.

The shift changed, and someone brought her a sandwich and a cup of soup, which she ate with her left hand because she couldn't bear to separate her right from his warm grasp.

Boyd was tireless in his determination to make sure Case was given the very best care PortGen could offer. Whenever he had a free moment, he dropped by to give Case a reassuring word.

Toward evening of the second day after the fever's grip had taken hold, Boyd appeared again to check his patient and consult with the nurses. Still in scrubs, dark blue this time, he looked tired and worried, yet somehow managed a reassuring grin when Prudy lifted her head from the mattress where she'd laid it for only a moment.

A quick glance at the readout on the freestanding monitoring device had him grinning. "One-oh-three," he said with a quiet note of satisfaction. "Down three quarters of a degree, and his BP's edging lower."

Prudy felt relief shimmer through her tired muscles. "He's been quieter this afternoon. I think he's past the worst of it."

"And how about Prudy? How's she doing?"

She shrugged, then winced as a muscle in her neck protested.

"Sit forward a minute," Boyd ordered as he stepped behind her. His hands were fully as big as Case's and made as powerful by Boyd's years as a carpenter. They were also wonderfully talented, she realized, sighing with pleasure as his fingers gently worked out the knots in her shoulders.

"Stace said you haven't been home for two days," he said quietly.

"I'm fine." She let her lashes drift closed. Her body craved sleep, but her mind wouldn't release control.

"Women," Boyd muttered as he rotated his thumbs to unravel the last of a stubborn knot. "I'm heading home in about twenty minutes. I want you to come with me."

"I would only worry myself sick at home."

Boyd sighed. "I'm beginning to regret letting you be assigned to him, you know. I guess I wasn't thinking." He broke off, and silence settled. "You always blustered so whenever his name was mentioned. I didn't realize you still—"

"I don't," Prudy cut in. "Not that way. It's just—" Pain welled in her heart. "For old time's sake, you know? I loved him once. It's hard to see him like this."

"I think it must be more than that. Your assignment demands you put in one shift per day. You've been staying here around the clock."

"He doesn't thrash around so much when I'm here."

"Prue, you've got to take better care of yourself now. As you know very well, my stubborn friend." She heard a tired burr of frustration in his tone and smiled.

"I'll take a break, just as soon as he's out of danger."

Boyd's sigh was heavy. "I'm his doctor, Prue, and I'm officially informing you that our patient is on the mend." He leaned forward until his head was close to hers. "Or don't you believe me?"

"I'll have a cot brought in so I can stretch out," she compromised. "Will that get you off my back?"

"A cot? Prue, you need—"

"Get your hands off my wife, MacAuley, or you'll be doing surgery bending over." Case's voice was raspy and weak, and his eyes had the unfocused look of a man who wasn't quite tracking. Nevertheless, Prudy sensed danger. Before she could reassure him, however, his eyes closed again. But the scowl on his face remained, a silent warning from a healthy male animal to a perceived rival.

"Well, what do you know?" Boyd marveled with a chuckle. "Big tough cop's still hooked on his ex-wife."

Prudy allowed herself a precious moment of hope before shaking her head. "No, he's hooked on sex. There's a difference."

"Don't kid yourself, Prue," Boyd said as he gave her shoulders a final squeeze. "A man in serious pain doesn't have a lot of energy to devote to anything but the basics."

"Like surviving." She let her gaze rest on that hard scowl. It was impossible not to remember the feel of his mouth on hers. Impossible not to long to experience that incredible feeling again.

"Yes, like surviving," Boyd said with gruff gentleness. "And love."

Prudy blinked, then swiveled her head in his direction. "I must be having an auditory hallucination here, because I thought I heard my cynical friend, Boyd MacAuley, mention the L-word without blanching."

"Very funny," he muttered, his face turning a dull red.

"Actually, it's just about the nicest surprise I've had in a long time." She reached out to touch his strong arm with her fingertips. "If anyone deserved to fall gloriously, wonderfully in love, it's you."

Boyd looked startled—and endearingly shy—as he nodded once, then all but jogged out of the room. Once in the hall, he swung back to poke his head back through the doorway and level a finger at her.

"A cot, stat. And you've got to promise me you'll use it."

Prudy smiled wearily. "Scout's honor, Doc."

As Boyd trotted away out of her line of sight, Prudy's smile vanished. Fortunately, she'd never been a scout. Contrary to Case's opinion of her, she didn't take well to lying, and the truth was, she wouldn't be able to rest until Case's temperature dove a couple more degrees. Then—and only then—could she be sure he was out of the woods. A woman couldn't sleep when the one man in the world whose existence made her life worth living was hovering in a danger zone.

Chapter 11

Don Petrov prowled Case's hospital room, his frown nearly as black as the thunderclouds gathering outside. It wasn't quite 6:30 a.m. Case had been up since five.

Already restless and bored by six, he'd been damn pleased to see his partner walk in. One look at Don's worried eyes, however, and he'd known this wasn't a social call. According to one of Petrov's snitches, Arturo Cardoza was mouthing off big time, threatening Case with everything from emasculation to cement boots.

Case had enough experience with whacked-out junkies to know how empty those threats usually were. To his surprise, however, Petrov seemed to be taking them seriously—very seriously. Case bit off a sigh and waited for his partner to work through the worst of his frustration.

On a scale of one to ten, Case rated the way he felt at about a two—lousy, in other words—but at least his head was clear again, most of the feverish haze gone with only a nagging headache lingering in its wake. Like most things in his life, however, the return of his senses was a mixed blessing. On the one hand, his thoughts were his own again. On the other, those thoughts were pushing him close to a dangerous edge.

Every instinct he possessed told him he'd be a fool to get hung up on Prudy again. A gold-plated sucker, that was him. Or maybe he was one of those stupid chumps who got off on dodging bullets, in this case the nine-millimeter, emotional variety—high-grained, hollow point slugs in a compact, streamlined casing, guaranteed to fragment upon impact and rip his heart to shreds.

"Dammit, Don, will you settle in one spot? You're giving me a headache with all that stomping."

Petrov stopped dead and glared his way. "Fine. You agree to let me put a man on the door and I'll stop stomping."

Case ground his teeth. "It must be the water in this place," he muttered. "Damn near everyone who comes in here is set on arguing with me."

Petrov ran a ham-sized hand through his wiry hair, his lower lip already pushing out. "Did it ever occur to you that you might be the problem?"

"The hell I am!" It had been a mistake to shout, he realized, as a violent pain in his leg stole his breath.

Petrov turned white, his gaze darting to the open door as though searching for help—or escape. "Hold on, I'll get a nurse."

"Forget it," Case ordered, still heaving for breath.

"Case, I know you have this little problem accepting help but—"

"Bull!"

"Dammit, Case, it's no crime to be sick."

"I'm not sick, and I don't want to hear another word about my lousy, stinking blood pressure. I keep telling MacAuley that hospitals always get me riled up, but he just grins and tells me to relax." He snorted. "Relax, hell. This place is worse than the squad room."

Petrov let out a windy sigh, then shrugged and dropped into the chair where Prudy usually sat. "So how's 'Little Red'?"

"Bossy."

Petrov chuckled. "'Bout time she got a little of her own

back on you.'' The amusement in his eyes faded. "Have you two patched up your differences, or are you still being a stubborn jackass?''

Case narrowed his gaze. "My relationship with my ex-wife is off-limits, even to you.''

"Don't ask me why, but she's still crazy about you. Me, I'd be walking on air if I had a sweet lady like that mooning over my body.''

Case snorted. "You run like hell the minute a woman gets that 'picking the date' look in her eyes.''

Instead of shooting Case the grin he expected, Petrov frowned down at the big hands splayed on his thighs. "Maybe that's because I'm still in love with the one I let get away.''

It took a hefty slug of surprise to jar Case into total silence. But, for a moment, he couldn't think of a thing to say. Petrov glanced up, his eyes clouded.

"You remember that summer I busted you?''

"I have a vague memory of it, yeah,'' Case drawled, his tongue firmly in his cheek.

"I busted someone else that summer, too. For soliciting tourists on the Embarcadero. She was older than you by a half dozen years or so, a flower child from Kansas down on her luck.'' He paused, apparently lost in thoughts of the past. Several moments passed in silence until, finally, he sighed heavily and began to speak again.

"She was about Prudy's size, with about two feet of curly black hair and big brown eyes that pleaded with me to let her go.''

"Did you?''

Petrov shook his head, his jaw tight. "Couldn't, even if I'd wanted to. She'd made the mistake of coming on to the mayor's brother-in-law.''

"Ouch.''

"Yeah.'' Petrov's grin was brief and devoid of humor. "She had a clean record, and a lawyer friend of mine got her off with a suspended sentence. I kept tabs on her, helped her get a job as a waitress.''

Case thought about all the times Petrov had showed up at

Chino, determined to befriend a scared kid with a belly full of hate and a determination never to trust anyone again.

It had taken Don months to hack away at the giant boulder firmly settled on sixteen-year-old Case Randolph's shoulder. There'd been no preaching, no blame. No lies. Just a steady friendship and a quiet belief in a kid everyone else had written off.

"What happened?" Case asked when Don remained silent.

"We lived together most of that year." Don rubbed his callused fingers over a wrinkle in his rumpled gabardine slacks, then slowly made a fist. "I bought a ring. Nothing real fancy, you understand—not on the kind of money I was making then. Found it in a little antique shop on Montgomery."

"She turned you down?"

"I never asked her."

"Scared?"

Petrov shook his head. "Stupid."

Two nurses passed the door, laughing softly at a joke only they knew. Petrov glanced their way, then sighed. "One night, while my partner and I were patrolling Market, I saw her crossing in front of us about two a.m. with a man I didn't know. A well-dressed dude, like one of those slick young brokers on Montgomery. I'm ashamed to say I lost it. Reamed her out right then and there. Turns out the guy was her brother from Topeka, trying to talk her into going home to Kansas."

"She was pissed?"

"No, I could have handled that. But she just accepted my apology with this funny little smile and told me she understood. It was only later, when I got home and found her packing, that she told me she couldn't love a man who didn't trust her."

Petrov got to his feet slowly, like an old man with aching bones, and offered Case a piercing look. "It's a funny thing about being too quick to judge, Case. It ain't worth spit when it comes to keepin' a man warm at night."

Petrov didn't expect an answer. Case didn't offer one. But he did stare at the empty doorway a long time after Don had disappeared.

His thoughts were not restful.

Prudy picked up the pale blue hospital gown from the floor where Case had flung it after snatching it from her hands.

"I'm warning you for the last time, Case Randolph. Put on this gown, or I swear I'll have Hollis Royden and some of the other orderlies hold you down while I put it on you myself."

Case folded his arms over his chest and gave her a defiant grin. "Now that has possibilities, love, but if it's all the same to you, I'd rather have privacy when you are doing such deliciously sexy things to my body."

Prudy drew an exasperated breath. "You were asleep when that dear little lady from the gift shop came in to deliver the flowers from Molly and Thad. I was the one who had to calm her down when she caught sight of you in all your…magnificent male glory—and clean up the mess when the poor darling dropped the vase."

There was mischief in his eyes as he shrugged. "It was as hot as a sauna in here. Who could blame me for kicking off the sheet? Besides, it's not my fault the lady lives like a nun."

"Case, Miss Pitcher is eighty years old—and never married. I was afraid she was going to go into cardiac arrest on the spot."

His mouth quirked at one corner, and his eyes glinted with mischief. With his temperature hovering close to normal and the post-op pain easing its excruciating bite, he was definitely feeling better. Not to mention that he was growing impatient to be released from the confinement and boredom of traction.

"Sounds to me like she should be thankin' me for putting a little spice into her life."

Prudy snorted. "You're impossible."

"Come over here and tell me that."

"Promise you'll put on this gown and I will," she demanded sternly.

"How many kisses will you give me if I do?"

"I'll give you a fist in the belly if you don't." She moved closer, holding the gown in front of her like a shield.

"Lord, but I love that pugnacious streak in you, Prudy my

sweet. Gets me hot every time." His raspy voice was laden with a slow, seductive promise that had her mind zooming to an image of that long, lean body under the sheet.

Naked. Aroused.

Her mouth went dry. She imagined herself touching him, her hands gliding with delicious slowness over those gleaming bronze shoulders and down his heavily muscled arms, her fingertips tracing the roped sinews under the warm skin.

Ruthlessly, she banished the image from her mind. Case was her patient. She was his nurse. And *in charge*. By the time she left for home this evening, one of them was going to be wearing that gown. And it was *not* going to be Prudence O'Grady Randolph.

"Hold out your arms," she ordered when she reached the bed.

"Kiss first," he demanded, cocking his head. Tendrils of shaggy black hair whispered against his neck, adding a primitive beauty to his stark features. Prudy felt her fingers flex against the gown, already imagining the springy softness of his hair under her fingertips.

"One kiss, no hands," she bargained with a stern look that had his grin chasing away the lines of strain around his eyes.

"Not fair," he protested.

"Take it or leave it, buster."

His mouth twitched, but his eyes had taken on a glimmer of sexual heat so fierce it seemed capable of searing her skin with only a look. "You never used to drive such a hard bargain, Prue."

"Maybe I've learned from my mistakes." And suffered, she added silently.

"Maybe we both have." The sudden deepening of his voice had emotion swelling inside her. Did he regret ending their marriage? she wondered before she warned herself to end such dangerous speculation.

"Close your eyes," she ordered, determined to lighten the mood. She was feeling particularly tired and had an appointment with Luke Jarrod in a little less than an hour for her monthly checkup.

"Not a chance."

She sighed dramatically, unintentionally drawing his gaze to the swell of her small breasts beneath the psychedelic print of her shirt.

"Pucker up, then."

Case laughed at the face she made, but his blood was already stirring. She was such an unpredictable bundle of femininity, with a buttermilk freshness to her face and the body of a sinner hidden beneath the shapeless smock and pants.

"With pleasure, nursie."

Her eyes flashed, just as he'd expected. A spurt of excitement ran through him, followed by another, more complicated emotion he couldn't name.

"Call me that again, and you'll be eating that pillow behind you."

"Okay, I'm ready," he said, bracing back his shoulders. He enjoyed sparring with Prudy, but he enjoyed kissing her even more. Much, much more.

A smile crossed her lips before she leaned forward, aiming the kiss for his forehead. He'd been ready for her this time and had his left hand fisted in her hair before she could draw back.

"Oh, no, you don't," he grated before fitting his mouth to hers.

Prudy stiffened against the quick surge of pleasure even as she felt her lips softening. How could she resist what she wanted so desperately? How could she deny the need for him that flared so wildly whenever he touched her?

Still, she tried, bracing a hand on his shoulder and pushing. Growling deep in his throat, he drew back far enough to scowl at her.

"No hands," he reminded her, his voice wonderfully husky and his eyes half-closed.

Before she could remind him of the big hand threaded so tightly into her hair, he took her mouth again. She felt heat rising from his body, a sigh from her own, as she let herself sink into the delicious swirl of sensation.

Case felt his breath catch at the back of his throat as she

oh, so carefully eased closer. And then, as the hardened tips of her breasts brushed his bare chest, his breath stopped altogether. His blood flowed hotter, faster, surging toward and pooling at the juncture of his thighs, a brutal hardening already in evidence under the thin sheet.

She moaned, a soft, eager sound that made his heart leap and his need turn acute. As he licked her mouth with tiny, hot strokes, savoring the taste of her, he remembered the times he had taken other women to bed, hoping that one of them—just one—might be able to fill the emptiness inside him. It hadn't worked. Each time he'd so much as touched another female, he'd thought of Prudy and regretted it wasn't her in his arms.

But now—

"Glad to see you're bouncing back so well, Randolph, but don't you think you should be saving your strength for your job?"

The question was drawled in a well-deep voice that Prudy didn't recognize. Even as she jerked backward, it was obvious from the sudden grin spreading over Case's face that he did.

"Hiya, boss. Nice of you to stop by, but I wish you'd waited about an hour."

"I can always go grab a cup of coffee," the man drawled, propping his shoulder against the doorjamb.

"Works for me," Case answered, shooting Prudy a mischievous look that had her blushing from the roots of her hair to the V of her smock.

"Don't listen to him," she told the now-grinning stranger in the doorway. "He's still recovering from fever-induced delusions."

She decided the man had a nice laugh. "So what else is new?"

"Prudy, meet Captain Bill Walters."

"A pleasure, ma'am," Captain Walters said as he came forward to offer her his hand and an engaging smile. Short and lean and the color of ebony, the man projected an aura of power and kindness. Prudy judged him to be in his mid-fifties and supremely fit.

"Thank you," she murmured, returning his smile with one of her own.

"You're even more attractive in person than on TV," he said, holding her hand so long Case started to glower.

Prudy fervently wished she could have passed on that particular fifteen minutes of fame. Everyone from the boy who'd filled Gray Lady with high test at the pump only this morning to the checker at the convenience store on the corner of her street had mentioned her brief claim to fame on last week's morning news broadcast, which had been aired again at six and eleven that night, of course. God forbid that any of the regular viewers should miss any little tidbits about the infamous Case Randolph, cop extraordinaire.

"I was hardly at my best that night."

"It was a rough few hours for all of us," Walters said as he released her hand.

Case snorted something under his breath that had his superior officer winking at her before he turned his attention Case's way.

"I stopped by to pass on the results of the official inquiry into the shooting."

"Excuse me," Prudy murmured with the intention of slipping away to give the two men a few minutes of privacy.

Case stopped her with a scowl. "Since when does a nurse leave her patient in his hour of need?" he demanded, his gaze colliding with hers with an impact as solid as a punch.

"What hour of need?" she retorted.

He glanced at his boss before shrugging one shoulder. "Walters here has been known to ream a man a new—"

"Case Randolph!" she interrupted with a pained look. "Behave yourself."

Walters saluted her with a wry grin before turning a suddenly sober gaze in Case's direction once more.

"The board ruled that Cardoza fired first."

Case reacted with the barest flicker of his lashes, but Prudy sensed the relief flowing between the two men. During her years as a cop's wife, she'd learned a lot about the work Case and his buddies called "the job." One of the things they feared most, she'd soon come to realize, was having to draw their gun. Even worse was the fear of firing on someone who later might turn out to be innocent.

"Hell, I could have told you it was a clean shoot," Case grumbled.

"You did tell me, and in quite, shall we say, colorful language."

Case blinked. "I did? When?"

"Right before the paramedics shoved you into the wagon."

Case searched his mind, came up blank. "You were there?"

"Just arrived."

Though Walters was facing Case and not her, Prudy saw the flicker of emotion that crossed the man's seamed face and suspected he was recalling the way Case had looked at that moment.

"Captain," she began, only to have him shake his head.

"Bill."

She managed a smile. "Bill, about that man, Cardoza, the, uh, brother?"

Walters nodded. "A real piece of...work."

"Yes, well, I was wondering about the threats he's been making."

Case snorted, and she shot him a reproving glance before persisting. "In the interview he gave he seemed to really hate Case."

"Arturo Cardoza hates everyone," Case interjected, clearly annoyed at the turn the conversation had taken.

"He's also disappeared," Walters said quietly. Too quietly, Prudy decided as a shiver stuttered down her spine. "Petrov's snitch claimed he's left town."

"Is that good news or bad?" she asked carefully.

"Good," Case declared.

"Unknown," Walters offered, "which is why I intend to put a guard on the room until we sort things out."

Prudy realized that she was pressing a protective hand against her belly and let her hand fall quickly to her side. At the same time, a wave of guilt over the secret she was still keeping warred with the sudden worry aroused by Walters's words.

"That sounds like a very good idea," she said, offering the captain a grateful smile. From the corner of her eye she saw Case frown.

"Now, boss—"

"Stow it, Randolph. One of the uniforms will be here shortly, and as soon as I leave here, I intend to stop by the nurses' station and put out the word. No visitors unless okayed by the man at the door."

Chapter 12

After studying the latest X rays taken of Case's leg, Boyd decided to release him from traction a day early, earning him Case's undying gratitude. If all went well and Case mastered the use of crutches without trouble, he would be ready for release in two days—with strict orders to watch his diet and take the pills prescribed to nudge his still stubbornly elevated blood pressure into the normal range.

Prudy wasn't as thrilled as she'd expected to find her stint as Case's special nurse drawing to an end. Which was utterly illogical and very probably insane, she repeatedly told herself as she sat waiting in the cafeteria for Boyd to finish casting Case's leg. For her own peace of mind she had to distance herself from the man, physically as well as emotionally. The sooner the better.

How was a woman supposed to stop loving her ex-husband when she spent ten hours a day in the same room with him, and frequently longer? While he was all but naked under the sheet? How was she supposed to distance herself when her day was spent listening to his deep voice teasing her into a burst of temper, watching his grin flash lopsided and white in an all too masculine and familiar face? Fighting off a longing to settle against that big, warm chest and let him enfold her in his strong arms?

No, the sooner she returned to her comfortable rut, the better it would be. And then, when Boyd gave her a thumbs-up that Case was well and truly on the mend, she would tell him about the baby.

Since she knew, absolutely and without a doubt, exactly when she'd gotten pregnant, she also knew she was just entering her thirteenth week. Her body was changing every day now. Changes that thrilled and excited her. Changes that she'd soon be unable to hide under oversized shirts and drawstring slacks.

This morning she'd finally admitted the need to buy a new bra with larger cups to accommodate the added fullness of her breasts, and soon, the barely noticeable bulge below her waist would take on a more recognizable roundness.

A smile curved her lips as she pictured herself in a few months, her belly preceding her into rooms like the rounded prow of a ship. She would probably waddle like a duck, too, and suffer from vicious bouts of heartburn. And when the baby grew larger, she would be subjected to constant kicks from impatient little feet and pokes from tiny fists.

Knowing she shouldn't, she pictured herself perched like a contented Buddha in the corner of her sofa while Case rubbed lotion on her swollen belly. Simply the thought of those big calloused hands gliding lovingly over her flesh provoked an immediate response from her body. Her skin felt warmer and her nipples tingled from the sudden surge of blood. Between her legs a wonderful warm feeling was spreading, like a slow wave of liquid heat.

Oh, Lord, she thought, glancing around uneasily. She was losing it big time here. Time to regroup, Prudy, old girl, she told herself firmly. No fantasies while you're on duty. Especially when you're on duty with Case.

Biting her lip, she glanced at her watch. What should have been a simple and brief procedure, removing the traction pins and encasing his long leg in acres of plaster, was taking far longer than it should. Had Boyd run into complications? Perhaps a trauma he hadn't anticipated?

By the time she saw Boyd striding through the cafeteria doors twenty minutes later, she had worked herself into a fine state of worry.

"We had some problems with the cast, but your boy came through it like a champ," Boyd said, dropping into the chair opposite Prudy in a quiet corner of the hospital cafeteria, a cup of steaming coffee in one hand and two cherry Danishes in the other. "Told me to tell you to get your buns up to his room before he comes looking for you."

Feeling just a little shaky, Prudy opened the pint of milk she'd been staring at for almost an hour and poured the contents into a paper cup before letting Boyd see her relief.

"Case likes issuing orders almost as much as you do," she told him before taking a sip. The milk had lost its chill and tasted like liquid chalk. "I hate milk," she muttered when Boyd lifted an inquiring eyebrow.

"Stace says the same thing about oatmeal."

Prudy saw the love light in his eyes and tried not to be jealous. "From what I've seen, Tory is developing the same aversion."

Boyd stuffed half a Danish into his mouth and swallowed before offering her a crooked grin. "Yesterday morning our little angel dumped the whole bowl on the floor, then gave her mother one of those innocent 'it's not my fault' looks."

Prudy laughed softly. "I assume Stacy wasn't fooled."

"Naw, she's on to our daughter's tricks. I'm the cream puff in this parenting business."

Prudy watched his eyes soften and felt the jealousy she'd tried so hard to shake tighten its talons. Both Boyd and Stacy deserved the happiness they'd found together. More than most, in fact. And she was genuinely happy for her good friends. She just wished the success of their marriage didn't make the failure of her own hurt so much.

"Just think, in less than a month, you and Stacy will be basking on the beach on Kauai," she said brightly, desperate to divert her thoughts from her own troubling thoughts.

"Twenty-three days, but who's counting?" Boyd corrected with a wry grin.

"Sounds like you are, for one."

Boyd's laughter floated over the nearly empty room, reminding Prudy of all the years after he'd lost his first wife and child when he'd been hard-pressed to smile. It soothed her to realize that there really was such a thing as a happy ending—for a few fortunate souls, anyway.

"Are you sure Stacy still doesn't know what you're planning?" she asked, watching an elderly man and woman sharing a bagel and smiling at each other across a nearby table.

"Not a clue." He looked smugly pleased with himself and his plan to whisk his wife away for a belated honeymoon at a friend's place in Hawaii.

Gathering her courage, she managed to down another few sips of milk without gagging. For the baby's sake, she told herself while she waited for her stomach to settle.

"I admit I was worried when she found out she was pregnant," she said as she glumly watched Boyd polishing off the last of the empty calories he loved. "But it turns out your darling wife is one of those rare women who never experience the dreaded heaves when they're expecting."

"She is amazing, isn't she?" Boyd grinned, then apologized when she glared at him. "Sorry. I thought you were feeling better."

"I am. Sort of." She sighed. "I only get sick at night now." At 11:00 p.m., like clockwork. It didn't matter if she was awake or asleep.

"Look, if it's going to be too much to take care of Tory while we're gone, say so. I can ask my sister—"

"Don't you dare!" she hastened to warn him. "I've already moved heaven and earth to get the time off, plus I've been looking forward to spoiling that little darling for months now. Mark my words, I intend to do just that."

Boyd saluted her with a pleased grin. "Guess it's a good thing you're almost finished sitting on Case."

She shot him a startled look that had him adding quickly, "Metaphorically speaking, of course."

"Of course." She reached for her cup, squared her shoulders and finished the milk in two shuddering gulps. "Do you still plan to release him tomorrow? If he doesn't have problems when you get him up on crutches, of course."

To her dismay, Boyd suddenly frowned. "That was the plan, yeah, until I found out the guy lives in a third-floor walk-up."

Prudy blinked. "I...didn't know that."

In the years since the divorce, she'd never been invited to Case's apartment, though he'd given her the address and phone number. Not because he'd wanted her to use either, of course, but because he was a very organized and careful man. Unlike her, who was neither.

"There's no way in hell he's going to be able to manage two flights of steps on crutches with one bum hand," Boyd said after a moment spent scowling down at his coffee.

"Not without wearing himself out," she conceded.

"More like falling on his butt and breaking the other leg." He scowled. "Or his stubborn head."

"Maybe he could stay with Don Petrov," she mused aloud. Seeing Boyd lift his eyebrows inquiringly, she hastened to explain. "Don's a bachelor. Last I knew, he had a place in Lake Oswego."

"Stairs?"

"I don't know," she admitted with a sigh. "But Don's big enough to haul Case up a couple of flights without breaking a sweat."

"Provided Case would submit to such an indignity, which is doubtful."

Boyd leaned back and rubbed his flat belly with one huge hand. Like Case, he projected an aura of power, even when he was relaxed. A reminder of a time in the distant past when a man's survival and that of his family depended on his strength and vigilance.

"How do you think he'd take to the idea of spending the next month or so, until his wrist knits at least, at Dr. Markham's place?" Boyd asked suddenly.

"A convalescent facility?" She shook her head, a smile playing over her lips. "Not a chance."

"It's a nice place. Pretty nurses, too."

"Now that's a plus. And certainly important."

Boyd grinned. "Hell, yes, it's important. A good attitude is essential in rapid healing, you know."

"Yeah, I know. That's exactly what Case said when I caught him hyperventilating over the centerfold in the *Playboy* he was reading yesterday."

Boyd laughed. "Good man."

Yes, Case was a very good man, she thought with a pang of deep longing. Decent and honorable and, in his own gruff way, very kind. He held himself to enormously high standards—and became enraged if he fell short. He was more tolerant when it came to others—but not with her.

"I'll let you break the news to him before I head upstairs," she muttered as she pushed her chair back and picked up the empty milk carton.

"Afraid to take the heat?" Boyd teased as he stood.

Prudy thought about the precious little soul she sheltered under her heart and sighed. "You've got that right."

He laughed, but his expression remained thoughtful. "Prue, I assume you've been waiting to tell Case about the baby until we had him stabilized?"

"Well, yes. Partly. And partly because I haven't quite worked up enough courage."

Boyd glanced down as though deep in thought. "Would it be too much to ask you to hold off a little longer? Just until we get his BP down to a normal range?"

"Boyd, pregnancy isn't something I can hide indefinitely. Besides, he has a right to know."

"I couldn't agree more, especially from a father's point of view. But as his doctor, I'm still concerned about the hypertension. The last thing we need is for the man to have a stroke."

"That's extremely unlikely, though, right?"

"Yes, but it has happened. Last May as a matter of fact, to a man who was a year younger than Case. Came in with a hot appendix. Had a stroke on the table. Fortunately he survived. Case might not be so lucky."

Prudy took a deep breath. "All right, I'll wait to tell him until you give me the okay."

Prudy stopped by the ER to touch base with the members of her team before returning to the sixth floor. As she approached six-twelve, the strapping blond patrolman sitting by the door glanced her way and grinned.

"Best cover your ears. The language is pretty raw inside," he whispered as she passed.

She answered him with a quick grin before rearranging her face into stern lines. Inside the room, Boyd and Case were glaring at each other.

"No nursing home," Case said with a note of finality in his voice.

"You talk to him," Boyd muttered, his gaze drifting Prudy's way. "Make him listen to reason, or so help me, I'll fill him so full of Valium he won't be able to move."

"You can try," Case countered with a lazy grin, earning him a dangerous look from Boyd's dark gray eyes.

"Lord save me from testosterone run amok," she muttered.

"Now, Prue, Boyd and I were just having a discussion. He stated his position, I stated mine, and my superior logic won out."

"Superior, my ass," Boyd muttered.

"That's it," Prudy declared with a frown. "I'm calling Don Petrov and telling him he's about to get a bad-tempered, immature, impossible houseguest."

Boyd grinned. Case scowled. And then suddenly his eyes took on a devilish gleam and a slow grin folded twins creases into his hard cheeks.

"Sorry to spoil your plans, sweets," he said in that low silken growl that invariably warned of imminent trouble. "But Don's place only has one bedroom."

"So you can sleep on the couch," she muttered, cursing the impulse that had her speaking before she'd checked with Don.

"Damn thing's too short."

"Rent a bed and put it in the living room."

He shook his head, his eyes laughing, and Prudy wanted to smack him in that impossibly stubborn chin. If there was anything more exasperating than that smugly arrogant look of his, she'd yet to see it.

"That's where my partner keeps his exercise equipment."

Prudy began to pace, one corner of her mouth clamped between her teeth. The solution, when it came, was so brilliantly simple she couldn't resist a pleased grin.

"Okay, we'll switch places. I'll move into your apartment, and you can stay at my house."

Case nearly laughed at the pleased look shining in her lush brown eyes. But he'd already pushed her as far as he dared.

"Won't work," he said, enjoying the way her eyes flashed when she turned her gaze his way.

"Why not?"

Case eased higher on the pillow. Propped on two pillows, his leg throbbed like holy hell inside the heavy plaster, but he'd sworn off the pain pills that scrambled his reflexes.

"Geraci? You out there?"

The patrolman appeared instantly. He didn't quite snap to attention, but Prudy saw the respect in the young man's alert blue eyes.

"Right here, Sarge."

"Explain to Ms. Randolph why it would not be a good idea for her to move into my apartment."

One side of Geraci's mouth twitched, but his expression remained rigidly impassive. "It wouldn't be safe, ma'am. Not while that bast...while Arturo Cardoza is still making threats against Sergeant Randolph."

Prudy drew a calming breath. Every time someone mentioned Cardoza's name, she recalled the eerily chilling look in the man's eyes as he'd stared into the TV camera. She was grateful that Case was finally taking the man's ravings seriously, at least.

"But that has nothing to do with my living at Case's apartment for a few weeks."

She saw Geraci shift his gaze in Case's direction, presumably to find out just how much to reveal. Though she'd deliberately turned her back on Case, she felt rather than saw his nod.

"It does if Cardoza decides to carry out his threat by torching the place," Geraci explained quietly. "Or possibly by slipping a letter bomb under the door."

"Looks like there's only one solution, Prue," Case said with an amused smile. "I'll have to stay with you."

"What could I say, Stacy?" Prudy asked as she smoothed the crazy quilt over the fresh sheets on her bed. "It makes sense for Case to stay here until he can handle a weapon again."

Across the room Stacy glanced up from the pumpkin-colored chrysanthemums she was busily arranging in an antique vase on the dresser.

Seated at her mama's feet, Tory was busily pulling "treasures" from the bright red chest Prudy kept just for her. Every few weeks, Prudy changed the contents, trying to find new and interesting things for the toddler to discover. At the moment, Tory seemed fascinated by one of Prudy's old wallets, crowing with excitement each time she managed to open another compartment or undo a Velcro tab.

"But I thought that horrible man Cardoza had left town," Stacy said as she smilingly acknowledged her daughter's chattering.

"Don heard from one of his snitches that he's back. And even nastier than ever."

"It's too bad they can't just arrest him for threatening a police officer."

"Case says it's not against the law to threaten someone, even a cop."

Stacy's expressive face registered concern. "Do you have a gun in the house?"

Prudy shook her head. "Case wanted to leave me one of his when he left, but I refused. I hate guns. Too many years of working in the ER, I guess. I've seen firsthand the damage a bullet can do to the human body.''

Prudy gave the quilt a final pat before sweeping the bedroom with a critical gaze one last time. Case would be sleeping in her bed. She intended to sleep on the futon in her sewing room cum library cum artist's studio.

The clothes she'd collected from Case's apartment on her way home yesterday, with Geraci's assistance and protection, were now neatly stowed in two drawers of her white wicker dresser. Case's shaving things and toiletries had joined hers in the master bathroom. She'd packed a small bag with clothes for him to wear home tomorrow.

"Ready to gorge yourself?" Stacy asked, her sudden grin as mischievous as her daughter's.

It had become a tradition between the two women to share a batch of carob brownies from the health food store when either one or the other was under stress.

"Ready and willing," Prudy declared as she scooped Tory into her arms. The little girl giggled as Prudy blew a kiss into her ear.

"Tickles," Tory protested, rubbing her ear against her shoulder as Prudy carried her into the kitchen.

While Stacy retrieved the milk from the fridge and glasses from the cupboard, Prudy settled Tory into the high chair she'd picked up for her small neighbor one day last spring at a garage sale, along with a Portacrib and an assortment of toys. Soon she would have to start accumulating the other things she would need for a baby. The prospect brought a soft smile to her face, and she realized she could scarcely wait.

"Here you go, tootsie. Your very own gooey brownie."

"Bwownie," Tory repeated before pushing the entire square into her mouth.

Laughing, Prudy hastily retrieved a clean bib from her towel drawer and fastened it around Tory's chubby neck. "You look like a contented chipmunk."

"Her pediatrician says she's not fat, just short for her weight," Stacy said with a exaggerated sigh.

"Tell me about it," Prudy muttered, glancing down. She

was wearing her favorite T-shirt, the one with splotches that reminded her of rainbow sherbet gone berserk.

"Don't worry," Stacy soothed, dropping into a chair. "You aren't showing yet."

Prudy pulled out two chairs, sat in one and rested her bare feet on the other. "Without my clothes I am," she admitted, reaching for a brownie.

Stacy poured milk into the happy-face mug Tory considered hers whenever she visited her Aunt Prudy. "Hold on to the cup really, really tight so it doesn't spill," she reminded her daughter gently as she set it carefully on the high-chair tray, then glanced up. "Boyd said he asked you to hold off a few more weeks before telling Case about the baby."

"I have to admit I didn't put up much of an argument."

Prudy glanced at her toes. Case had told her once that she had cute feet. And that he'd fallen in love with her because she was the only woman he'd ever met who hadn't bored him after the first few dates. Her lips curved at the rueful grin he'd given her then—right after the pressure cooker had exploded, spraying burned beef stew all over the ceiling.

It had been his fault, of course. He was the one who'd insisted on dragging her off to bed the instant he'd come waltzing in the door. To celebrate his promotion to detective.

They'd feasted on peanut butter sandwiches, then swabbed the kitchen clean between kisses, and ended the evening by making love on the kitchen table. She still remembered how his laughter had boomed when they'd nearly tumbled to the floor during a particularly innovative maneuver.

But the laughter they'd shared had stopped after she'd lost the baby he'd never wanted her to conceive, the baby he'd feared he'd never be able to love. It had been at the same table, in the same kitchen, a year later that he'd told her he could no longer live with a woman he couldn't trust.

Heart aching, she traced a swirl of oak grain with her fingertips, trying not to remember. A futile effort.

"Case has a picture of me on his bedside table," she said softly. "A snapshot taken on one of our first dates. I saw it when I collected his clothes."

Stacy stopped chewing and stared at her. ''Obviously, he's still in love with you.''

Prudy pressed her index finger against a stray crumb on the raffia place mat before conveying the morsel to her mouth thoughtfully.

''Then why, in all the years since the divorce, hasn't he ever called me? Or sent a Christmas card?''

''Maybe for the same reason Boyd quit medicine for three years. To find a way to come to grips with the past so that he could move on to the future.''

''He didn't want a future until he met you,'' Prudy corrected softly.

Stacy's eyes clouded, and Prudy suspected her friend was remembering the long, lonely months she'd spent thinking Boyd had rejected her and her love.

''I hate to see you looking so sad,'' Stacy murmured gently. ''It's so unlike you.''

''It's all Case's fault,'' Prudy said with a jaunty grin. ''He has a talent for bringing out the worst in me.''

''I didn't say it was bad,'' Stacy scolded. ''Your feelings are your feelings.''

Prudy took a deep breath. ''Well, my feelings are about to change. I've spent eight years regretting one mistake. I don't intend to wallow in guilt one more second.'' She threw her shoulders back and forced a grin. ''If Case doesn't want me and our baby, it's his loss.''

Arturo Cardoza eased open the fire door at the end of the corridor just far enough to get himself a good look. His breath hissed spittle between his dry lips as he caught sight of the baby-faced cop sitting by a door about halfway between him and the nurses' station near the elevators.

His belly burned with hatred as he eased the door closed again. He'd figured they'd put a guard on the bastard that had gut-shot Felix. Hell, cops protected their own.

But then, so did he, he reminded himself as he made his way down the stairs, the gun he'd retrieved from Felix's hidden cache in his place in the San Juan islands a comforting weight in the pocket of his windbreaker.

He felt a familiar gnawing in his gut and knew he'd have to score at least a nickel bag soon. Maybe more, if he got lucky enough to snatch him a purse filled with more than supermarket coupons.

A sudden noise on the stairs below him had him freezing in mid-flight, his hand diving into his pocket to close around the nubby grip of the nine millimeter.

"Ah, c'mon, babe, just one quick feel for your honey," a deep voice wheedled below.

"No way, I'm already late for my shift," a woman's high-pitched voice answered.

Cardoza heard the click of the door opening, followed by another flurry of argument, which ended abruptly as the heavy fire door thudded shut.

Still, he waited while the need in his gut grew. Like the rats him and Felix used to hunt in the alley where they'd lived before the state had scooped them into separate foster homes, he'd survived because he was cautious. More cautious than Felix, even if his brother had been the smart one. Everyone always said they made a good team, him and Felix.

Arturo felt rage bunching inside him again, seething hot. Felix had always taken care of him. No matter what. Felix had loved him.

In his mind he saw the face of Felix's killer. Those hard, unforgiving eyes. The mouth that had shouted for Felix to freeze. A credit to the force, the paper had called him. A cop's cop.

Soon he'd be a *dead* cop, Arturo reassured himself as he decided it was safe for him to move again.

The sun was shining when he left the hospital by the service entrance, searing his retinas with the sudden glare. Felix had died at night, in agony, his belly blasted open and bleeding.

Arturo didn't particularly care when Randolph died. Fate would guide him to the right time and place, just as it had nudged him earlier into taking the back stairs instead of the elevator.

Oh, yes, fate was on his side. And Case Randolph was going to die.

Slowly and painfully, begging Arturo to end his suffering.

Arturo grinned as he headed toward the park and the easy pickings it offered for a man with fate on his side. As he walked, he kept his mind off the hunger gnawing at his insides by imagining how wonderfully long it would take for a man as big as Randolph to bleed out his life.

Chapter 13

After fifteen days and the same number of nights, Case was released a few minutes after ten on the sixteenth. Anticipating the great event, the nurses and support staff on Six West voted hands down to award him the dubious distinction of being their most difficult patient—ever.

After much serious discussion, they settled on a suitable prize—a couple of bedraggled roses scrounged from discarded bouquets and plopped into the plastic urine collector he'd used during his stay.

Prudy was given the honor of making the presentation and was quite pleased with the impromptu speech she'd delivered with a perfectly straight face.

Case had had the last laugh, however, when he'd grabbed her instead of the "prize," pulling her against him for a long, ravishing kiss that had left her breathless and panting.

By the time Willie Geraci had helped Case into Prudy's Volvo, wished them well and then returned to his patrol car behind hers, she was already wondering how she was going to get through the next six weeks or so without losing her mind.

All the way home, Case told her when to signal, when to brake, when to reduce speed to keep from snagging a ticket. When she threatened to dump him—and his back seat driving—on the nearest street corner if he said one more word about her driving, he started in on Gray Lady herself, ticking off all the reasons why the old Volvo was ready for the salvage yard.

"Hell, it's got be a good fifteen years since we bought the blasted thing."

"If you will recall, I wanted a convertible, but you insisted on this one because it was *safer*," she reminded him as she accelerated up the on ramp to the crosstown freeway.

"Yeah, well, now it isn't, dammit! It's a wonder the DMV doesn't order you to pull the plug on this bucket of rust."

"I'm fifteen years older, as well, Randolph," she informed him tightly when her patience finally gave out. "Guess that means I'm ready for the scrap heap, too."

She heard him snort, then risked a glance his way and caught the flash of heat in his eyes even as his hard mouth softened into a roguish grin. Oh, yes, he was a handsome devil at forty-five and as hard as a hickory nut inside and out.

"Honey, you are about as close to perfect as the weaker sex can get."

The purr in his voice had her blood warming, but she made herself scowl. "Weaker sex, my sainted aunt."

"Now, don't get your Irish up, Red." He patted her knee with his left hand, then let it settle against her thigh. Through the thin barrier of her slacks, she felt the strength in his hand—and the promise.

"I see you're still using the same old moves, slick," she muttered, glancing down.

"You used to like my moves, remember?"

She still did, but she wasn't about to cede him an unfair advantage by telling him so. Not until she knew exactly what kind of move this was.

"Keep your hands to yourself, Randolph," she muttered, then was acutely disappointed when he complied.

Mill Works Ridge was still shrouded in morning fog when

she pulled into the carport and shut off the engine. Instead of following her into the dead-end driveway leading to the row of carports, Geraci parked at the end. He or another officer would be watching the back of Mill Works Ridge while another had been assigned to the front. While Case was in residence, the two of them would be under the watchful protection of the Portland PD. At least, while they were inside the house.

She'd put her foot down when Case had wanted to have an officer assigned to accompany her whenever she left the house. As for him, he wasn't going anywhere—except to bed, as soon as she got him inside.

The air was nippy, and she shivered in her lightweight jacket as she hurried around to help Case out of the passenger's seat. Already half in, half out, he scowled up at her when she urged him to use her as a crutch.

"Don't hover," he snapped, his jaw taut.

"Lord save me from male pride," she muttered, earning her another dangerous look.

While he braced his good hand on the roof of the car and balanced on his good foot, Prudy retrieved his crutches from the back seat.

"Left one first," she instructed.

Once he had the crutch tucked securely under his left arm and had found his balance, she handed him the right. With his hand in a cast, he had only his fingertips to manage the handgrip, a test of his patience and dexterity. Consequently, it took him several minutes to inch his way up the walk while she trailed behind, ready to catch him if he overbalanced.

"Hold on while I get the door," she said, hastening to open the screen. As she fitted her key into the lock, she heard a plaintive meow coming from the direction of the hedge separating her property from the MacAuleys'.

"Hey, Sunshine," she called, earning her another sorrowful cry. "Don't try to con me, miss. I know you've been fed already this morning, and very well."

She threw open the back door to the sound of another feline protest, then stepped back to allow Case to precede her. As he maneuvered carefully over the threshold, he banged his elbow on the jamb and nearly dropped his crutch. Curses rolled from his throat with the force of shotgun blast. Behind him, Prudy bit her lip to keep from laughing.

"If you'd just let me help you—" Prudy chided before he interrupted.

"I can do it, dammit."

"Fine," she retorted, her jaw already aching from the struggle to keep her mouth shut. "Go ahead and break your fool neck. See if I care."

The man was impossible.

Stubborn.

Infuriating.

And adorable, with his hair mussed from his angry fingers, and his face flushed from the exertion of hobbling from the carport to the house.

He'd lost weight during his hospital stay, but the magnificent shoulders stretching the seams of his faded blue sweatshirt were still packed with plenty of muscle and his butt still filled out the ratty old sweatpants very nicely.

Too nicely, she decided as she felt an inner softening. *Get a grip, Prue.* Sex appeal and roguish charm were a poor substitute for love and trust.

Once inside the kitchen, Case paused to draw a much-needed breath before taking a tighter grip on his left crutch. Each step forward was costing him another chunk of his strength. The stamina he'd always taken for granted had been badly eroded by the gunshot wound, followed by the two weeks he'd spent flat on his back.

"Damn," he muttered under his breath as he inched across into the kitchen, each slow step infuriating him more.

"Enough," she said softly as she placed her small body squarely in his path, her chin set and both hands braced on her curvy hips.

She looked like a miniature drill sergeant, Case thought, biting back a shaky grin. Perfectly capable of bending a whole squadron of muscle-packed, rednecked marines to that stubborn will of hers.

In spite of the pain clawing the length of his leg and the swimming in his head, he was tempted to hook his good arm around that tiny waist of hers and snuggle her close. More than once while he'd been tied to that blasted bed, he'd staved off pain and boredom by remembering the sweet, soft give of her body as she eagerly adjusted to his.

At the moment he was too weak to do more than scowl at her, however, as she gently relieved him of the right crutch. After propping it against the refrigerator door, she tucked her shoulder under his arm and slipped her left hand around his waist.

As she took the crutch's share of his weight, Prudy felt the moist heat of his sweating skin, and the tension in the muscles of his chest and hip. Heat and power and a strong man's vulnerability—it was a potent combination to tempt a woman to ignore common sense.

She nearly laughed aloud at the thought. When did her feelings for Case have anything to do with common sense?

Her emotions tangled, pulling at her.

When they reached the living room, he stopped suddenly, breathing hard. "Rest a minute, then we'll get you to bed," Prudy said.

"Forget that," he muttered through clenched teeth. "Help me sit."

Prudy surveyed the room, decided the key lime chair was the most comfortable and helped him across the room. Once she had him settled, she placed his crutch on the floor within reaching distance, then piled several throw pillows on the ottoman in front of the chair. His face was pale, his eyes closed, as she gently positioned his leg on the pillows. Even that easy movement caused his facial muscles to grow taut with strain, and his breath to hitch.

"Can I get you something to drink?" she offered, aware that he would refuse her suggestion of a nap. "And maybe a snack? I made cookies before I left to pick you up this morning."

"With nuts and chunks of chocolate instead of chips?" he asked hopefully, his eyes still closed.

"Yes," she said tersely because she was suddenly remembering other times, other batches of cookies, made once by a young wife desperately in love with her big, strong, enigmatic husband.

"Coffee, too," he ordered, then opened one eye as he added a gentler, "Please?"

"Sure." Throat tight, she fled to the kitchen and opened her cookie jar.

Eyes still closed, Case heard the clink of china and the whoosh of the refrigerator door opening and closing. Familiar sounds in a familiar house.

It smelled the same, too. The odd spices she collected like other women collected diamonds, then never remembered to use, beeswax from the candles she loved and used constantly, and perfume. Chanel No. 5.

Too drowsy to exert his usual control, he let his thoughts drift backward, to the first time his sweet, shy bride had worked up the courage to try her hand at seduction. She'd come sashaying out of the bathroom, wearing only a smile and a whisper of Chanel.

Wiped out by a particularly exhausting night shift, he'd been sprawled on the bed, desperate for a solid chunk of uninterrupted sleep. It had taken his tired body about fifteen seconds to react to the signals she'd been sending out, another fifteen or so for his mind to sort through his options. Sleep or let her seduce him?

Making love to Prudy had won, no contest.

Making love to Prudy would always win, he admitted with a soul-deep sigh. Even in the damned hospital, when he'd been half-dead with pain and weakness, he'd responded to her like a randy teenager every time she'd touched him.

His fate had been sealed the first time she'd opened her heart and her body to him. She'd become a part of him then, as necessary as air and water.

For a man who rated deception of any kind right up there with murder and rape, he'd sure done his share of lying to himself these past eight years. Eight years of telling himself he was over her. Eight years of nursing his anger like a love-sick martyr.

Eight years of acting like a gold-plated jerk.

Hell, he thought with sleepy disgust. He was damned lucky the woman hadn't kicked his teeth in long ago.

Prudy returned to find Case asleep, his face pale and taut with pain and, she suspected, exhaustion. As quietly as she could manage, she set the tray she carried on the coffee table and hurried to retrieve a blanket from the linen closet.

Countless times in the past, she'd come home from a swing shift at the hospital to find him stretched out on the couch, waiting for her, his face lined with exhaustion and, far too often, the frustrations of the job he loved, yet cursed.

Gently, so as not to wake him, she smoothed the light cover over the big strong body that rarely failed him. Even asleep, he projected an aura of toughness and discipline. Yet, there had been moments in the years they'd spent together when she'd felt a startling vulnerability in his touch or his kiss, when, for reasons he'd ruthlessly kept hidden, he'd reached out to her with his defenses lowered.

Their lovemaking then had taken on a sweetness that wrapped around her heart and drew her inside him. The loneliness she'd glimpsed there had torn at her soul. The loneliness of a man who carried his own burdens and walked his own road. The loneliness of a man who still carried scars that had never really healed. Scars that she herself had unwittingly ripped open.

Remembering Don Petrov's hoarsely uttered account of Case's childhood, Prudy's heart twisted. The two women he should have been able to trust most had turned on him, lying to save themselves. Consigning him to two and a half years of misery because he'd cared about his sister.

How it must have hurt him.

Just as it must have hurt him when she'd lied to him. No wonder he'd stopped loving her.

Prudy closed her eyes as a wave of anguish coursed through her. God, how she wished she could go back in time and undo what she'd done. But she couldn't. That one mistake—which

Case had seen as an unforgivable betrayal—had cost her the man she loved.

The only man she would ever love...

Now that his mind was no longer dulled by medication, Case woke up as he always did, instantly alert and aware of his surroundings. A quick glance at his watch told him he'd been asleep for less than an hour. On the other side of the room Prudy was curled into the corner of the sofa with her head pillowed on the back. Her eyes were closed and the steady rise and fall of her breasts under the soft shirt told him she was fast asleep.

The coffee he'd requested and a plate of cookies sat in front of him on the chicken crate table. Evidently she'd dropped off into a doze while waiting for him to surface again.

With her face in repose, exhaustion had settled over her like a veil, blurring the vitality of her features. It wasn't a simple lack of sleep he was seeing, either. The purple shadows under her eyes were the kind that didn't appear overnight. Even the gold of her freckles seemed to have dulled.

Damn, what had he done?

Worn her out, for one thing, he decided, taking in the weary droop of her pretty mouth. And pushed her into an impossible situation, for another.

He had a passing acquaintance with guilt. Only a sociopath reached the age of reason without collecting regrets. Though he reckoned his own collection was bigger than most, he rarely spent much time looking back. What he couldn't change he shoved in a corner someplace and moved on. Or so he'd always figured.

He glanced down at the long stretch of white plaster protecting his leg while it healed. The media called him a hero. A brave man. An exemplary public servant.

In plain truth, he was a selfish son of a bitch.

He'd had the entire hospital in an uproar because he'd been furious to find himself helpless and vulnerable. No, dammit, he wasn't anywhere close to hero material. Not when he'd been scared to the bone to realize how close he'd come to bleeding out his life on a dirty street.

Most of that night was a blur—all but one vivid memory. He must have blacked out shortly after taking the slug. When he'd fought his way back to consciousness, he'd been lying on his back in a blaze of slashing light from the emergency vehicles, surrounded by people—curious onlookers, paramedics working with swift efficiency, his partner spewing out orders. At first he'd been numb, then consumed by rage, and then, finally, wracked by an agony so excruciating it took his breath. Not because his body hurt, but because he'd been so sure he would never see Prudy again.

He closed his eyes for a moment to ward off the memory of that soul-jarring moment. Something had changed in him in that one split second, something he'd been trying to deny ever since. Hunger came closest to describing it, he guessed now. Hunger to recapture that special feeling they'd shared before hurt and anger had blasted it to smithereens.

Her soft sigh had his eyes snapping open and his senses on alert. Though still deeply asleep, she stirred restlessly, rubbing her cheek against the back of the sofa where it rested. Below her coppery bangs, her pale brow knitted into a frown, and she whimpered as though in pain. Though barely audible, the sound tore through him like a murderously sharp blade.

"Prue?" he called softly, reluctant to wake her, yet too worried to remain silent. "Honey, are you okay?"

His only answer was the brief fluttering of her thick eyelashes, followed by another, longer sigh through lips that parted slightly, drawing his gaze. Her skin seemed translucent, and so delicate he could see the fine network of veins in her temple where her pulse throbbed steadily, a reassuring sign that should have eased some of the tension clawing at his rigid muscles. Instead, he felt a need to hold her small body close.

Holding his breath, Case leaned forward and used his good hand to ease his leg to the floor. It took him a moment to find the crutch on the floor, another to lever himself to his feet.

Graceful he wasn't, but by using the crutch like a cane and hopping on his uninjured foot, he managed to get himself from the chair to the couch without ending up on his butt instead. After propping the crutch against the coffee table, he pains-takingly maneuvered himself back against the cushions. As soon as he was steady, he eased her into his arms, tucking her head beneath his chin.

Lord, but she was thin, he realized with a pang of chagrin. As thin as a shadow. Had she lost weight? He couldn't be sure. He scowled, fully aware now of just how self-involved he'd been.

After nearly a decade of deliberate silence, he'd barreled back into her life, had arrogantly talked his way into her bed, then spent weeks trying to convince himself he didn't even owe her a phone call.

Still, when he'd needed her, she'd been there. Holding his hand. Bullying him into letting them take care of him. Turning her life topsy-turvy to accommodate *his* wants, *his* demands.

Even as he asked himself why, he knew. Because she loved him. And God help him, he loved her.

He was pretty sure now that he'd never stopped.

Tightening his grip, he held her protectively against his chest. He felt the tension in her small body, the instinctive reaction of a small vulnerable animal sensing danger even in her sleep.

It hurt him to discover she was afraid of him, he realized as he soothed her with quiet words. Not physically, though he was twice her weight and a head taller, but emotionally, the one place where her defenses were so terribly thin.

Careful to keep the rigid cast on his forearm from pressing into her tender flesh, he massaged her back with his left hand, soothing the tautness from her spine. She made another sound, more a sigh of pleasure than pain, and rubbed her cheek against his neck, much as she'd snuggled against the pillow. Her breath was warm against his throat, and her breasts were soft.

"It's all right, sweets," he murmured, his throat tight. "I'll make it up to you, I promise."

Prudy surfaced slowly, leaving the dark, lonely depths of sleep for the sudden warmth and security she felt enveloping

her. Though she was far from alert, her senses told her that
she was being held in a man's steely, strong arms, cradled
with great care against a man's wide, hard, warm chest.

It felt so good to be held, she realized, snuggling closer into
the expanding warmth. To borrow strength from someone
stronger, someone braver.

In some part of her sleepy mind, she knew she was dream-
ing of Case again. A wonderfully vivid dream this time. He
was whispering to her in that deep, sexy purr that never failed
to arouse her, murmuring gruff endearments that made her
smile.

"Such a sweet mouth..." she thought he said before the
man in her dream began kissing her. On the tip of her nose,
the tender spot behind her ear, on the corner of her mouth.
Tender kisses, she discerned with growing pleasure. Kisses
feathered against her lips by a hard, masculine mouth.

Eagerly, as she'd done so often before in her dreams, she
arched upward, her mouth hungry for more. He stiffened, drew
away from her.

"No, don't leave me again," she pleaded, looping her arms
around that strong masculine neck. It had been so long since
she'd felt safe, so long since she'd felt cherished.

She heard his voice, words her sleep-drugged mind couldn't
decipher, and then that stern, clever mouth was firming over
hers. Tasting, tempting.

Pleasure filled her, washing out the lethargy and despair,
buoying her spirits, renewing her strength. Moaning, she
opened her mouth. The wet velvet thrust of his tongue parted
her lips wider, then slipped inside to stroke hers, lightly at
first, and then more aggressively.

She was aware of another moan slipping from her mouth to
his, aware of the warm tendrils of desire uncurling inside her.
Like sensation returning to a sleep-numbed limb, prickles of
need ran over her skin. Beneath the thin shirt, her breasts tingled as the nipples engorged.

Between her legs, a hot liquid tension began building until
she ached to be stroked into an explosion of pleasure. She

whimpered when the kiss ended, her hands grabbing fistfuls of his hair in an effort to pull him closer again.

"Easy, sweets," Case murmured, his voice husky and lashed with strain.

Prudy felt her dream start to slip away as her senses sharpened. Frowning, she sought to reclaim the lovely sensations feathering just beyond her reach. Reluctantly she opened her eyes to find her still-parted lips only inches from Case's unsmiling mouth.

"Something wrong?" he asked when she continued to stare at him.

"You were kissing me," she managed after lubricating her dry throat with a hasty swallow. "I thought it was a dream," she added when one side of his mouth edged upward. His hard cheek flirted with the dimple that lurked there, bemusing her.

"At least you didn't call it a nightmare."

As though held in check until this moment, his grin slashed white. Beneath the dark brows that always appeared angry, even when he wasn't, his sapphire irises were suddenly shot with silver.

"Your coffee's cold," she said when she realized she was in danger of melting against him again. "I'll just pop it into the microwave for a couple of minutes."

He shook his head. "I don't want coffee."

"Tea, then," she said, easing farther into the corner of the couch.

He used the hand that had been doing such delicious things to her nerve endings to push back the thick lock of hair tumbling over his forehead.

"What I *want* is to know what you want. And I don't mean to drink."

Prudy blinked, her gaze locked on his. The teasing glint was gone from his eyes, and his jaw was tensed, the way it always was when he dealing with feelings he refused to put into words. Her senses went on alert, though she curved her lips in a smile.

"It would help if you rephrase your question in more specific terms,'' she said lightly, though her stomach was now doing somersaults.

"You. Me. For the next month or so. How do you want to play it?"

"You're the patient, I'm the nurse," she ticked off firmly. "You do what I say."

His mouth quirked, but the tension in his face refused to ease. "Fair enough—if I stay."

She drew a breath. "Case, we've been through all this—"

"Straight talk, Prudy. I was only thinking about myself when I forced you into agreeing to take me in." He scowled, then raked an impatient hand through his hair. "Look, if you want me to go to that damned nursing home, I will."

Stunned, Prudy opened her mouth to respond, only to close it again when she realized she had no idea what she wanted to say.

His face took on a dangerous wash of red. "Don't look at me like that, dammit."

"Like...what?"

"Like you think I've lost it all of a sudden."

"You mean you haven't?"

"Probably," he muttered, glancing past her toward the front door. "Why pink?" he asked suddenly.

"Pardon?"

"The damn door. Why did you paint it pink?"

Puzzled, Prudy turned to look at the door, which was an ordinary ivory on the inside. It struck her then that he meant the lovely fuchsia enamel on the outside.

"Because I got tired of all the gray around me every winter."

Prepared for one of his caustic remarks about her "whims," she was amazed when he merely nodded.

"Did you mean it, what you said the night I stayed?" He drew a fast breath. "About not having a special guy in your life right now?"

"I'm not dating anyone special, no," she hedged.

He cleared his throat. "So the timing would be good."

Prudy felt the blood pounding in her head. Case hadn't been

this awkward since the first few weeks of their courtship, when he'd tripped over his words and all but growled at her when asking her for a date.

"Timing for what?" Her voice was only slightly breathless, a remarkable feat given the aching tightness in her throat.

"Starting over."

"You and me?" she probed carefully.

"Hell, yes, you and me," he all but shouted at her. "From square one. No baggage from the past. No heavy expectations for the future."

Prudy felt her hands begin to tremble and pressed them tightly together. "Why now?" she asked, almost afraid to hear his answer.

"Because I'm crazy about you, that's why!" The growl was back in his voice, and her heart soared. "I love you, Prue. God help me, I always have."

"Oh."

"Oh? That's all you can say?"

"Well, I guess I could say you have good taste."

His teeth ground together and his brows formed an angry line over his arrogant nose. "You're enjoying this," he muttered.

"Yes," she said, her voice shaking. "I'm loving it. And you."

He started to reach for her. She forestalled him with an upheld hand. "I made you a promise once, that I would never lie to you again, and I meant it. I need to know that you believe me, truly believe me. That if we do this, you won't be holding back your trust. Otherwise, it'll never work."

His eyes darkened. "I believe you."

"No matter what 'evidence' you might have to the contrary?"

His gaze flickered. "You're asking a lot of a man who makes life or death decisions based on the evidence he sees with his own eyes."

She touched his stubborn jaw. Hope was just a fragile thing. As fragile as trust. "I'm asking for what I need, Case. If it's more than you can give, then, please, tell me now, while I still have some defenses left.''

His throat worked as he swallowed. "I want to be with you. If that's your condition for allowing me into your life again, I'll agree.''

Prudy felt a moment of utter joy, which was quickly dampened by an echo in her head of his careful wording. "There's a big difference between agreeing to a condition and unconditional love.''

She was close enough to see the shadow of impatience that crossed his face. "Prue, I can't predict the future, or how I'll feel about some phantom 'evidence.' I know I love you and I want you and I'm willing to accept what you tell me without reservation.''

His gaze probed the depths of her eyes. "Windows to the soul," he'd quoted her once in all seriousness. "Now I'm asking you to believe me. Can you?''

Keeping her gaze steady on his, she answered as honestly as she could, "I'm afraid, Case. Afraid I'll say something that strikes you as false and you'll start to look at me with those same...cold eyes. I can't...go through that again. It hurts too much.''

He drew a deep breath, the only sign of emotion he was willing to reveal. Or perhaps couldn't prevent.

"Tell you what. Why don't we start out with baby steps this time? Use this time to get to know each other.''

Her smile felt rueful on her lips, and just a little shaky. "Baby steps I can manage.''

His grin was unexpected and irresistible. "Then we have a deal?'' he demanded, holding out his left hand.

She felt like shouting, yet reminded herself they'd only made it over the first hurdle. No longer the blissfully naive girl he'd married, she knew there would be others. Higher ones, perhaps. Telling him about the baby would be the highest of all. One she knew she wasn't yet ready to attempt.

She needed a few more weeks to prepare him. Just a few more. Until he was medically sound and she was stronger. *But he's just told you he'll believe you, no matter what,* a voice niggled.

It shook her to realize that for all her fine words about unconditional trust, she couldn't quite make herself believe him. But she would, she told herself. Just as he would believe her. All they needed now was time.

"No deal," she murmured impishly. "Not until you kiss me."

"Bossing me around already?" His grin was lopsided and just a little wary.

"You bet, hotshot. Care to argue?"

The light that came into his eyes drew her closer, even though she was sitting perfectly still. "No argument," he said, lifting his hand to her face. His thumb lightly brushed the corner of her mouth.

"You've been eating my cookies, haven't you?"

She blinked. "I...how did you know?"

He showed her his hand. There was a speck of chocolate on his thumb. "Evidence," he said, his mouth kicking up at one corner before he licked his thumb. She watched his mouth, fascinated by the combination of hard determination and flagrant sensuality.

"Ready?" he demanded, his eyes smiling even though his mouth remained somber. And irresistible.

"Ready?" she echoed, blinking.

"For your kiss?"

Bemused, she nodded. Somehow she'd lost track of their discussion, and she'd definitely lost control of the situation. His eyes were still open, still smiling, as she let hers flutter closed. His mouth was gentle on hers, his lips soft. The kiss brief.

She frowned when it ended and opened her eyes.

"Baby steps, remember?" he said, the smile in his eyes replaced by a devil's triumph. Oh, yes, she'd lost control, all right. And suddenly, it felt wonderful.

Chapter 14

Case took another swig of breakfast coffee and waited for the caffeine to kick in. Across the table, Prudy had been busily pushing granola around the bowl for the past five minutes.

Hell, he thought as he studied her bent head. Maybe she was having second thoughts about letting him back into her life already. It was possible. After all, she had a soft heart, and he'd done his damnedest to play on it. He felt a moment of panic before he ruthlessly leveled it. Whatever was bugging her had a cause, just as every crime, big or small, had a motive. It was his job to dig deep enough to find it. Like clues in a particularly thorny case.

Hell, he was a detective sergeant, wasn't he? And a damned good cop. Taught by the best. Hadn't Petrov ragged on him about that often enough? All he had to do was stop chewing on the "maybes" and get to the "what is." Once he'd peeled away the right layers, he'd be able to deal with the truth she was so reluctant to reveal.

"Did I say something wrong?" he probed cautiously. Better to shift her attention to him in order to put her at ease.

"When?"

"Uh, this morning?"

She shot him another look. "Let's see," she mused, her lips twitching. "First you said—no, *demanded*—'Kiss me good morning,' which was actually more of a growl. That was a few minutes after seven. At seven-fifteen you asked me if I intended to stay in the bathroom until hell froze over, then—"

"Ouch," he muttered, shifting. "Guess I've gotten a little set in my ways—"

"More like encased in stone."

Case winced. "That bad, huh?"

"Worse."

Case hid his relief behind a conciliatory nod. What she said made sense, all right. And, yeah, she probably had cause to complain. His mood *had* been marginal at best since he'd settled in.

From her perspective, it had probably been a rocky three days since his arrival. From his perspective, it had been a lousy two nights. He figured he'd slept a total of fifteen minutes. Not so much because of the pain, which he'd handled as he usually did by ignoring it, but because she'd insisted on sleeping in another room.

It should have been easy to explain his frustration to the woman he still considered his wife, no matter what that damned piece of paper full of lawyer's jargon in his safety-deposit box might proclaim.

It wasn't easy at all. In fact, it was damned impossible.

"Would it help if I promised to reform?" He tried a grin.

"Define 'reform,'" she demanded cautiously.

"Uh, promise to let you help me more."

He knew he was manipulating her, playing on her compassion and kindness to evade revealing his true feelings, but he told himself it was in a good cause. After all, patching together their marriage was what counted, right?

"Help you how?" she asked after a moment's reflection during which she chewed on her lip and watched him closely with those soft brown eyes.

Case searched his mind. How many times had they argued in the past three days? A couple of dozen? Fifty? A hundred?

Most of their "discussions" had centered around his pride, which she considered excessive. So maybe it *was* shaded a bit toward stiff, but he'd been trying. Hadn't he? Except when she wanted to wrap his leg and arm in plastic before she'd let him near the shower. No plastic, no shower. As for his pathetic attempts at feeding himself with his left hand, well… Stifling a sigh, he decided he'd be a model patient—even if it killed him.

"I'm not going to let you feed me," he grumbled, then caught himself when she frowned. "Okay, you can cut my steak, but I can eat the damned thing myself."

As he hoped, she laughed, and for an instant, her eyes had sparkled at him the way they used to, when they were both young and crazy in love. He felt his chest expand as he leaned across the table to beg a kiss.

She responded eagerly, her lips clinging to his and her small hands framing his face with a heart-stopping possessiveness. But when the kiss ended, and they drew apart, the uninhibited joy he'd expected to see in her eyes was gone, replaced by that same wary look he was coming to hate.

A look he swore held secrets.

Prudy opened her eyes to the hazy gray light of dawn. Because she wasn't by nature an early riser, she knew something had pulled her from sleep. For an instant, she was afraid the morning sickness had returned, but after a few deep, testing breaths produced nothing more than a little giddiness, she realized that something else must have disturbed her.

Had Case called out to her?

Alarm jolted through her as she left the sewing room and padded down the hall to the bedroom.

Case was still deeply asleep, lying on his back, his casted arm lying across his belly, his other arm under his pillow. His ebony hair was tousled around his head and lay in lazy waves over his brow, a dramatic contrast to the yellow pillowcase. The tiny hoop in his left earlobe caught her gaze, reminding her of the dangerous role he sometimes played, working undercover in the line of duty.

His face, too, showed the toll exacted from a man by a job that stayed with him around the clock, day in, day out. Only a man with a will of iron could survive that kind of pressure—not to mention the danger and constantly having to mingle with the dregs of mankind—with a large chunk of his humanity intact. She traced the strong, stubborn line of his jaw with her gaze.

Awake, Case projected an aura of barely restrained energy and impatience, a man who seemed to be moving even when he was perfectly still. Asleep, he was adorable. A larger, stronger version of the irrepressible, adventurous boy he must have been.

She smiled as she remembered the time she'd teased him about the slight pouting frown he invariably wore as he slept, as though he resented each and every moment his body forced him to be unproductive.

It was those deep-set, arresting blue eyes that marked the most striking change in him when he awoke, she'd finally decided as she allowed herself to edge closer. So watchful and penetrating when they settled on your face, as though he were looking beyond the masks people wore to the vulnerable nakedness within. Only a rare individual could endure that unflinching, measuring gaze without withering. Only those with nothing to hide could survive unscathed. Yet, when those eyes softened into a smile, he had a way of making a man relax or a woman purr.

She loved those eyes, she realized. And feared the truths they sought. Beautiful eyes in an interesting, compelling face. A man's face, more angles than curves, more carved than molded.

His thick eyelashes lay straight and black against his cheeks, perfect half moons against his permanently bronzed skin. Boldly drawn, his eyebrows formed twin slashes of angry black above a nose that was a trifle too long, yet surprisingly straight, as though his wild ways had spared that one part of him.

That wonderfully, exasperatingly stubborn jaw she loved was darkly shadowed by a night's growth of whisker stubble that she knew would feel erotically rough and virile against her cheek. She'd seen pictures of him in his early twenties wearing a beard he'd grown on a vacation he and Don had taken to the wilds of Canada. Black as sin, it had hidden the hard line of his jaw and covered the character lines that had slashed deep on either side of his mouth even then. Though neatly trimmed, the beard had made her uneasy, perhaps because it gave him the look of a man unable—or unwilling—to be tamed.

Only the fear of waking him kept her from leaning closer to touch the large, warm chest only inches away. Bleached several shades lighter than the ebony of his hair by the same sun that had layered his skin with bronze, the furry pelt covering his pectoral muscles would feel soft and springy under her fingertips. Or her breasts, she thought as they began tingling.

Nestled in the enticing thatch of chest hair were flat, masculine nipples she longed to touch with the tip of her tongue, knowing that when she did, his breath would hiss into that wide chest and his muscle-tracked belly would go slab hard.

Slowly, feeling desire unfurling warm tendrils deep inside her body, she allowed her gaze to follow the trail of dark body hair bisecting that same corded belly to the spot where it flared again to encompass his sex.

She pouted a little to discover the sheet angled across his hips, obscuring the impressive contours of his masculine physique.

"Feel free to explore any area you find interesting." His voice was still rusty from sleep and lashed with amusement that had her face heating even as she jerked her gaze to his face.

"I was worried you might be in pain," she said, and then felt her blush deepen. "In your leg, I mean."

His mouth took on an endearing slant. "No pain."

"Good."

He withdrew his left hand from beneath his pillow and used it to capture hers.

"I could use a good-morning kiss," he murmured, his eyes

still a drowsy midnight blue between lashes as black as the witching hour.

She allowed her lips to curve as she leaned forward to press a quick kiss on his muscle-padded shoulder.

"How's that?"

His grin was slow in coming and definitely menacing, arousing fast little spurts of excitement in her blood.

"You do like to live dangerously, don't you, sweets?"

She started to scoot backward only to have him tug her closer.

"Now, Case, your blood pressure—"

"Is fine. Or it will be as soon as I get a decent kiss."

"Define decent," she demanded, but she was already inching closer.

"Sit first," he ordered imperiously. And then, somehow she was on the bed, angled across his hard, warm body. The instant her breasts slid over his chest, his breath hitched. Beneath the thin cotton nightshirt her nipples puckered into hot nubs, and her own breathing faltered.

His hard fingers cupped the back of her head, guiding her mouth to his. As soon as their lips met, pleasure exploded inside her, and she moaned.

She felt his mouth curve before his lips were feasting on hers, tasting, nipping, teasing her lips apart to allow his tongue to taste deeper.

"Sweet," he whispered, his voice husky and moist against her mouth an instant before the kiss turned hungry and demanding. Now his tongue stroked and swirled around hers until she was sucking on him. Needing an anchor, she slipped her hands around his neck, and pressed closer.

He groaned, shifted, until she felt his hand splayed against her derriere, his fingers kneading as they inched the nightshirt higher.

"Oh, Case," she managed when they drew apart for air. "We shouldn't."

"The hell we shouldn't," he grated as he released her just long enough to fling off the covers.

"Dammit," he muttered when he tried to use his right hand to rid her of her nightshirt.

"Let me," she said when he started to glower. After raising herself to her knees, she quickly slipped the shirt over her head and tossed it to the floor.

His face grew taut as he ran his gaze the length of her body. Aware of the changes the baby had made, she held her breath. Would he notice? His eyes were intense, his expression absorbed. Unreadable.

The blush of heat that had left her face returned. "You're…staring," she whispered in an agony of suspense.

"Admiring," he corrected, lifting his gaze to hers. "You're amazing."

"I am?"

He nodded, his pupils very dark. "You're rounder. Softer. Sexier." His mouth kicked into an enticing comma at one side. "Your breasts are fuller and your skin is so white and…tempting." He reached out to flatten his hand against her side. The contrast of his darker skin against hers was unexpectedly poignant, and she swallowed.

"I want to make love to you, Prudence O'Grady, but I'm afraid I'll rip you in two, I want you so much," he murmured, echoing the same words he'd uttered to her when she was twenty-three and a virgin.

"You won't hurt me," she said as she'd said then.

His smile was as gentle as his hand as he began stroking her. Pleasure feathered along her skin wherever his fingers touched, sensitizing her, arousing her.

"Come here," he ordered, his voice raspy with need.

With a soft, eager sigh, she snuggled against him, luxuriating in the blissful feeling of skin against skin. Careful not to jar his injured leg, she ran her hand along the corrugated slope of his belly, loving the hard, mean contours of unyielding bone and steely muscle.

His breath whistled through his teeth as her fingers burrowed into the soft curls below his navel, then withdrew.

"Don't stop there," he said in a gravelly whisper, his free

hand fisting in her hair. "God, baby, I love your hands on me."

Prudy ran her fingertips over the hair-roughened concavity of his belly, her touch moving closer and closer to the little dent in the middle. Beneath her skimming palm, his muscles spasmed, out of his control.

He muttered a low plea that exploded the last remnants of hesitation and she let her fingers burrow lower. He was fully aroused. Painfully aroused.

"Yes, baby, yes," he grated when she allowed her hand to measure the full length of him.

She pressed a kiss to his belly, then encircled him with her fingers. He was hot and hard, yet surprisingly silky. Satin over steel. Fierce and proud.

Case felt her small hand close around him and a pleasure such as he'd never known flooded through him. She was sweet and still slightly shy, his lady, which made her tentative caresses all the more arousing.

He choked out her name, his control eroding more with each slow, gliding stroke of her palm, each gentle exploration of her fingers. Sweet Lord on high, he wanted to be hard for her, strong for her, to give her the same wild pleasure she was giving him.

When he could bear it no longer, he began moving, thrusting against her hand. Her fingers tightened, squeezed, and he had to suck in hard to keep from yelling the house down.

"Prue," he pleaded, unable to keep his hand from tugging on her hair. "Take me inside you, baby. Now, before I explode."

It was a heady experience to be in control, to be the one to open herself to his hard upward thrusts, to decide when to settle over him, enveloping him in the warmth of her love.

With one strong movement of his hips, he buried himself to the hilt, his hand on her hip, his neck arched backward. She cried out in joy and pleasure and let him take over, his thrusts coming faster and faster, a frenzy of need matched by her own.

The culmination came quickly, seizing them both with the same intensity, their cries blending with the same wild pleasure as their bodies. She collapsed against him, her face pressed to his throat and her breathing labored.

Still sheathed in hot velvet, he closed his eyes and brought both arms around her. He felt the fragile cadence of her heartbeat, strangely in sync with the body-jarring rhythm of his own, as their breathing slowly settled into a more normal pattern.

Outside, the morning birds heralded a new day, their cheerful cries blending with the distant hum of morning traffic. Below the ridge, a barge, plying its slow way upriver, signaled a course change with a single blaring blast.

Prudy sighed at the commonplace sounds, so familiar to her that she'd stopped hearing them. But now, lying sated and boneless in Case's sheltering embrace, she felt reborn. Attuned to every sight and sound. Deliciously alive.

Still partially aroused, Case rubbed his nose against the silk of her hair, inhaling the intoxicating scent of flowers. From the living room came the muted bonging of the big old grandfather clock, into which he had stumbled, usually nose first, more times than he could count, compliments of Prudy's penchant for rearranging the furniture without telling him. He counted the chimes. Six o'clock. Damn, but it was good—so very good—to be home. She could paint the house puce with a garish green door. He didn't give a damn. Just as long as he had his own key.

"Good thing you're not on duty today," he murmured, idly stroking her back.

Prudy started to nod dreamily, then let out an anguished sigh. "But I am," she cried in a mournful tone. "Marge had a hot date with an airline pilot who's only in town for the day, and she promised to trade me three days for her one." She closed her eyes, unwilling to move, yet knowing she had to get up and shower. "Little did I know how much I'd be missing if I left."

His laugh was delightfully rich, its vibrations tickling her tummy where it was pressed against his groin. "You never could think ahead, my sweet Prudy." And it was one of the things he loved most about her, he silently added, that adorable impulsiveness.

The reply she'd planned dammed in her throat as she felt an odd flutter in her belly. Like a quick little hiccup. Frowning, she held her breath. In less than a heartbeat, it came again. Her heart swelled with joy as she realized her baby had just delivered its first kick.

"Prudy? Is something wrong?"

She felt Case's arms tighten and burrowed her head into the warm hollow of his strong throat. If only she had the courage to take his big strong hand and press it against her womb. But the thought that he would hate that soft little flutter as much as she loved it held her back.

"No," she whispered as her eyes stung from the tears she dared not shed. "Everything's fine. Just fine."

Or it would be soon, she promised herself.

It had to be.

Boyd threw down his cards and shot Case a disgusted look across the dining table, the usual clutter of Prudy's treasured collectibles cleared away to accommodate the poker players. "Count me out, you lucky so-and-so."

"Man cheats, sure enough," Luke Jarrod muttered, his gaze fixed on the cards fanned out in one huge hand.

"Up yours, cowboy," Case drawled with a lazy wink in Prudy's direction.

"Behave yourselves, boys," she chided before tipping Case's beer bottle to her mouth.

Case watched her lips close around the slick neck of the bottle and felt his body stirring beneath the cutoffs he'd taken to wearing to accommodate his cast.

Luke glanced up. "Slow down there, girl. No alcohol, remember."

Prudy's hand shot to her waist, and bright flags of color slashed her delicately molded cheekbones. Luke shot her another look, then directed his gaze at Case.

"She's been, um, having some stomach trouble. Acid, I think."

Case arched an eyebrow. "So *that's* why you're down to one cup of coffee a day." He winked at Luke. "Don't screw with the lady's one cup of morning coffee. She was slicing cantaloupe when I did, and for a minute there, I thought she was gonna relieve me of my, um, masculine charm."

He arched Prudy a teasing look, his gaze moving quickly over her and assessing all points of interest. Once the game ended and everyone left, it would take five minutes, tops, to sweet talk her into the bedroom. Another five to peel her out of those baggy sweats, he promised himself as he watched the sway of her world-class backside as she walked toward the kitchen, carrying four empty beer bottles and an empty bowl that had once held about a bushel of potato chips.

"How about scaring up some more of that clam dip, while you're at it?" Don called after her with a wheedling tone.

Pausing, she looked back to offer Don a severe look. "Now, Don, it wasn't but two nights ago that you were sitting right there on our sofa complaining about your cholesterol level."

"Ah, Prue—"

"Don't 'ah, Prue' me, Petrov," she scolded, shaking her head. "It was bad enough having Case come through my ER. I don't want to show up some morning and see you there, too."

Don scowled. "Hey, I'm not the one with the Superman complex who thinks he's faster than a speeding bullet."

"No, you're the one who's going to have a stroke if he doesn't get his cholesterol count *and* his weight down," she countered before disappearing into the kitchen.

"Women sure do like to have the last word," Petrov muttered to the table at large.

"Course, in this case, she just might be right," Boyd commented with a pointed look at Petrov's midsection.

"Hell, no, she's not right," Petrov declared, huffing. "A man in my line of work needs more bulk than most. Ain't that right, Case?"

Case took his time answering. He hadn't given his partner's expanding gut much thought—until he'd heard Prudy warning him about the chances he was taking with his health, "given his family history of strokes."

Hell, he'd known Don for more than half his life and knew squat about his family history. But then, Prudy had taken the time to ask questions and listen to the answers.

His lady was at her best taking care of others, he realized. A born nurturer. A natural mother.

He felt his gut twist. No kids, he reminded himself as he grinned across the table at his partner.

"Come to think about it, I have noticed you slowing down a step or two lately." The guilty look in Petrov's soulful eyes had him cursing his lack of tact. Unfortunately, now that he'd taken the leap, Case also knew Don's masculine pride would suffer more if he cut him any slack. Women nurtured; men razzed.

"Not to mention the trouble you've been having getting behind the steering wheel," he added in a lighter tone. "Or that you've got to lengthen the seat belt after I've used it."

"Bull!" Don exclaimed as he glanced toward the curtained windows. "Too bad Stan Morey is stuck outside in the unmarked. I've cleaned him out of more beer money than any other guy at the station."

"Any more word on that guy, Cardoza?" Boyd asked before bumping up the pot another twenty-five.

"Nothing worth squat. He was staying in a flophouse down by the warehouse district until a few days ago. Led the man we had on him a wild-goose chase over to Vancouver, then up and disappeared."

Luke glanced up. "Back home in Arizona, scum like that has a way of ending up buzzard bait."

Case grinned. "Spoken like a true cowboy."

Luke snorted. "Up yours, double, Randolph."

"Man has a point, though," Don said before folding. "Too bad we've gotten so damned civilized in the past hundred years."

* * *

In the kitchen, Prudy slathered hot mustard onto another slice of pumpernickel before slapping it onto the mound of ham, cheese and salami.

"Shoot, I forgot the onions and peppers," she muttered, shaking her head.

"Give that one to Boyd," Stacy said, opening another bag of chips. She and Tory had stopped by to share a cup of tea with Prudy while Boyd was losing his shirt in the other room. Tory was now asleep in the Portacrib in the spare room. "Peppers keep him awake. Besides, I'll be happy to eat his share."

"I thought you were craving sardines instead of peppers this time around," Prudy said, slicing the sandwich into two neat halves before adding them to the already laden tray.

"Both, actually. How about you? What are you craving these days besides those koshers you devour by the gallon?"

"Sex," she admitted, then blushed when Stacy burst out laughing.

"I thought there was a special glow about you these days."

Prudy brushed back her hair and wondered how soon the poker game would break up. Now that she and Case were sharing a bed again, she was anxious to be in it.

"I feel as giddy as a bride," she admitted with a soft laugh. "And deliriously happy."

Stacy nodded. "I know the feeling."

Prudy glanced toward the door before confiding, "The baby's started kicking. Just little flutters so far, but definite kicks. I was so excited the first time I felt it." She drew a breath. "I feel like I'm cheating Case by not sharing this with him."

"Have you mentioned this to Boyd?"

Prudy nodded. "Yesterday, at the hospital. He's still worried about Case's blood pressure and asked me to wait another few weeks before I tell him."

"Oh, Prue, this has to be agony for you." Stacy frowned. "Are you sure you're in any shape to take Tory while we're gone? Yesterday, when Boyd told me about the surprise he had planned and that you'd volunteered to take Tory, I was so excited I wasn't thinking straight. But now—"

"Not to worry," Prudy interrupted with a breezy wave of her hand. "I have it all planned."

"Uh-oh, why do I think I don't want to hear this?" Stacy muttered to the knife in her hand.

"No, really, Stace. It can't miss. I saw Case's face when Molly finally talked him into holding little Casey. At first, he had this panic-stricken look in his eyes, and then he just…fell in love. I swear, I saw it happening. I just know it'll be the same with Tory."

Stacy bit her lip, then sighed. "Prue, much as I dislike raining on this rainbow parade of yours, I feel compelled to point out that there's a great deal of difference between a newborn who's all sweet smelling and cuddly, and an almost-two hellion in training pants."

Prudy licked the mustard from the knife before tossing it into the sink. "I know that, but Tory's such a love, even when she's being energetic—"

"A holy terror, you mean."

"Now, Stace, she always behaves like a perfect little angel when I have her here alone."

"That's because she's not here twenty-four hours a day." Stacy rolled her eyes. "Trust me, there's a lot of devil in that particular angel."

Prudy considered Stacy an exemplary mother, but her friend's tolerance for mischief was far lower than her own. After all, she'd had years of training in pediatric psychology and behavior. How much trouble could a tiny wisp of a little girl cause, anyway?

Chapter 15

"I should get up and shower," Prudy murmured as she rubbed her cheek against Case's hard chest.

Sated and drowsy after an hour of lovemaking, she lay stretched out on top of him, carefully keeping herself positioned to one side to avoid putting weight on his cast. Lightly caressing his bony ankle with the toe of one foot, she lay with her other leg slightly bent, her knee resting on his warm, muscular thigh. Beneath her, his long, rangy body felt like well-padded satin molded over steel. His heart was still beating more rapidly than usual.

"You have time yet," Case lifted a lock of her hair and let it sift through his fingers, his touch as reverent as though he were testing the grain of rare and expensive silk. She smiled at the lovely feeling of contentment she felt whenever she was in his arms.

"It's raining," she murmured, lifting her head to glance out the window at a sky darkened by cumbrous slate clouds, nearly indistinguishable from the pearly twilight of dawn. Lazy beads of moisture clung to the eaves before falling like iridescent teardrops to the ground. The rhythmic dripping sound soothed

Prudy, making her feel languorous. Or was it the steady, reassuring thud of Case's heartbeat that filled her with a sense that everything was right in her world?

"It's November. It always rains this time of year." He lifted his head to plant a warm, wet kiss on her responsive mouth. Prudy felt a small flutter of pleasure skip-hopping down her spine and let out a long sigh.

"Do you like that?" he asked, looking smugly male and very sexy with his rumpled dark hair and lazy, devilish grin.

"Hmm, I'm not sure," she pretended to ponder. "Maybe if you did it again."

Their mouths met in a sweetly tender kiss, with just the tips of their tongues touching. He made a sound in his throat, half groan, half growl, and deepened the kiss, his tongue stroking and darting, then caressing the already swollen curve of her lower lip. Beneath her thigh his body surged. When the kiss ended, she drew back to look at him. In spite of the inclement weather of the past few days, his previous weeks in the sun had obliterated the hospital pallor and deepened his tan. He looked relaxed and happy. A virile, vital man in his prime.

"Have I told you recently how crazy I am about you?" Her voice had a sultry tremor that had his vivid blue eyes taking on smoky centers.

"Not since last Sunday night, right before you slipped in the fact that our happy home was about to be invaded by Patton's army."

She choked on a laugh. "Now, Case, Tory doesn't mean to cause trouble. She's still a baby."

The corners of his mouth dipped into a frown, but his eyes were still hazed with desire. "She's a menace," he grumbled, his hand stroking her breast.

"She's not. She's just missing her mommy and daddy, that's all."

"She throws tantrums. She cries. She refuses to eat. Then when she does eat, she throws up."

Prudy had to bite her lip to keep from laughing at the memory of Case's stunned expression when the banana he'd spent an hour coaxing Tory to finish made a fast return trip—all over his favorite T-shirt. To his credit, he'd handled the mini-disaster with self-deprecating humor instead of fury—after she'd reassured him that he hadn't somehow poisoned Tory by mistake.

"She's only been here three days. Give her time to adjust."

"Hell, what about me? I'm the one going through a shock. I don't know squat about kids."

Prudy managed a teasing pout. "How come, if you don't know anything about kids, Tory keeps bringing *you* her books to read instead of her doting Aunt Prudy?"

"Because she's female, and all females are born with a need to work their wiles on a man whenever possible. Like you, sweet witch."

Before she could protest, he covered her mouth with his in another draining kiss. His hand was warm and gentle on her breast as he fondled the sensitive flesh. The nipple hardened beneath the skillful manipulation of his callused fingers, and she sighed against his lips.

"Ah, sweets, I love it when you beg," he teased in a throaty rumble.

"I'm not…oh!"

With one easy motion, he rolled her to her back, careful to keep his casted leg from crushing hers. In the month since he'd left the hospital, he'd regained an impressive amount of strength. Other than the casts on his arm and leg and his still-elevated blood pressure, he was healthy enough now to live on his own.

"Case," she murmured, "we can't."

"Can't what?" He sponged her nipple with his tongue, and she gasped.

"Can't…aah." She lost her train of thought when he took the tip of her breast into his mouth. His tongue played and stroked, kissing the hard little nub into hot pleasure. Sinking fast, she watched his jaw flex as he began sucking gently, his morning whiskers wonderfully erotic against her skin. His eyes were closed, crinkling the corners, and his lashes were inky crescents on his hard cheekbones.

Even in the dim morning light she could see a light frosting of silver in the tumble of ebony hair that had grown even longer during his enforced convalescence. She ran her fingers through the softly waving thickness as she held his head to her breast, hoping the pleasure would go on forever.

She whimpered when he lifted his mouth, only to sigh when his mouth closed over the other breast. Again, he licked and sucked, using his lips and his tongue to finesse the nipple into nearly unbearable heat.

Rolling her head side to side she choked out a strangled plea. She needed him inside her, filling her. Yet he continued to lavish attention on her breasts, his tongue devilish and talented, driving her deeper and deeper into a velvet madness.

She felt the pressure deep inside, building and easing, to the rhythm of his mouth. Her breathing was labored as she writhed beneath him, driven now by primitive urges beyond her control. Finally, when she knew she would die from the longing, he drew back, his breathing as rapid and harsh as her own. His face was taut, his eyes blazing as he nudged her legs apart.

Conscious of the heavy cast that hindered his movements, she braced her hands on his shoulders and arched upward as he slowly thrust into her. He was thick and hard, sliding into the slick sheath with a maddening slowness.

"Case, please," she choked out, her nails sinking into the heavy muscle padding his shoulders.

With a deep groan, he thrust harder, knotting the tension inside her tighter until finally, like a shower of hot rain, the tension shattered. She heard her own cry of ecstasy, felt him shudder.

He cried her name as he came, collapsing against her damp skin, his breath coming in great gasps.

"If that doesn't send my blood pressure into the stratosphere, nothing will," he muttered against her throat.

Prudy chuckled, her hands clutching his hard buttocks, preventing him from withdrawing. "I think you're definitely on the mend," she murmured, kissing the top of his head. His body glistened with a sheen of perspiration, as did her own.

"I guess that's what the manuals mean when they refer to

afterglow,'' she murmured, trailing one hand up the curve of his spine. His skin was slick and hot, and she allowed herself to imagine them making love under a hot island sun.

"What manuals?" His voice was as drowsy as his expression.

"Sex manuals."

He growled something sightly obscene, and she giggled. "Want me to describe in clinical detail what just happened?"

"Not on your life, witch. I like my own version." He dropped a kiss on her mouth, then rolled to his back.

"Which is?"

"Whatever deity really runs this universe of ours designed one man for one woman. I just happened to be lucky enough to get the most luscious pick of the litter."

Prudy blinked, then snorted. "Gee, Case, you sure know how to make a girl feel loved."

His laugh was deep and throaty. She was seriously thinking about shoving him off the bed when he turned his head and looked at her. The expression in his eyes had her throat closing and her heart pounding.

"Tell me the words you want, Prue, and I'll say them. As many times as I have to convince you."

"Oh, Case," she whispered, emotion welling inside her until she was shaking. "I was only teasing."

He touched her face. "I'm only half-alive without you, Prudy. I admit it's taken me a while to figure that out, but I never want you to doubt it."

Prudy took a deep breath, trying to ease the sudden knots in her insides. Her heart was thudding so loudly she knew he had to hear the din. Fear for Case's health warred with a terrible need to tell him the truth. And yet, how could she live with herself if Boyd was right about the risk?

"I love you, too," she whispered, her voice breaking. "And when the time is right, there's something important I need to…share with you."

Curiosity edged out the wary sincerity in his eyes, and she nearly groaned aloud. "How about now? I doubt I could get much more…receptive."

She shook her head, aware that she shouldn't have broached the subject. "I thought I heard Tory stirring," she hedged as she sat up.

"Couldn't have," he said, turning to his side. "She's not screaming."

As though on cue, Tory let out a shrill "Mommeee."

Prudy winced, and Case groaned. "Ten more days," he muttered as she pulled on her robe. "And then we can give her back."

It was less than a week before Thanksgiving, and although the sun shone with summer brilliance, the air had a definite bite. Still, it was a glorious day for a toddler to play outside—and a rare chance for said toddler's honorary aunt to grab a moment of silence for herself.

The MacAuleys were due home in three days, and Prudy had to admit she would be very glad to see them. Taking care of Tory *and* a man chafing at the days of enforced inactivity had pushed her to the very limit of her patience, yet at the same time had her mourning the fact that her patient would soon be released by his physician to resume his job.

To his credit, Case had helped her with Tory as much as his limited mobility and dexterity had allowed, entertaining the child with stories and puzzles and gentle bouts of rough-housing on the living room floor every evening before bed, but Prudy had been the one who'd had the bulk of the responsibility for Tory's safety and well-being.

The little vixen, she thought as she finished stowing the last of the breakfast dishes in the dishwasher. In spite of Case's grumbling, it hadn't taken Tory more than a few days to win him over. Little by little, his defenses had crumbled until he was behaving more like a devoted uncle than an unwilling observer. Prudy doubted that Case had yet to realize that he was crazy about this little one—and as protective as an alpha wolf watching over his cub.

Even Don, when he'd stopped by a few nights earlier with some files for Case to review, had mentioned the affection that seemed to flow between his usually reserved partner and the tiny sprite with the big green eyes.

"What'd I tell you, half pint? Putty in her hands," Don had whispered in Prudy's ear as he'd hugged her good-night.

Smiling to herself, Prudy stood at the kitchen window, drying her hands and watching Tory toddle after the soft red ball Case had just tossed toward her. Arms outstretched, she'd giggled when the ball had skittered off her tiny hand, her small face alive with delight at having her new playmate all to herself. Beneath the fuzzy white stocking cap, Tory's cheeks were pink from the wind.

As Tory bent to pick up something lying on the grass, Prudy noticed that the little girl's jacket was unzipped. She was about to open the window and yell at Case to zip it up, when he called Tory to him.

Laughing, the little one obeyed instantly, toddling to the lawn chair where he was sitting with his casted leg extended and his crutches lying next to him. Prudy chuckled when she saw the large brown feather clutched tightly in Tory's chubby fist.

While Case awkwardly zipped her jacket with his left hand, then tugged the cap more firmly around her ears, Tory chattered a mile a minute in a jabberwocky jargon uniquely her own. Yet Case listened to her intently, as though understanding every word.

He looked so cute sitting there with his head bent attentively, his gaze fixed on the little girl's animated face. The hand with the cast was pressed protectively against her tiny waist in a gentle hug.

Suddenly he laughed, and she grinned. Very gently, he took the feather she held up and used it to tickle her neck. Squealing in surprise, she grabbed for the feather.

Prudy felt her eyes filling with tears as Tory climbed onto Case's good knee with the confidence of a child who knows she's loved. She bobbed her head as though lecturing him, then settled back against his broad chest, popped her thumb in her mouth and waited.

For a story, Prudy realized as Case took the feather from

her fingers and began to talk, his head bent so that his mouth was close to her ear. Telling her about the bird that had dropped the feather, no doubt. Case's stories were always grounded in fact, yet told in an endearingly droll way that Tory seemed to love.

This was what she wanted, she realized, biting her lip. What she'd dreamed about since she was a lonely little girl cringing under her mother's endless criticisms.

A home shared with a man she loved and who loved her, and a child to nurture and adore. Her eyes filled with tears as she realized how very close she was to having that dream come true.

Tonight, she would tell him, she decided, her heart suddenly fluttering with an acute case of nerves. Tonight, after she'd done her daily check of his BP, if it hadn't suddenly elevated again, she would snuggle next to him and place his big hand on the gently swelling curve of her belly. And then, when he felt the baby kicking, she would tell him that he was going to be a father.

It would be all right, she told herself, watching Case brush a kiss against Tory's rosy cheek. Hadn't he said he loved her? She knew without his saying the words that he loved little Casey and Tory.

Why wouldn't he love his own child? The child that already existed.

Yes, she thought. After tonight, there would be no more secrets between them. No more worry. No more fear. After tonight, they would be able to look forward to the birth of the baby with joy and love.

As Prudy watched, entranced by the mental image of Case telling stories to his own child in that same gently loving way, Sunshine crept from beneath the hydrangea hedge and sashayed toward the man and child sitting in a patch of sunlight, her furry cat's tail twitching at the end like a little flag, heralding her approach. Aware that Case was less than fond of cats, Prudy had taken pity on him and fed Sunshine at the MacAuleys. She doubted Case had ever seen the fluffy yellow creature.

He was about to see her now, she realized as the plump feline launched herself directly at Case's lap. With Tory snuggled close to Case's chest, there was perilously little room left for a cat of Sunshine's size, especially given her state of advanced pregnancy.

"Oh, no!" Prudy cried softly as Sunshine started to slip. Naturally, the cat stopped herself the only way she knew how—with her claws.

Case jerked, then let out an outraged male bellow that Prudy figured had to have been heard in every house on Mill Works Ridge.

An instant later, two policemen converged on the backyard, one from the front, one from the back, weapons drawn and eyes glittering.

The look on Case's face as he explained the reason for his shout of alarm had her pressing her fingers to her mouth to keep from bursting out laughing.

"At least we know the guys who are supposed to guard you are alert," Prudy murmured, careful to keep a smile from her voice. Case had been prickly ever since he'd come inside.

Seated at the kitchen table, his bloody sweatshirt lying in a heap on the floor where he'd flung it, he flexed his bared shoulders, then winced as Tory shifted on his knee and jammed a sharp little elbow into his gut.

"If I had the use of both my hands, that cat would be history," he groused as he watched Prudy lay out bandages and disinfectant on the kitchen table.

"Ow-ee," Tory said solemnly, poking a tiny finger at the longest and deepest scratch crisscrossing his chest. In spite of the hydrogen peroxide Prudy had splashed on with a liberal hand and a lot of amused clucking, most of the scratches were still oozing blood.

"Tory, climb down now and let me take care of Uncle Case's owees," Prudy ordered in a brisk but gentle tone.

Her nurse's voice, he thought with a silent grimace. For some reason, that superefficient, I'm-in-charge tone struck him as being completely at odds with his sweet, amenable Prue.

Yet he accepted that she was a woman with her feet firmly planted in two different worlds, one in that of medicine, where quick thinking and an iron set of nerves were prerequisites, the other here, where she became the impetuous, hobby impassioned, sometimes slightly scatterbrained redhead he adored.

"Towy help."

Case smiled down at the little squirt bobbing her head with fierce determination. She was a stubborn one, all right. With dimples and green eyes that drew a man in before he had time to think. What was there about a man that made him a damn sucker for a female with dimples, anyway?

"All right, you hold the salve for me, okay?" Prudy offered Tory a smile before pinning him with a glance that warned him to behave.

"Hurry up, it's darn cold in here."

"The thermostat is set at seventy-two." Prudy swiped away the blood with a cotton ball moistened with alcohol. The sudden sting had him sucking in hard.

"Bad Sunshine," Tory said, her wispy eyebrows drawn together in a frown.

"Sunshine was just trying to sit in Uncle Case's lap, too," Prudy explained as she took the antiseptic salve from Tory and spread it on a large gauze pad. "She didn't mean to scratch him."

The hell she didn't, the mean little bastard, Case thought, but he kept his mouth shut. Two weeks of censoring his language whenever Tory was within earshot—which was most of the time—had him hesitating before he spoke more times than he cared to admit. And yet, it hadn't been nearly as bad as he'd expected, having a little one hanging around.

Of course, Tory was special. Cuter than most kids, he figured, and bright as a new penny. Like Molly had been the first time Geoff had brought her up to Portland to meet her black-sheep uncle. He remembered the pressure in his chest when Molly had reached out a tiny hand to touch his face, and then how she'd grinned, as though she liked what she saw.

At the time he hadn't wanted to put a name to the emotion

he'd felt. He knew now it had been an odd kind of hunger. The kind a man feels for something he's always longed for, yet has been forced to deny himself.

Forced by what? he wondered now.

Fear that he'd be as lousy a father as his own? Fear that a child of his would grow up feeling worthless and inadequate in the same way he had? And for reasons he'd never fully understood? Therein lay the rub, Case decided, that he'd never been able to define exactly which of the numerous mistakes his parents had made were the ones that had turned him into the man he'd become.

Unless a guy could pinpoint a mistake, how the hell could he keep from repeating it?

Looking back on his youth, Case felt as if he were trying to make sense of the underside of one of Prudy's tapestry projects, another of the countless hobbies she'd once taken up and never finished. Threads going every which way in a confusing tangle. Knots everywhere. Strings hanging. Damn. And like one of those tapestries, Case had been hurtled into adolescence and the harsh weave of adulthood with knots all through him and emotional strings dangling, a half-finished project his mother abandoned and that his father helped shove into a closet.

He wouldn't do that to a kid of his own, dammit. He just plain wouldn't. Until babies started being born with instructions printed on their soft little butts, Case wanted nothing to do with parenthood. There were enough screwed-up kids in the world. In his line of work, he stumbled across them every day.

"Ouch!" he muttered as the tape Prudy was applying tugged on his chest hair.

"Sorry," she murmured, her browner than brown eyes laughing into his.

"No, you're not," he accused, feeling his libido kicking in.

"Ow-ee aw gone," Tory said, patting the sparkling white bandage.

"All gone, and you were a big help to Aunt Prudy, too," Case agreed, dropping a kiss on the little girl's head before he realized Prudy was watching. He lifted his gaze to hers and scowled, daring her to make a sarcastic comment. Instead of laughter, however, he saw the shimmer of tears in her eyes.

"Prue?" he asked, his voice coming out more gruff than he wanted.

"Let me put this away and I'll make us some tea," she said as she methodically returned her first-aid supplies to the large metal box sitting open on the table.

Case wasn't fooled by her casual air. Her face had grown pale, and her lower lip was clamped between her teeth in the way she had when she was trying not to cry. He didn't need a cop's instinct to tell him something was wrong.

Forcing a smile, he tipped Tory's face up to his and asked solemnly, "Tory, sweetheart, will you be my special friend and run get a sweatshirt from the bedroom for me?"

"Kiss first," she demanded, puckering her lips.

"Whatever you say, Princess," he said, playing out the little ritual they'd fallen into sometime during the past few days.

She giggled as his lips brushed hers, then returned the kiss with a wet, smacking sound.

"The blue sweatshirt in the bottom drawer of the white chest, okay?" he said as she slipped from his knee.

"'Kay," she returned, her fat little legs already churning.

"Talk to me, Prue," he demanded when Prudy started to follow Tory from the room.

"Tonight, I promise," she said, her gaze averted.

"Now. " He hooked his good arm around her waist and drew her to his knee. "What's wrong, honey?"

"Case, I'm too heavy!" she protested, even as she was slipping her arms around his neck.

"You're light as Tory's feather." He linked his arms around her waist and held her fast. "And don't try to change the subject."

The troubled look in his eyes nearly tore Prudy in two, and she had to look away. "You're so good with Tory. I couldn't help thinking how you would have been with—" She stopped, suddenly appalled at the mistake she was about to make.

"With the baby we lost?" he said quietly.

Prudy nodded, too surprised at his use of the word *we* to speak. Always before, on the rare occasion when he'd mentioned the miscarriage, he'd referred to the child as hers.

Case saw the sudden flicker of her long lashes and realized he was inching across a line he himself had drawn. "I thought we'd gotten past this. Maybe I was wrong."

She gave him a startled look, her brow pleated in a puzzled frown. "Past what?"

"I behaved like an ass after you...miscarried." It hurt to dredge the words from his soul where he'd shoved them after the baby's funeral. "If I could take back the words I said to you then, I would, but—"

"Oh, Case, don't," she said, fresh tears flooding her eyes. "There's something I have to tell you, something—"

"What the hell was that?"

Prudy blinked, startled by the sharp note of surprise in his voice. Her breathing stuttered to a halt when she realized he was staring down at the spot where his wide forearm was pressed against her belly—where the baby had just kicked.

Chapter 16

Prudy had seen shock before—in patients confronting their own mortality, in frantic relatives struggling to accept intolerable news, even, on rare occasions, in pain-hardened medical professionals. But this was the first time she'd felt it shudder through a man's body with the force of a mortal wound.

She saw it in his eyes a split second later, a jolt of hot realization followed by a searing accusation, as he leveled those piercing blue eyes on her face.

"You're pregnant." His voice was flat and utterly cold, the words spoken through a jaw so hard it was edged in white.

A wave of clammy dread ran through her as the stinging words reverberated inside her head. Where was the joy she'd hoped—prayed—to hear in his voice?

"Yes, Case, I'm almost five months' pregnant," she said quietly, her own joy still struggling for life as she took his hand and pressed his broad palm against her womb. As though feeling his mama's desperation, the baby responded with another hard kick, connecting right below the pressure of his father's big hand.

"Feel how strong he is? Just like his daddy."

Her pale lips trembled into a smile, and her shiver of delight shot through him with the same shattering force as the nine-millimeter slug that had torn through his thigh, feeling as if it splintered bone and shredded flesh. A baby. A child.

Dragging in a sharp breath, Case nearly staggered, as dazed as if he'd just been sucker punched. He jerked his hand free from her grasp, his mind struggling to reject the evidence of life that had just fluttered against his palm.

"Five months?" The question seemed to come from another man, a man with a voice made harsh by stunned incredulity and barely contained anger. "Is it mine?"

Very calmly, she stood and took a careful step away from him. "Yes, it's your baby. I conceived the night of Casey's christening."

"You said you were on the pill." He heard the harsh edge to his voice and flinched inwardly.

"I was," she said with a quiet sincerity he'd heard once before. Years ago, when she'd told him how sorry she was for lying to him. "But I'd had stomach flu the week before the christening and I couldn't keep anything down. Obviously, the hormone levels in my body were thrown off."

"You're saying the pill failed, a one in a hundred occurrence, and that's why you're pregnant? Is that your story?"

"More like two in a hundred actually, and I'm saying that, somehow, we made our very own miracle."

Miracle? Or betrayal?

Suddenly the years seemed to melt away, and he was fifteen again and shivering scared, waiting desperately in a dank, windowless room that reeked of stale urine and sweat. Waiting for his mother, counting on her to make everything right. His damned *mother*, the woman who'd given birth to him. Who'd preached family loyalty and responsibility all his damned life. Who'd berated him for his sloppy ways and careless habits while ignoring his paragon of a brother's flaws and his perfect little sister's dependency on drugs. His mother who'd been entrusted with his life, his future, and was supposed to love and protect him.

Bile rose in his throat as he remembered the look on his

attorney's face when he'd walked into that room to tell him he'd been tossed aside by the very people who were supposed to stand by him, no matter what. The way he'd been there for his sister.

So he'd turned to his father. Swallowed his pride and begged Jackson Randolph to say the words or pull the strings to keep him from being locked up.

Jackson could do it. Hadn't he bragged often enough about his high-powered clients?

His father had simply shaken his head and walked away.

Casey Randolph had been a dumb-assed kid when he'd been locked up, broken in spirit and about as empty inside as a person could get. Case Randolph had come out thirty months later an adult who'd seen humanity reduced to its basest form, resolving never to care for another living soul the way he'd cared for his mother and baby sister.

Fool that he'd been, he'd renounced that vow to make another—a vow that, at least to him, had been a sacred pledge that united him for life with Prudy, the one woman he'd believed could love him enough never to hurt him in the same soul-shattering way his mother had. He'd taken that risk because he had needed her. Because he'd trusted her. Because she filled his life with sweetness, and, when he was with her, he could forget, for a few cherished hours, the human depravity he encountered, day in and day out, while performing his job.

Now, for the third damned time in his misbegotten life, he had to face the fact that he'd been played for a fool. Sucker punched, hell. He'd gotten it half-right. The "sucker" part fit him like a glove. He had *trusted* her, dammit. And now, there she stood, with those big, innocent brown eyes silently pleading with him to overlook her deceit yet one more time, while he was the one being torn apart.

A miracle, she called it. Instead of a lie.

Yeah, there was a miracle, all right. A miracle that a woman taking a birth control pill, which was ninety-eight percent foolproof, suddenly popped up pregnant?

"I don't want it." The words were out before he could stop

them. A part of him longed to call them back, but he'd been down that road before and the hurt he'd found there had nearly killed him.

Her face lost all color, making the freckles stand out in stark relief. All that was left of the trusting boy he'd once been longed to pull her into his arms and beg her to understand. The man he'd made himself become refused to bend.

"Case, please, I know it's a shock, but—"

He cut her off ruthlessly, unable to bear the phony trembling in her voice. "All those fine words you said about trust. About how you needed me to believe in you, no matter what? All that crap about 'evidence.' You were setting me up, weren't you, Prue? Laying the groundwork for the moment when you'd spring your 'good news' on me."

"I wanted to tell you!" she cried, twisting her hands together in front of her belly. "I called the station—"

"What about the two weeks I was in the hospital," he grated, cutting her off. "You were there every day. Surely you could have found a few minutes to lay the truth on me then."

Prudy heard the sneer in his voice and wondered how she could have been so wrong about this man. He didn't have a loving heart. Or a hidden vulnerability. No, he was granite, through and through.

"Yes, I was at the hospital every day. Part of the time you were fighting off an infection, part of the time your blood pressure was off the scale. It's called hypertension and it can have some very nasty consequences if not treated. Like stroke, for instance. Now there's a lovely scenario for you. Paralysis of one side, inability to speak, a lot of other very unpleasant symptoms. But then, in your weakened condition, you probably would have died, anyway."

She turned and would have walked away, but his hand shot out to shackle her wrist. "Oh, no, you don't," he said in a silky voice that was more punishing than the harshest shout. "You're not running away from this before we come to an agreement about this godawful mess you've gotten us into."

"Is that how you view the conception of a child? As a

godawful mess?'' Prudy forced the question through lips that were suddenly numb.

"Dammit, Prue, I was never anything but straight with you about this baby thing.''

"I know that, Case.'' She licked her lips but felt nothing. "I've told you the absolute truth. I neither intended to get pregnant or thought it possible that I could. But when it happened, I wanted to shout my thanks to God.''

"Yeah, well, I feel like shouting, too. But not with joy.'' His mouth twisted. "I don't want to be a father. Maybe that makes me a selfish jerk. Fine, I'll accept that. What I can't accept is the way it happened.''

Prudy forced herself to breathe. His hand was still clamped around her wrist, tight enough to send pain spiking up her arm. She refused to pull away or even ask him to gentle his hold. No, in some odd way, she welcomed the pain.

"Let me get this very clear in my mind,'' she said, measuring her words with great care. "You're telling me you think I deliberately deceived you when I said I was on the pill.''

His gaze flickered. "I don't know what I think. I need time—''

"Aunt Pwudy? Unca Case mad?'' At the plaintive sound of Tory's questioning voice, Case jerked his gaze toward the door where the little one stood, his sweatshirt gripped in one hand and dragging the floor behind her, her green eyes wide and solemn as her gaze went from one to the other.

"No, sweetheart, Uncle Case is just tired,'' Prudy said, recovering first. A slight tug on his hand made him realize he was still holding on to her arm and he released his grip.

"Unca Case need a nap?''

"Yes,'' Prudy murmured as she scooped the toddler into her arms. "Give Uncle Case his shirt, and then you and I are going to go next door to check on Sunny, okay?''

"'Kay.'' Tory grinned, revealing tiny white baby teeth. "Kiss first,'' she said when Case reached out to take the shirt dangling from her hand in front of his nose.

"Anything you say, Princess.''

Case took the sweatshirt and dropped it on the table, then

used his good hand to push himself to a standing position. Suddenly he was towering over Prudy and Tory, bare chested and intimidating. His bronzed skin was a variety of textures, smooth over powerful muscles except where the soft hair curled, corrugated over his trim midriff, puckered over the scar on his shoulder.

His face was dead sober as he leaned down to accept Tory's smacking kiss. "We'll finish this tonight, when she's asleep," he said quietly to Prudy as she tightened her hold on the laughing little girl.

"It's finished, Case. You've made your point. You don't want to be a father. Fine, I accept that, and I hereby absolve you of any responsibility for this baby."

"Prue—"

"I think it would be best if Tory and I stay at the MacAuleys' until they return."

"Not a chance. Not until we've thrashed this thing out."

She knew that Tory's presence was the only reason his voice was quiet and his hand at this side. He wouldn't hurt her physically. At least not intentionally, she amended as she reflected on the throbbing in her wrist where his hard fingers had clamped like a vise.

"I'll arrange for another nurse to stay with you."

His jaw flexed. In his eyes a dangerous light kindled. "The hell you will," he grated, his mild tone belying the violent red tinge suffusing his face.

"Fine. You offered once to go to a nursing home if that's what I wanted. I'd appreciate it if you'd be gone by the time Stacy and Boyd return."

She strode past him to the kitchen door. Tory chattered nonstop as Prudy pulled it open and walked outside into the midday sun. The air was crisp, and she cradled Tory closer.

Sunshine was curled atop a wooden picnic table near the porch. As Prudy moved past, the spoiled creature opened one eye, as though taunting her before resuming its feline dream.

After setting Tory on her feet on the MacAuleys' back stoop, Prudy retrieved the spare key to their back door from its place under the cat's water dish.

"In you go, sweetpea," she said as she unlocked the door and pushed it open.

"Mama?" Tory cried eagerly, racing through the silent kitchen, her tiny sneakers squeaking on the tile.

Prudy felt her lips curve in a sad smile. *Mama.*

"No, sweetpea, Mama and Papa aren't home yet," she called as Tory went racing through the living room. "Remember what I told you this morning? Three more days."

And two nights.

Without Case. Alone.

Except for the baby she carried under her heart.

Her baby. No matter what, her child would always know he or she was wanted, she vowed fiercely as she went to find Tory.

How odd, she thought later as she sat rocking Tory to sleep in Stacy's chair. In all the years she'd spent as a nurse, she'd never believed that it was truly possible for a heart to actually break.

She knew now that it was.

"Whew, it's damn cold out there tonight," Petrov grumbled as he lumbered past Case, who'd just opened Prudy's front door in response to his partner's impatient pounding. "Raintree's pulling the stakeout duty out there tonight, poor sot. Told me the car heater's busted in his unmarked and that he's freezing his butt off."

Case glanced across the street where a plain gray sedan sat like a sore thumb. Hell, why didn't Raintree just put a sign in the back window, telling Cardoza the damned address? He made a mental note to give Walters a call in the morning.

"Maybe he'll shiver off a few pounds of that fat gut he's always trying to lose," Case grumbled as he shoved the door shut.

"Naw, he's got a dozen cream-filled doughnuts keepin' him company." Petrov glanced around, rubbing his own well-rounded paunch, the gleam in his eyes conveying that he wouldn't be adverse to sinking his teeth into a doughnut himself. "Speaking of which, you got anything to eat?"

"There are some chips in the cupboard, and there's beer in the fridge," Case grated as he crutched his way back to the ugly green chair he was beginning to hate after having spent so many hours in it with his leg elevated. He felt reasonably certain the upholstered buttons on the cushion had made permanent imprints on his ass. "Bring me another cold one while you're at it."

"Will do." Petrov was halfway to the kitchen before he stopped dead in his tracks and swung around. "I assume Prudy's not sleeping since you've decided to throw a party in the middle of the night?"

"I have no idea what she's doing."

"Where is she? Working night shift again?"

Case bit down hard on his back teeth. "Last I heard she was hiding out next door. Pissed off."

Petrov lifted one ponderous eyebrow, but kept his mouth shut as he continued on to the kitchen. Good thing, Case decided after a moment's intense reflection. Otherwise, he knew he'd have to smash a fist into his partner's smart-ass mouth—preferably the fist still wrapped in five pounds of plaster cement.

Case had only had five or six beers, well below his usual limit when he really set his mind to tying one on, so it surprised him all to hell when he had trouble sitting down without toppling over. Somehow, his crutch slipped from his right hand, throwing him off balance, and he was forced to catch himself with that same hand on the arm of the chair. Pain shot to his elbow, taking his breath for a beat. The second he was able to expand his lungs again, he blistered the walls with curses.

By the time he'd collapsed onto the pea-soup green cushion and dropped his other crutch, Petrov had returned, a beer in each hand, a bag of chips tucked under one elbow.

"Looks like you've taken up a new hobby while you've been on leave," he said, handing Case the frosty bottle.

"What the hell are you talking about?" Case muttered before lifting the bottle to his mouth for a long swallow.

"That," Petrov said, gesturing with the bag of chips toward the empty bottles. "Drinking like there's no tomorrow."

"So I've had a couple. What about it?"

"A couple of six packs is more like it. I happened to notice the pile of empties in the recycling bin."

Case glared at him. "What are you, some kind of recruiter for AA?"

"Nope, just someone who's been where you are." Don took a sip, his gaze still fastened on Case's. "Numbing your brain with alcohol won't help worth squat."

"Can't hurt," Case muttered before draining the bottle. "Get me another one, will ya?"

Tossing the chips onto the coffee table, Petrov settled a hip against the back of the sofa and regarded Case steadily, his expression about as revealing as a stone.

"Sure, I'll get you another one. Right after you tell me why you rousted me out of bed in the middle of the night."

Case shrugged. "I need a ride to my apartment."

"You gonna tell me why, or are we gonna play Twenty Questions?"

"She's pregnant," he said, the words coming hard.

Petrov didn't turn a hair. "I assume you're referring to Prudy?"

"Very funny, Petrov."

"How come you're not laughing?"

Case stared at the watercolor on the wall. It was a primitive of a one-room schoolhouse and a playground full of kids. It took him a minute to recognize the signature as Prudy's. Another hobby, he thought wearily, and then wondered why he hadn't noticed the painting before. Dumb question. When Prudy was around, he had eyes for nothing else.

"I want you to fix it with Walters to keep a man on her until we get enough on Cardoza to haul his ass in."

Petrov glanced at the window overlooking the access road. "Piece of cake. Walters thinks Prudy's a dynamite lady. Told me so himself right after he ran into her at the hospital. Said he caught her giving you a little TLC in your room and was wishing he'd been the one who'd taken a bullet by the time he left.''

Don took a long swig of beer, then swiped at his mouth with a beefy hand. "Watch your back, Case, old man. With a woman like Prue, there are always a lot of guys standing in line, ready, willing and able to fill in as your replacement.''

Case had to work at keeping his temper clamped tight. Petrov would be old and feeble before he'd hook Case Randolph into reacting to such a blatant stab of jealousy.

"MacAuley's due back tomorrow," Case said, scowling down at the expanse of battered plaster sheathing his leg. His damn thigh itched like holy hell, and so did his shin.

"I'll give him a day to ditch the jet lag, then threaten him with major bodily harm unless he cuts me out of these casts.''

"Whatever you say, partner." Petrov took another swig of beer, then straightened. He flexed his oxlike shoulders, then ambled over to the window overlooking the lawn between Prudy's place and the one next door.

"Light's still on in one of the rooms next door," he said as he pushed aside the drape for a better look. "Think I should check it out?''

Case glanced at the grandfather clock and saw that the hands were edging toward two. It occurred to him now why Prudy was always climbing out of bed in the middle of the night to go to the can. And why she wore those sloppy clothes he hated.

Yeah, he was some great detective, all right. How many times had he made love to her since he'd come to stay at her place? A dozen? Two dozen? In the daylight, with the lights blazing. By the light of a full moon streaming into the bedroom.

He'd mapped that small, lush body with his hands and his mouth so thoroughly he could close his eyes and see every tiny detail, from the small cluster of freckles just above her right breast to the crooked little toe on her right foot.

Damn his poor besotted soul, he'd even swirled his tongue over the curve of her belly. And like a blind rookie on his first case, he hadn't seen the evidence that was right there in front of him.

Evidence.

I need to know that you believe me, truly believe me. No matter what "evidence" you might have to the contrary.

I believe you.

He waited for the anger to hit again, needed to feel its bite. When it didn't come, he scowled.

"Well?" Petrov pressed. "Should I go over, or what?"

"You do what you want," Case growled as he fished for his crutch. "I've got packing to do."

Arturo stood shivering in the scant windbreak offered by a thick cluster of man-high rhododendrons at the edge of the woman's lawn and peered through the rain-slicked leaves. Like a beacon in the darkness, a bright orange orb suddenly flared inside the cop car across the street. Arturo snarled. The overweight pig inside the vehicle was taking another drag on his cigarette, the sixth he'd smoked since Arturo had started keeping watch around midnight.

Disappointment clogged his chest, making him feel as if he'd swallowed a sponge. The way he figured, he had another night to blow before he could kill the son of a bitch. Timing was everything, and now that Petrov had shown up, Arturo didn't want to take any chances. *Damn pig.* What was he doing here at this time of night, anyhow? Arturo grinned at the possibilities. Maybe him and Randolph were takin' turns screwing the broad.

Felix would have been proud of the way Arturo had kept his cool, in spite of the hot fear that had churned in his gut as Petrov had lumbered past his hiding place on the way up to the house. Damned if Arturo hadn't split a gut, not to mention that he'd nearly panicked and slit the bastard's throat. The funniest part was, Petrov had never even realized he was there. He'd just shuffled by, coming within inches of Arturo's hiding place.

Dios mio, pigs were stupid. And lucky. If it hadn't been for not wanting to blow all his plans, Arturo would have had himself a little pig-sticking party. Too bad. But first things first, and killing Randolph was definitely at the top of his priority list. Besides, he couldn't afford to bring down any heat on himself right now, not when he was so close to getting the bastard.

Hauling in a deep breath, Arturo remembered Felix's favorite saying, "Good things come to he who waits." Petrov's unexpected arrival had spoiled Arturo's plans for tonight, but there was always tomorrow. He had everything worked out to a gnat's ass, and next time, Petrov wouldn't happen by to save Randolph's neck. Nothing could save him, Arturo thought with a greasy grin. 'Cause he had himself a foolproof plan.

These stupid pigs were creatures of habit, the same gray car parked across the street every night and them changing shifts as regular as clockwork. Tomorrow night, he'd make his move just a few minutes before the next cop was supposed to come on duty.

Child's play, he thought with a huff of laughter. Slip up to the open car window, come in slightly from behind. In two seconds, maybe less, he'd have the bastard's throat slit. All he'd have to do was circle the block to come up on the gray sedan from the rear. He would wait then, crouch by the left front door until the pig inside rolled down his window again to let out some of the smoke.

Arturo's fingers itched as they fondled the switchblade in the pocket of his jacket. He'd bought it in a hock shop a few days back, with money he'd taken from a barmaid leaving a joint down on Powell Street. Teach her to walk across a dark parking lot when she got off shift on payday, he thought with a smirk. Not that she'd be going back to work anytime soon. He'd roughed her up pretty good before tossing her down on the asphalt between two parked cars for a quickie. Party time. A guy deserved to have a little fun on the side, right? Six months from now, he'd send her one of them greeting cards that was blank on the inside. In big, block letters, he'd write, *Hi, Sweetheart. Welcome to the world of HIV.*

Since buying the switchblade, he'd spent hours honing it to a razor's edge, and he'd given careful thought to the method he might use to gut Randolph. Only question was, which would be most fun, pig-sticking or gut-shooting? He'd nearly had an orgasm as he'd imagined the squeal the bastard would let out, either way. In spite of the cold, Arturo broke into a sweat at the thought.

It was supposed to be tonight, dammit. Would have been, if that big ape partner of Randolph's hadn't suddenly shown up around two.

Arturo had spent fruitless, frustrating weeks prowling the neighborhood where Randolph lived, waiting for the bastard to show. It had taken him longer than it should have to remember the TV picture of Randolph's pretty, redheaded ex-wife crumpled on the couch of the hospital waiting room. He took comfort in reminding himself that he'd been out of his mind with grief for weeks after Felix's murder. How could a man think clear when his brother had just been gut-shot by a no-account, low-life pig?

But he was calm now. And he knew where the cops had hidden the murderer. Tonight. Tomorrow night. What did it matter?

Yes, he thought, smiling into the ink of night. When the time was right, he would strike. He had the plan imprinted on his brain and a vial of coke in his pocket in case he needed to calm his nerves.

He'd take care of the guard first, then slip inside that whore-pink door and kill the woman. Or should he rape her first and make Randolph watch? Excitement raced through his reed-thin body as he pictured the anguish in the pig's eyes as Arturo thrust again and again into the woman's body. Oh, yes, he would rape her first, he decided on a vicious wave of lust. Then he'd take his time with Randolph, taking pleasure at making him crawl and beg.

He was still thinking about the various indignities he would savage on the man when the pink door opened and Petrov lumbered out. Arturo froze, his hand already dipping into his pocket for his nine millimeter.

Pausing on the top step of the porch, Petrov scanned the yard, flipped a wave at the candy-ass across the street, then headed down the steps and started walking—not toward his own four-wheel drive parked at the curb, but toward the house next door.

Puzzled, Arturo watched him knock. Saw the porch light blaze, heard Petrov bark his name in apparent response to a request from within, saw the door open to reveal a small woman in a robe.

He sucked in when he recognized the fiery red hair.

Randolph's whore.

Petrov disappeared inside the house, and Arturo stood frozen, listening to the frenzied pounding of his own heart. Something was wrong. The bitch was supposed to be in her own house, tucked up next to Randolph. That was the plan, dammit.

He felt fury crowding his always-aching head. No! he raged silently. He wouldn't be denied the revenge he was due. He'd promised Felix. Felix expected to be avenged.

When the time was right, a voice commanded, *you'll know.*

Arturo relaxed, calm again. Fate was on his side. When the time was right, there would be no more obstacles. No more surprises.

When the time was right, he would be ready.

Arturo Cardoza was very, very patient.

Chapter 17

Petrov dropped the receiver onto the hook and shot Case a pleased look. "Markovitch found Cardoza's address. A seedy midtown hotel."

Case absorbed the news with the grunt that had become his preferred method of communication these days. Words—forming them, stringing them together to make some kind of sense—took too much energy. Since he'd slept a grand total of approximately six hours in the past fourteen nights, he didn't have much to spare.

"Desk clerk said Cardoza pays his rent regular and doesn't cause trouble." He lifted an eyebrow.

Case snorted. He yearned for a cigarette. Just one drag. Anything to take the edge off.

Petrov sighed. "Said he hasn't seen Cardoza for a couple of days. Rent's due again tomorrow. Markovitch plans to sit on the place till he shows."

Case nodded and reached for the rubber ball he kept in his top left drawer. While he methodically squeezed it with the fingers of his right hand, still pathetically weak from the time in the cast, he flipped through the reports in the file they were amassing on the kingpin of Felix Cardoza's ring, a slippery Mexican expatriate strongman known only as *El Hefe*. With Felix planted six feet under, their investigation was now centered on his second-in-command, a *mestizo* named Aguilar they hoped would lead them to the top man.

It was sometime later when Case realized he was simply staring at words on paper, his mind replaying the images of Prudy's white face and disillusioned eyes the day she'd walked out on him.

Dammit, why had she looked at him as though he'd torn out her heart and ripped it apart when he'd been the one sucker punched?

He'd seen her only twice since then. Once at the hospital when Boyd had cut him free of the casts, and yesterday, when he'd stopped by her house to check on the surveillance that Walters had agreed to keep in place, even though Case was no longer living there.

She'd been preparing her flower beds for the winter and her backside had wiggled at him as she'd backed out from underneath one of those puffy bushes she was so crazy about. Her face had been rosy from the wind, and she'd looked about sixteen in faded jeans and an old University of Oregon sweatshirt.

When she'd swiped back her hair, she'd left a streak of dirt on her cheek. It had been more provocative than the fancy makeup she sometimes used.

It had steamed him big time to realize he still wanted her. Still found her the most desirable woman he'd ever met, bar none. Which was why he'd acted like more of a jerk than he really was, he told himself as he glanced over at Markovitch's desk on the off chance she'd left her spare pack of cigarettes within reach. No such luck.

He'd wanted to ask Prudy how she felt. And if she intended to stay at Mill Works Ridge or find another place. He'd figured to find out if she was planning to take time off after the baby was born, and if she had a good obstetrician. Instead, he'd ragged at her for wearing herself out, then compounded his insensitivity by telling her she looked like hell.

He'd expected her to explode, had actually anticipated the fire he'd seen in her eyes. But she'd simply smiled and went inside.

Damn, he'd never felt so alone.

The phone shrilled. "For you, Sergeant Petrov," the civilian receptionist called over the usual squad room clatter. "A Ms. Randolph."

Case nearly gave himself a whiplash jerking his head in his partner's direction. "What the hell?"

Petrov spared him a pitying glance before grabbing the receiver. "Hiya, half pint. How's the mom-to-be today?"

Case sucked in air and tasted anger along with the stale remnants of smoke and mildew. He felt his gut knot as Petrov laughed softly.

"Well, I'll be damned," he exclaimed softly into the phone. "A little girl. You're sure?" He laughed again. "Yeah, I guess if the picture shows no outside plumbing, it's a pretty good bet."

Case felt the knot in his belly climb to his throat, all but shutting off his ability to breathe. A little girl. His own sweet little princess, with Prudy's red curls and freckles. He started to smile, then froze.

It took more than circumstance to make a father, more than he had to offer. The word that hovered on his tongue was foul and an accurate reflection of his mood.

"How about you and me catching dinner tonight?" he heard Petrov asking softly, his mouth pressed close to the receiver. "You choose the place."

Case refused to care.

"Hell, yes, I love steak. I'll bring the wine." Don listened, frowned. "Okay, sparkling apple juice for you, wine for me."

Case squeezed the ball in his right hand so hard the tendons in his forearm threatened to snap. Shake it off, he told himself. Prudy was free to entertain another man, even if she was carrying his child. Just as he was free to date another woman.

Any woman.

A leggy blonde maybe, or a sultry brunette. The new tenant on the second floor in his building had been giving him the eye for the past week. Crandall was her name. Marcia or Marie, something like that. A real put-together woman, all right. Had a body made for sin and a mouth that could summon the dead.

Case pictured himself poised between Marcia's athletic thighs and waited for his body to react. Instead, he felt a wave of disgust hit his gut and spread like acid.

"See you at seven, half pint. Take care now." Petrov hung up the phone, his expression smug.

Case flipped another page in the file and scanned the raw data. "How about you and me run over to that bar on the waterfront where Aguilar's compadres hang out, see if we can pick up something," he said, giving Petrov a measuring look.

"Works for me." Petrov stretched, then flexed his shoulders. "Can't tonight, though. I'm busy."

"Yeah, I heard."

Petrov pushed back in his chair until the front legs left the scarred floor and the spring protested. "You seen Prudy lately?"

"Last week." Case closed the file.

"You think she looked haggard? Like maybe she isn't sleeping regular?"

Case scowled down at the cigarette burns scalloping the edge of his desk. "She looked okay," he said, but his mind was busy sifting through his memories of that morning.

"Getting pregnant at her age the way she did, it has to be hard on her."

Case grunted. He'd thought the same thing. Then tortured himself through a sleepless night with endless images of Prudy in hard labor, trying to push his baby into the world. Screaming. Growing weaker. Dying. He'd been soaked with sweat by the time he'd shoved out of bed around five and fixed himself a stiff Scotch. It hadn't helped.

"Told me they did this test. Amnio-something to see if the baby was okay. Did an ultrasound, too. It's a girl."

Case watched Detectives Potts and Yourzek shepherding a cuffed Viking gang member with greasy hair and wild eyes toward one of the interrogation rooms. Down the hall, someone shouted an obscenity. The phone shrilled incessantly.

The job had gotten him through the rocky days after they'd lost their baby. Their *first* baby, he corrected. Nature's way of reversing a mistake, the doctor had told him. He remembered wondering how a baby could be a damned mistake.

"This amnio thing," he said casually, keeping his gaze on an ant crawling over the blotter. "Did it show anything... wrong?"

When Don didn't answer right away, a chill ran down Case's spine and he jerked his gaze toward his partner. Don waited until their gazes meshed, then shook his head.

"Your baby's fine, Case. It's the baby's mom I'm worried about."

Case had rarely seen that naked look of concern in Petrov's eyes. The last time had been the night of the shooting as he'd bent over Case's bleeding body, ordering him to "hang on, dammit."

"Spill it, Petrov! You know something."

"Nothing specific. I just remember my own mother. She was forty-two when she had my last sister. Died two days later. Hemorrhaged on the way home from the hospital. Of course, that was damn near forty years ago. Medical science has come a long way." Don cleared his throat. "The night I drove you home when I went over to check on Prudy next door, she asked me to recommend a good attorney. Seems she was wanting to make a will to provide for the baby in case something happened to her during delivery."

"She knows I'd make sure the baby didn't want for anything," Case grated.

"Does she?" Don shrugged. "From the few things she let slip, I got the impression you'd washed your hands of both of them."

Case felt his jaw bunch. "Dammit, Don, I was ready to use protection. She's the one who told me it wasn't necessary." He drew in air. It didn't help the pressure in his chest. "She knew how I felt about being a father, and yet—"

Don's voice cut across Case's at the same instant his chair

hit the floor with a loud thud. "Yes, she knew," he grated, his eyes blazing. "And while she was puking her guts out when you were in surgery, she told me about the pill and the stomach flu. It didn't occur to me not to believe her."

"She lied to me."

"Did she? Or was she simply afraid to tell you? Afraid you'd react exactly the way you did. Afraid you'd take this precious gift she was offering you and toss it onto the garbage heap."

"Careful," Case warned, knotting his fists.

"You blew it, partner. Big time."

"The hell I did. The evidence—"

"Circumstantial. Not worth squat. Besides, I saw Prudy's face when MacAuley told her you'd probably survive. The woman all but worships you, you stupid, selfish bastard. Or did. Last I heard, she was working real hard on changing that." Don reached into his drawer for his police issue .38 and clipped it to his belt before getting to his feet. "But then, you make it easy, don't you?"

Case searched his mental dictionary for a name foul enough to call himself. Nothing in his impressive collection came close.

"Petrov," he called as Don headed for the door.

"Yeah?" Petrov asked, pausing.

"Keep that dinner date tonight and you're a dead man."

Petrov grunted. "Like hell."

Case drew a tortured breath. "I'm going in your place."

Don studied his face impassively. "Why?" he asked at last.

"Because she's having my child, dammit. If anyone takes care of her, It should be me."

"Won't wash, Randolph."

Case swore viciously and glanced around to make sure no one was listening. Thanks to the Viking raising hell over in one corner of the large room, no one was looking in Case's direction. When he returned his gaze to Petrov, the man didn't so much as lift an eyebrow. "Because I'm responsible."

"Puny reason."

"I care for her."

"Bull. A man who really cares for a woman doesn't call her a liar."

"I didn't—" Case felt his shoulders slump. "Dammit, Don. I love her, and I broke her heart. Somehow I have to make it better."

Prudy was running late. She'd taken a nap after speaking with Don and had slept longer than she'd intended. It had been nearly five by the time she'd surfaced, awakened by the pummeling of a small fist against the inner wall of her uterus.

"Thanks for the wake-up call, Chloe," she murmured, pressing her hand against the now-pronounced bulge below her navel. Her daughter, she thought as she checked on the cherry cobbler she'd slipped into the oven earlier. Her very own precious little girl.

She'd decided on the name just that morning while looking at the Polaroid photo taken by the ultrasound tech. Her daughter had a delicate profile, as pretty as a cameo. Her heart warmed at the memory of the thrill that had gone through her when she'd looked at the screen and seen the baby moving.

The sense of awe she'd felt at that moment was still with her. After half a lifetime spent longing for a baby of her own, then grieving when she realized her chance was lost, she was truly, gloriously, wonderfully pregnant.

"We're having company tonight, Chloe," she murmured, smiling at her reflection in the oven door. In honor of the occasion she'd donned one of her new maternity shirts, a lilac cotton with a huge purple zigzag across the front. "He's a nice man. Big as a house, but with a soft heart. You'll like him."

She glanced at the clock, saw that she still had ten minutes until Don was due and decided to toss the salad now. The table was already set. She was using her wedding china and the Waterford crystal she'd inherited from her mother. And, of course, the sterling candlesticks Don had given her and Case as a wedding gift. He'd been Case's best man, of course, the only member of Case's "family" to attend. About the worst duty he'd ever pulled, he'd told her later with a rueful grin.

Case had been a nervous wreck. He'd sworn the starched collar of his tux shirt was strangling him—right before he'd suddenly developed a firm conviction the wedding band he'd bought her was the wrong size. Even after he and Don had arrived at the church, he'd spent a solid hour trying to bully Don into kidnaping his bride so that they could elope.

She would always remember the panic on his face when she'd started down the aisle. And then suddenly, he'd grinned—and winked. She'd known then that everything was going to be all right.

Ancient history, she reminded herself. A closed chapter in the frenetic life of Prudence Jane O'Grady Randolph.

Time to move on to a great future.

"It'll be a lovely party," she murmured, her voice echoing into the silent kitchen with false gaiety. The same false gaiety she found herself projecting in the ER these days.

Oh, yes, she was a laugh a minute, all right. Upbeat, cheerful. Laughing at Hollis's corny jokes. And why not? Her health was good, the baby was healthy and growing rapidly and she was financially solvent. All was right in her world.

Or it would be. Her baby wasn't going to have a mother wallowing in misery. Or pining for a man who wasn't worth the tears she couldn't seem to stop shedding.

Fake it until you make it, she'd read somewhere.

Tomorrow after work she was going shopping for nursery furniture. And while she was at it, she intended to buy herself a new bed. Something esoteric. A waterbed, maybe. Or a giant tester with a feather tick.

She smiled down at the lettuce she was tearing and wondered if they still made beds with canopies. With lots of ruffles and lace, the kind she'd always dreamed about when she'd been a lonely little girl. A bed fit for a fairy-tale princess and her brave and handsome prince.

The kind of bed Case would hate.

A crushing pressure squeezed her chest, and she had to force air into her lungs. Why was it so terribly hard to stop loving a man who deserved only her contempt? The way he'd reacted to the news of the baby and how he'd treated her afterward were inexcusable.

Why, he was more generous to common criminals than he'd been to her. The woman he'd claimed to love. He'd condemned her without a fair hearing. And it hurt. So very much. If only he *had* treated her with the consideration he did a suspected criminal. At least with them, he extended the courtesy of informing them that everything they said might be held against them.

"I refuse to cry over the man," she muttered, swiping the sudden tears from her lashes with the back of her hand. Nodding her head for emphasis, she reached over to switch on the small tape player next to the toaster. The music that suddenly blared was metal, Case's favorite.

She muttered a curse, and punched the eject button. By the time she'd flung Stench into the trash and found a Mozart tape, the doorbell was pealing.

"Coming!" she yelled, patting a stray lock of hair into place as she hurried through the living room. Like the rest of her life, the stubborn curl refused to be controlled and flopped onto her forehead again.

Chuckling ruefully to herself, she flung open the door, a gay greeting on the tip of her tongue. Her welcoming grin faded at the sight of Case standing on the threshold.

He was wearing tan slacks and a navy blazer over a pale blue shirt crisp with starch and open at the collar. His loafers were shined to a mirror finish.

His hair was clean and shiny and hanging loose to curl against his neck, exactly the way she'd repeatedly told him she liked best. His implacable jaw was shiny from a recent shave, and his eyes held a guarded expression. He held a bottle of sparkling apple juice in one hand and a bouquet of long-stemmed red roses in the other.

"Case?" Her voice was rendered breathless by surprise and a fast, sweet flutter of pleasure at the sight of him.

His eyebrows drew together. "Dammit, Prue, remember

what I told you? You're supposed to ask who it is before you open the door.''

The pleasure faded, sinking like a rock into the hole that opened in her belly. ''See that blue car parked at the end of the block?'' she asked, jabbing a finger in that general direction. ''There's a policeman sitting behind the wheel, watching us. There's *always* a policeman watching the front of this house, and one watching the back. It seems like a terrible waste of manpower to me, but that's not my problem.''

Anger crowded his eyes, and she welcomed the surge of strength it gave her. ''Sorry I can't ask you in. I'm expecting a guest for dinner and I have things to do.''

She moved fast, intending to slam the door in his face. He moved faster, using his shoulder to force it open. ''Your damned guest is already here. Me!''

''Let me clarify. I'm expecting an 'invited' guest.''

''Don isn't coming.'' He narrowed his gaze and set his jaw. She curled her right hand into a fist and wondered if she'd break her knuckles if she slugged him.

''Go ahead, give it your best shot,'' he challenged, thrusting his chin forward to give her a better target. ''I hope you break my jaw. That way I can put off saying the things I came to say.''

Her stomach lurched. No more, a voice shouted in her head.

''No thanks,'' she said, managing to keep her tone cool and disinterested. ''I already know exactly what you think of me.''

Knowing that it would be futile to argue with a man with steel in his eyes, she turned her back and headed for the kitchen. Behind her, she heard him close the door and follow.

''Prue—''

''Go away, Case.''

''No.'' His voice was edged with warning.

As she stepped into the kitchen, she spun around to find him less than an arm's length from her. As always, he seemed to fill the room with raw masculine energy, the kind that tugged at a woman's core and tempted her to forget all the reasons why he was dangerous.

''Not until you listen to me,'' he said in a softer tone,

though his body strained with an almost palpable tension. He took a step forward and at the same time reached past her to put the apple juice on the counter. Instinct had her retreating, before pride stayed her steps.

"Dammit, Prue, I'm not going to hurt you!" he grated, slapping the roses onto the counter with such force that one of the dewy buds snapped off and rolled onto the floor.

"You keep saying that, and then the next thing I know I'm bleeding!" she all but shouted. The baby protested her vehemence with a hard kick. Her hand went to her belly in an automatic gesture, as though to reassure her tiny daughter.

Case's face drained of color, and his mouth went slack. "God, what's wrong? Are you in pain?" He dragged air into his lungs, a gray tinge layering his bronzed skin. "Should I call someone—911? Or I can—"

"Case, I'm fine," she hastened to assure him. She felt the warmth of his hard hand against the top of hers and realized she'd sought to comfort him with a touch. The last time she'd done that, he'd jerked away. This time he'd clamped a hard palm over the backs of her fingers, as if to keep her hand anchored on his arm.

"You're sure?" he demanded, his gaze boring into hers. Cop's eyes. Measuring, testing, refusing to take anything or anyone at face value. Especially not her.

"I'm sure," she said softly, trying to pull away. "I'm not a consummate liar, Case. I just occasionally deceive the people I care about." She flashed a brittle smile and shrugged a shoulder. "You understand how it is. When I need to trick a man into getting me pregnant, maybe? Or to set him up." She leaned slightly toward him. "Or maybe because I'm responsible for his nursing care and I'm under doctor's orders not to upset him with unsettling news until his blood pressure stops spiking clear off the chart."

Case tightened his fingers. He couldn't let her go. Not yet. "Look, I felt blindsided, and I reacted. It's what a cop has to do to survive." He stopped when he realized he was trying to skate through without risking more than a dented ego. He stiffened his spine and gulped air. "What I said—"

"What you said is exactly what you felt. No amount of explaining can change that."

He saw the sadness in her eyes and the pain. But it was the lack of fire that hurt him the most. Prudy loved with the same exuberance she poured into everything else she did. Her work. Her crazy hobbies. Her friends. He knew now he'd come to depend on that love. Even when they were apart, he'd known she still loved him. His stomach twisted with the realization he was losing her.

Denial was like a hot coal in his throat. He couldn't lose her. He wouldn't!

"At the time, maybe, I did mean them," he confessed, measuring his words to give him time to find the right ones. "But since then I've given it a lot of thought, and I realize now why you're so upset."

"Upset." She said the word slowly, as though testing its feel on her tongue. "No, that's not quite right. Actually I was devastated." Her casual shrug tore at his heart. "But I'm getting over it."

He tasted fury, then realized it was tinged with desperation. "Prue, we can work this out." It was as close to begging as he would let himself edge, even for her. Hatred for his mother came like a savage smash to the gut, then faded as quickly as it came. His mother hadn't made him into the self-centered, unforgiving bastard he'd become. He'd accomplished that on his own.

"Prue, please. I swear I'll never doubt you again. Just give me the chance to prove it."

Prudy heard the urgency in his tone and, for a blessed moment, believed him. Then reality surfaced like the treacherous remnants of a shipwreck, waiting to snare the unwary. Or the very foolish.

"What about the baby, Case? Can you look me in the eye and tell me that you're happy about becoming a father?"

He tried, she realized numbly, but an infinitesimal flickering of his lashes gave him away. "Never mind. I already know your answer."

She tugged harder on her hand and he let her go. Away from him. Out of his life.

"No!" he shouted at her retreating back, but though she flinched, she kept on walking. She hit the swinging door with such force, it rocked on its hinges, then snapped closed behind her. He was about to charge after her when the wall phone near his shoulder rang.

Ingrained habit and a sixth sense he'd never doubted had him reaching for the receiver even as he glared at the swinging door that had just slammed closed behind her.

"Yeah?" he grated into the mouthpiece with barely contained fury.

"Case, listen up!" It was Don's voice, and it was lashed with fear that raised the hair on the back of Case's neck. "Dispatch just got a call from one of the plainclothes we've got sitting on Prudy. His voice was pretty weak and garbled when he called in, but dispatch got enough to know Cardoza attacked him with a knife, then left him for dead and headed for Prudy's place."

"Gotchya."

Case was reaching for his .38 even before he replaced the telephone receiver in its cradle. *Instinct.* It had saved his ass more than once, and he didn't question the prickling sensation that was still raising the hair at the back of his neck. Cardoza was already inside the house. Case could almost smell him.

He put his back to the wall and unsnapped the safety strap of his belt holster to draw his revolver. Elbows tucked against his ribs, wrists locked, he held the weapon pointed toward the ceiling, the blue-black barrel a scant inch from his nose.

Not a sound came from the room Prudy had disappeared into a few seconds earlier. Inching along the wall, Case kept his gaze fixed on the swinging door. The bastard was in there with her. Case would have bet his life on it, and the realization had him fighting down a panicky fear he'd never felt before. *Prudy.* Just the thought of that lunatic harming her or the baby—

Case cut the thought short. He had to stay focused. Prudy's life depended on it.

Police procedure ingrained in him by nearly twenty years of brutal experience, Case knew Petrov would already be on his way. He also knew that the cop assigned to watch the rear of Prudy's house had been alerted by radio and was probably moving in on the back door even now.

For the moment, however, Case was on his own.

Chapter 18

Everything inside Case urged him to bolt through the swinging door to find Prudy. Exercising the steely self-control he'd acquired through years of training, he forced himself to inch the door open instead.

"Join the party, pig," Arturo Cardoza wheezed. "Me and your little honey here were about to start without you."

Thinner than ever, his cadaverous features contorted in a rictus of hate, Cardoza stood near the dining room table, one bony arm pressed against Prudy's throat. In his other hand he wielded a knife, the blade of which was perilously close to her heart.

"Let her go, Arturo." Case kept his tone soft and unthreatening. "Can't you see she's pregnant?"

Cardoza sneered, the coke glitter in his eyes an obscene contrast to his muddy complexion. Sweat was already beginning to pearl along the man's greasy hairline. "A nice twist of fate, don't you think? Three lives in exchange for one."

Case eased into the room, both hands raised, with only the thumb and middle finger of his right holding the .38 in plain sight. Cardoza's liverish eyes glittered as he lasered a gaze at the gun. The door swung closed behind Case's tensed body with a soft *swish.*

"I'm the one you want. Let her go, and you can have me."

No, Case, don't! Prudy wanted to cry out, but the pressure on her gullet was too painful to allow more than shallow breaths.

"Oh, I'll have you all right. I've had a long time to—" A siren wailed in the distance, the sound cutting Cardoza short. "What the hell?"

The shrill sound quickly grew louder until it shook the walls, then quit abruptly. Prudy felt a relief so intense her knees started to buckle. At the same time pain shot into her breast. She felt a sticky wetness spreading over her skin, and her head started to spin. She knew she was about to faint and willed the icy queasiness to abate. No matter what, she had to remain alert.

"Call 'em off, Randolph, or I'll stick her. Now!"

"Take it easy, Arturo. That's just the ambulance coming for the guy in the car outside."

Prudy saw Case's mouth ease into a placating grin, as false as the calm in his eyes. Incredibly, Cardoza giggled. "Son of a bitch died chewing on a Twinkie."

"He's not dead. So far the only charge you're facing is assault and attempted murder. A good lawyer can plea-bargain that down to attempted manslaughter."

Case kept his gaze riveted on Cardoza's eyes. He figured Walters already had a sniper on station, or would have soon, and the SWAT team positioned. The dining room adjoined the living room. Where Cardoza stood at the far end of the table, he would be clearly visible to anyone outside the living room window. Case tried to remember if the drapes in Prudy's living room were open or closed, then remembered noticing that they'd been drawn when he approached the house.

His blood chilled. Until he got a clear shot at Cardoza's head or convinced him to let Prudy go, she was at risk. At desperate risk.

"Arturo, listen to me. What happened to Felix—"

"No more talk. Drop the piece, and kick it over here where I can reach it."

Prudy prayed with all her heart that Case wouldn't give up his gun.

"Let her go first," Case bargained. "She's not a part of this."

Cardoza's lips snaked into a maniacal smile that revealed rotting teeth. "She is, until I say she's not."

Case couldn't risk taking his gaze from Cardoza's face for even a split second, but he sensed Prudy's terror and longed to reassure her.

"At least let her sit down."

Before Cardoza could respond, spotlights hit the closed living room drapes, filling the room with a muted glow. The blare of a bullhorn cut into the silence. *"Cardoza, this is Captain William Walters, Portland P.D. Come out now with your hands in the air and you won't get hurt. You have my word."*

Case strained to hear the creaking of the back door as Don and the others slipped inside under cover of the noise. Somehow he had to get the bastard to turn his back to the kitchen door.

"An ambulance, huh?" Cardoza sneered. "I shoulda known better than to trust a cop."

"Captain Walters means what he says," Case assured him, edging to his right in the hope that Cardoza would move left, exposing his back to the door.

"One more step, and she's dead!"

Case froze. Prudy uttered a little cry, bile all but gagging her.

Suddenly weary of the game, Arturo stood straighter, feeling more powerful and clearheaded than he'd ever felt before in his whole life. He'd outwitted the whole frigging police department. Just like *El Hefe.*

It came to him then, the perfect way to punish the bastard. The same way *El Hefe* had punished an informer once.

Pleasure at his own cleverness rocketed through him, as hot as any sex he'd ever had. "Hey, lady, you're a nurse, ain't ya?'' he asked, keeping his gaze on the man with the cold eyes who stood only a scant six or seven feet away.

He heard Prudy gurgle something and eased the pressure on her throat. ''Yes, I'm a nurse,'' she answered, her voice hoarse.

''Take a look at this here purple spot on my arm and tell me what you see.'' Arturo kept his gaze fixed on the cop. He could feel the man's hatred. Like a line of the best white goddess, it gave him a savage high.

''It's Kaposi's sarcoma,'' Prudy said with a jolt of desperate fear. ''One of the first symptoms of HIV.''

''Doc down in 'Frisco figured I got me about six good months left. I was planning on spending them in Hawaii someplace, drinking Mai Tai's and ogling whores. Now, I guess I'd just as soon end it quick like.''

He moved slowly, nudging her along with the pressure of his knee against hers, keeping the knife snugged close to her tit. His destination was the green ottoman to his left. Careful to keep her between him and the wadcutter Randolph had in his hand, he eased his hold long enough to reach into his pocket for his nine millimeter.

''Hey, looky what I found,'' he singsonged as he pressed the barrel against Prudy's head, then slowly eased her to a sitting position on the ottoman. With his other hand, he dropped the knife into his jacket pocket, then rested his bony fingers against Prudy's neck.

''Cardoza, this is Captain Walters again. In ten minutes the phone will ring and I want you to pick it up, so we can talk about this situation we got here.''

Cardoza glanced at the old clock in the corner, then grinned. ''Is that what we got here, cop? A situation?''

Case remained silent. He knew that Walters's words were a signal. That they would be coming in *nine* minutes. Cardoza's back was to the door now, an easy target—if Case could only get him to lower the gun.

''Look, Cardoza—''

''No, you look, cop. And listen. I know there's a SWAT team out there ready to nail my ass. I also know the only reason you haven't tried to take me out already is 'cause of your whore here.'' He waited, his expression feral. Case knew he was waiting for a spark of emotion. Trying to goad him into making a mistake. So he gave him nothing.

"So you and me are gonna play this little game I seen once. When I give you the word, you lower that there wadcutter in your hand to your belly and pull the trigger.''

"No, you can't make him do that!'' Prudy cried, trying to twist toward him. But her head was wedged between the gun barrel and Cardoza's talonlike grip.

Case prayed that Cardoza would shift focus for only an instant, but the bastard only grinned wider. "Now, Randolph. Do it now.''

"Let her go first.''

"Not a chance.'' He shrugged. "I just figured you for a gambling man is all. Guess not.''

Keep him talking, Case reminded himself. "Who says I'm not?''

"What you said. See, a gambling man likes nothing better than playing the odds. In this case, betting that the men you got waiting to bust through the door can take me out before I can pull the trigger on this here Smith & Wesson.''

"What men?'' Case knew the question would win him a laugh, and it did.

"God, I admire you, Randolph. About to watch me spatter your honey's brains all over this pretty room and you can still laugh.'' He grinned. "What'll it be? You shoot first, or do I? Either way I figure you'll end up in pain. Your choice.''

Case stalled. "Give me a minute to think it through.''

He knew the chamber of the .38 was empty, so he was willing to shove the barrel against his belly, just as Cardoza demanded. But could he get a second shot off at Cardoza's head before the bastard pulled the trigger and killed Prudy? Especially now, when his arm, only just recently removed from the cast, was still weak and felt like lead from holding it in the air so long.

"Thirty seconds,'' Cardoza ordered, his voice slick with triumph. "And only 'cause I've always been partial to pregnant ladies." He trailed his dirty fingernails along the line of Prudy's jaw, and she flinched. Case felt a killing rage that took all of his control to squelch.

"Okay, you have a deal," he said, lowering his gaze to Prudy's white face.

"Please don't," she whispered, her voice thick with tears.

"It'll be okay, sweets," he told her gently, then prayed that what might be his last words to her weren't a lie.

"Keep your trigger finger alongside the cylinder so's I can see it, and lower that piece to your gut."

Case did as he was told, fighting to keep from gasping aloud at the hot needles racing up his arm as the blood returned to starved tissues.

"Wait!" Cardoza cried, his face suddenly blotched and twitching. "I almost forgot something else *El Hefe* taught me."

"What's that?" Case gauged the distance, counted down the seconds. He figured he had about another two or three minutes to go before the door burst open.

"Said cops always keep the chamber empty."

"*El Hefe*'s full of crap," Case grated. "But if you don't believe me, come look for yourself."

"I got a better idea. Spin the chamber and let's make sure. That way you still got a one in six chance of survivin'." Cardoza's giggle rang out again, and Prudy realized that the man was definitely psychotic, either from his illness or from frying his brains with coke. Her fear nearly choked the breath from her.

"Mr. Cardoza, please don't do this. Don't make my baby an orphan. It's a little girl, you see, and she needs her daddy so much. Please, I'll do anything—"

"Shut up or I'll shoot the both of you *right now!*"

Case knew a moment of terrible weariness before he very carefully, very slowly brought his left hand down to spin the chambers of the .38.

"Put the end of the barrel against your belly, right above your belt buckle," Cardoza taunted. "Right where your slug hit Felix."

Case did as he was told. He hadn't prayed since he was a kid, but he prayed now. That Prudy would be safe, that he would live to see his daughter born. He squeezed the trigger. The hammer clicked on an empty cylinder and Prudy sagged with relief.

Case's jaw clenched. Sweat glistening on his skin, adding luster to the bronze.

"Now isn't this fun?" Cardoza cackled. "I'll tell you what. Let's do it again. And just to make it interesting, why don't you open the cylinder and take out four of those shells."

Case hoped the bastard hadn't ever heard the children's story about the little rabbit that begged not to be thrown in the briar bushes, pretending to be terrified. Removing the shells from the chamber would give Case an opportunity to stall for time. "No way, Arturo."

"Do it!"

"That wasn't part of the deal." Case longed to look at the clock, but he didn't dare let Cardoza know he was watching the time. "I'd rather just shoot myself, do it fast and clean. Don't make me sweat, man."

"Open the damn cylinder."

Hoping that Arturo would think he was stalling because he was trying to prolong his life, which was about as true as true could get, Case delayed as long as he could. Opening the cylinder. Shaking out the shells into his cupped hand, replacing one. Spinning the chambers.

"Throw them other shells on the floor," Arturo ordered, spitle flying. The look of anticipation in his eyes was frightening. Case could almost feel the man's blood lust.

"Case, please don't do this," Prudy pleaded as he opened his hand and let the blunt-nosed shells fall to the carpet. "Please, please don't."

Unable to bear the thought of Case pulling that trigger again and again until the hammer finally crashed down on a live round, she clamped her arms around her belly and prayed.

"Tell me you forgive me for hurting you," Case whispered hoarsely, his finger snug around the trigger, the barrel of the gun pressed to his flat abdomen. He was going to do it, she realized in rising panic. The man she loved—adored—was going to pull that trigger again and again, until he snuffed out his own life. To save hers. And their baby's.

"Please, Prudy. Before I go, I need to hear that you forgive me."

Forgive him? Prudy stared at him through a blur of tears. Of course she forgave him. But she couldn't say the words, knowing that as soon as she did, Case would pull the trigger.

Terrified, she saw his eyes go cold and empty and the muscles in his arm flex. No matter what, he was going to take his own life to spare hers.

"I forgive you!" she cried on a strangled sob. "Oh, God, Case, I love you so much. Of course I forgive you!"

Only the iron control Case was exerting on the muscles of his back kept his shoulders from sagging. He allowed himself one long, last look at Prudy, praying he'd stalled long enough, and pulled the trigger.

The hammer clicked. Cardoza giggled. "One down, three to go."

Case felt sweat pooling between his shoulder blades and on his forehead. His hand itched to whip the .38 toward Cardoza's grinning face. But the odds weren't right. Not yet. Still with each pull of the trigger, his chances of being able to turn the gun on Cardoza and fire a live round were getting better. Maybe, just maybe, luck was going to be on his side this time. Maybe, just maybe, there was a God up there, looking down, who'd decided to spare his life so he might be able to hold his daughter in his arms. Maybe—

"Don't even think about it," Cardoza warned, his gaze narrowing. To emphasize his point, he tapped Prudy on the temple with the gun barrel.

Horribly, acutely aware of Prudy's soft sobbing, Case tensed to pull the trigger again. Sweat ran down his face, streaming into his eyes, beading over his lips.

Two more minutes, please, Case prayed, but the look in Cardoza's eyes told him he was out of time. And out of luck.

Ignoring Cardoza, Case leveled his gaze at Prudy's face as

he tightened his finger. "I love you, Prue, and, as God is my witness, I would have loved our little girl. I—"

"Pull the trigger now," Cardoza screamed. "Now."

Prudy cried Case's name, and it was her voice he heard as he pulled the trigger. The report of the gun was deafening. Simultaneously, Case felt as if a mammoth iron fist plowed into his gut. Then he felt nothing at all.

It had been a nightmare. Angry shouts and exploding gunpowder. Prudy didn't remember leaving her chair, didn't recall falling to her knees to run expert hands over Case's bloody torso. The hole in his abdomen had been surprisingly small in the front, but the exit wound had torn away huge chunks of tissue.

The paramedics had been brilliantly efficient, already preparing to transfuse him with plasma as soon as they'd been given the okay to enter the house. Shoving her fear and all sense of modesty aside, Prudy had stripped off her new maternity smock to make a bandage. Ordering Petrov to turn Case gently onto his back, she expertly applied pressure, praying silently as the lilac cotton became saturated with blood.

It was only later that she realized some of the blood covering her hands and forearms had been her own, dripping from a bullet graze in her neck. The men rushing through the door had startled Cardoza sufficiently to spoil his aim.

"One minute more," Petrov had bellowed as he'd bent over his partner's inert body. "All we needed was one lousy minute more."

Boyd had pushed him aside to direct the paramedics, then climbed into the ambulance for the fast trip to PortGen.

Now, three hours later, wearing Petrov's shirt over the bandage Marge had applied to the cut on her breast, her maternity jeans still spotted with Case's blood, Prudy sat with her arms folded over her belly, rocking back and forth in her chair. Next to her, Don sat stony faced and solid, his big hands wrapped around a paper cup. The coffee it held had long since lost whatever warmth it had managed to retain during the trip from the far end of the hall to the waiting room.

Like the first time Case had been in surgery—God, had it only been three months ago?—the small area was filled with hard-faced men and several women, one of whom, a lovely dark-haired detective who'd introduced herself as Andrea Markovitch, had spent the past few hours hovering over Prudy like a big sister. Bringing her soup and hot tea all the way from the cafeteria. Gently nagging at her until she'd finished both.

Captain Walters had been as attentive and caring as any father, his dark eyes filled with boundless compassion. It had been the captain who had burst through the door one step ahead of Don an instant after the bullet had ripped through Case's belly. Until ballistics issued a report, no one knew for sure which of the half dozen bullets they'd pumped into Cardoza's torso had burst his aorta, killing him instantly.

She still remembered how gentle Walters had been as he'd helped Stacy pull her away from Case's bleeding body. And how reassuring his deep voice had been as he'd led her outside to the car assigned to speed her to the hospital in the ambulance's wake.

"Excuse me," a tech Prudy recognized from the blood bank called softly from the door. "If there's anyone here who is type AB positive, we need blood donors."

"That's Case's type," Prudy murmured.

"Yeah, I know," Petrov acknowledged, his voice clipped.

Next to her, Markovitch was already retrieving her purse from under the chair. "I'm AB positive," she said as she leapt to her feet.

"Me, too," one of the other detectives called, already rolling up his sleeve.

Petrov watched his two colleagues leave before heaving a sigh. "Guess that's a bad sign, them wanting blood."

"Not necessarily," she hedged, aware that all eyes had suddenly swung her way. "AB isn't as common as O positive," she explained, raising her voice slightly. "The blood bank might just be running low." Even as she said the words, even as her mind registered the looks of cautious relief directed her way, she knew they weren't true.

Case was in trouble. Even with Boyd and Chief Surgeon

Dr. Ivans fighting to repair the damage. She felt a sob well up in her throat and fought it down.

"Honey, you need to rest," Don urged when the clock on the wall ticked past another hour of waiting. Endless, agonizing waiting.

"I'm fine," she murmured, her words coming automatically, like the breath that flowed in and out of her lungs.

"Sure you are, but you've had a rough day. Why don't I find you an empty room someplace where you can stretch out for a few minutes?"

Prudy shook her head. "I keep seeing the look in his eyes when he...when he knew he was going to pull that trigger." She drew a ragged breath. "During our marriage he must have told me a hundred times that he loved me." When they'd made love, when she'd done something to please him. When he'd left her a tissue rose. "In my head, I knew that he meant it, but until he looked at me in that split second before..." She couldn't go on. Instead, she drew another ragged breath.

"He threatened to kill me if I didn't let him take my place at dinner," Don said with a harsh laugh.

"That...sounds like Case." When had Don taken her hand in his? she wondered, managing to cast him a wan smile.

"He loves you, honey. Deep down, to the bone, loves you. And he would...he *will* love that little one you're brewing."

"Oh, Don, he saved my life." Her voice caught on a wracking sob that all but doubled her over.

"Honey, Case wouldn't want you to take on like this."

"He put that awful gun to his belly and pulled the trigger. He had to know what it would do to him." She shivered. "Oh, God, what he must have gone through in those last few minutes."

Don winced, but his gaze remained steady. Comforting. Buoying her. "He'll make it, Prue. He has too much to live for not to."

Case survived the surgery.

Dawn was breaking when Boyd came to tell her Case was being moved directly from the OR to ICU. While the others asked questions, she saw only the bleak look in his red-rimmed eyes.

"It was a hell of a patch-up job, but all the parts are back where they belong," he said in answer to Bill Walters's quiet request for a prognosis. "I don't know if it was luck or skill, but he managed to put that bullet in the one place where his chance of survival was slim instead of none."

Prudy winced, but kept her gaze riveted on Boyd's face. "How many times did you lose him on the table?" she asked quietly.

His gaze flickered. "Twice."

"Good God," one of the detectives muttered, his voice barely audible.

"He's fighting. That's all I can say. The next forty-eight hours are critical. If he makes it through, I'd say he has a decent chance."

"Any idea what kind of odds you'd put to the word *decent?*" Don asked gruffly, his eyes suspiciously bright.

Boyd hesitated, regret and worry stamped as heavily on his face as the usual post-op weariness. "If we get lucky and infection doesn't set in, he might manage fifty-fifty."

Prudy couldn't fault Boyd for wanting to give Case's friends a handful of hope, but she was far too aware of the real odds. Two in ten, maybe. "I want to see him."

Boyd tugged the surgical cap from his head and ran his fingers through his hair. "As soon as they get him settled, I'll have someone come down to fetch you."

"No need. I'll wait upstairs." Right outside the double doors to the ICU. *Inside,* if the charge nurse didn't object.

"I'll walk you up," Don insisted quietly, and she knew not to protest. In his own way, he needed to feel as though he were doing something for Case. Something Case would want him to do.

At the other end of the hall Don had just pushed the button for the elevator when the doors drew open and Marge stepped out. "How is he?" she asked as soon as she saw Prudy standing there.

"Fighting. I'm on my way to ICU now."

Marge nodded. "I found this in his jacket pocket when I was looking for personal effects to lock up."

Prudy stared at her wearily for an instant before glancing down at Marge's outstretched hand. There on her palm were two roses—one white, and one a delicate pink. The pink one was smaller, she realized, her heart stopping. Just the size for a tiny little girl.

It was a good twenty minutes after Prudy arrived at ICU before Rosemary Bogan left the small cubicle where Case lay utterly still, his face as bleached as the sheet covering him.

"He's stable," Nurse Bogan murmured when she reached the desk where Prudy sat watching a bank of monitors registering his vital signs. The too-rapid beeping of the heart monitor and the steady flashing of his pulse, temperature and blood pressure readouts testified to his enormous stamina. The fact that he was breathing on his own, without the aid of a respirator, buoyed her slightly. But she'd already seen his chart and, consequently, knew exactly how tough the battle facing him really was.

"If you see old Pruneface Fister sticking her head in here, duck, okay? I'm only supposed to let immediate family in here, and only for five minutes every hour."

Prudy nodded as she rose from her chair, though she'd already been aware of the rules. "Thanks, Rosie. I owe you one."

The purple-and-pink sneakers she'd slipped into after her nap because she'd thought they'd give Don a laugh when he showed up for dinner were silent on the ubiquitous white linoleum as she entered the small cubicle.

PortGen had recently upgraded its critical-care equipment, and everything gleamed, even the rails of the bed. As quietly as she could, she eased down the rail, then moved closer.

"Oh, Case," she whispered. "You have to get better. Chloe and I need you so much."

Needing to touch him, she took his limp hand in hers and pressed it to her belly. "Chloe's sleeping now, but it won't be long before she's practicing her place-kicking again." She watched his face, desperate to see an indication that he could hear her. A flicker of his blunt eyelashes, an upward kick at the corner of his mouth. Something, anything. When he didn't respond, she felt a wave of disappointment so intense it took her breath.

"You *will not* leave me," she said fiercely through a sudden wash of tears. "You hear me, Case Randolph? I don't intend to raise this child alone."

Leaning forward carefully so as not to jar him, she brushed her lips over his forehead, his cheek, the relaxed curve of the mouth she loved.

And then she settled down in the chair next to the bed and waited.

Case felt only pain, coming in waves, so severe he knew death would be a blessing. Only the soft murmur of a familiar voice kept him from screaming. He couldn't make out the words, but they tempered his agony. His breathing seemed easier then, his will to fight stronger.

At first, he clung to the sound as a lost child clings to a kindly rescuer's hand. Gradually, however, he felt himself longing to make sense of the soothing sounds. The longing grew until he found himself struggling to sharpen his senses. But every time he tried to open his eyes, his strength failed, and he sank into the black void where his only hope was that same soft voice.

Boyd planted his feet and crossed his arms over his chest. He'd been delegated by half the nurses on staff and his wife to force Prudy to leave Case's side long enough to get some sleep.

"Prudy, you need some downtime. Go to the cafeteria and eat breakfast. Take a shower and a nap. I promise I'll give you a holler if he wakes up."

Prudy shook her head. Her shoulders were stiff from sitting in the same position, holding Case's hand against her tummy. Chloe had done her part, kicking her daddy's wide palm often.

The little dickens had even given him a couple of good punches. Once, Prudy was almost certain his mouth moved.

"I need to be here," she said, ignoring Boyd's frown. "And I have been eating."

"Junk food from the machine."

"No, Boyd. Real food. Rosie's taken it upon herself to make sure I eat."

Boyd sighed. "Lord, but you make a man crazy sometimes."

Prudy was about to tell him to get lost, when she heard a faint whisper. "Like it...though."

"Oh, Case, you're awake," she cried, her heart leaping. But his eyes were already drifting shut.

"Hot damn, he's gonna make it," Boyd cried softly.

Terrified to let herself hope, Prudy held his hand, her body braced as if for a blow. Case's fingers tightened slightly around hers, and then, even though he didn't open his eyes again, one corner of that arrogant mouth twitched at one corner in a ghost of a grin.

"Yes," Prudy whispered through tears of the wildest joy she'd ever known. "He's going to make it."

Epilogue

Prudy was halfway up the walk from the carport to the back door when she realized disaster had struck while she'd been at work. The lovely flower bed she'd left that morning was now a muddy mess. Bits of her pampered petunias and marigolds were strewn like confetti atop the rubble of overturned stones and broken foliage.

In the middle of a particular gooey puddle was her darling, soon-to-be-a-year-old daughter, barefoot, wearing her best sunsuit, now smeared with mud, and a floppy sun hat, happily chattering away to a bedraggled yellow marigold that she was apparently attempting to replant in a hole scooped out of the muck.

Crouched nearby, clad only in cutoffs, Case was using a small trowel to dig another hole for his daughter. Mud was smeared on his cheek and liberally streaked across his big chest. The scar on his leg had faded, but the one on his back was still more red than pink, a gruesome reminder of the pain he'd endured—and of the fight he'd waged to survive.

Prudy never failed to send a fast prayer of thanksgiving aloft whenever she was reminded of that horrible time when she and Chloe had nearly lost him. Even though she'd gotten rid of the blood-soaked rug in the living room and rearranged the furniture several times, she still sometimes saw him lying there so terribly still.

But he'd survived. And since the moment he woke up in ICU, he'd made it a point to show how much he trusted and loved her.

"Case Randolph, what in the world do you think you're doing?" she demanded as she quickened her step. She worked only part-time now, usually Saturdays like today and the odd day during the week.

He glanced up, his grin flashing white and his sapphire eyes lighting. "Hiya, sweets. How was your day?"

"Not nearly as much fun as yours, I see," she said as she dropped her purse and shopping bag onto a nearby lawn chair.

A sleepy meow from the butterscotch tabby curled into the grass under the seat protested the sudden noise. The smallest of Sunshine's only litter of kittens and slightly lame, Buttercup had attached herself to Case during his convalescence, and her antics had helped ease some of the frustration he'd felt during yet another bout of reduced mobility.

"Sorry, BC," she muttered as she marched by.

"Uh-oh," Chloe piped up, grinning. "Mama's mad."

"Naw, Mama never gets mad at us, darlin'. You and me, we're special." Case leaned over to take a pretend bite out of his daughter's chubby shoulder. "And you're sweet."

Chloe giggled, patting her daddy's cheek to leave a fresh daub of mud, and Prudy felt a lump forming in her throat. Her family, she thought. The two people she loved most in this world. Her adorable, redheaded, blue-eyed daughter and the impossible, adorable man who'd fathered her. Knowing that she'd nearly lost him had made every day they'd had since doubly precious.

"I distinctly remember asking you to weed this bed, not destroy it," she chastened as she leaned down to accept her husband's kiss. Not once since he'd awakened in ICU had they wasted an opportunity to show their love for each other. And their gratitude for the second chance they'd been given.

"Weeded *and* watered," Case said smugly, his fingers haphazardly combing long black hair glinting like polished ebony in the April sunshine. Ebony now liberally threaded with silver. Stress highlights, he called them. From the trauma of fatherhood.

"*Very* watered." She gestured with the toe of her yellow sneaker at the pool of muddy water.

Case's proud grin folded his hard cheeks into the sexy creases she adored. "Chloe wanted to do it herself. I admit she got a little carried away, but she was so pleased with herself at learning how to turn on the hose." His gaze found Prudy's and she felt the inevitable shiver of pleasure. "Sort of reminds me of you when you get involved in a project."

Prudy tried to keep her expression stern. "Are you implying that my projects turn into messes like this one?"

His eyes crinkled. "Heck, no. Some of them turn out pretty good. Just look at me. You set about teachin' me to do daddy things and you have to admit I learned fast."

Chloe lifted her head and beamed at her father. "Daddy," she declared firmly.

Prudy laughed. "You two are incorrigible."

"But lovable, right?" Though his manner was teasing, Prudy saw the flash of insecurity in his eyes before his lashes swooped it away. She realized now that Case had never felt totally accepted or truly loved in the whole of his life. Even now, she sometimes caught him looking at her with doubt in his eyes.

Once, after they'd made love and he was lying drowsy and off-guard in her arms, she'd asked him about that look. At first, he'd laughed it off, but when he'd realized she was going to nag him until he chipped another piece off that protective barrier he kept around his deepest feelings, he'd admitted that he had trouble believing he deserved to be so happy.

Consequently, she made that her latest—and most important—project. So far it seemed to be working.

"Lovable *and* sexy, but don't let it go to your head."

His eyes took on a gleam she recognized. "It's not my head that's the first thing affected when you show up, my love."

"I assume you've forgotten that I invited Don and the MacAuleys and Grandvilles over for a prebirthday party for Chloe this evening."

Case looked abashed. "Guess maybe I did at that."

"Uh-huh." She folded her arms and tapped her foot. "Guess you know you owe me big time, Randolph."

"I do, huh?" He got to his feet in that lithe big-cat movement uniquely his. "How about a kiss for starters?"

Her heart speeded. "That might work, I suppose."

"What time is the horde descending?" he asked as he drew her into his arms.

"Our *guests* are due at six."

He lowered his head and nuzzled her neck. "Chloe missed her nap. Probably needs one before company comes." His tongue found the sensitive spot beneath her ear and she gasped. "Mommy and Daddy need a nap, too."

"Case—"

"It's been a damn long day without you, love," he murmured between nibbling kisses. "And I have this project of my own that needs some work."

Blatantly, he rubbed against her, letting her feel the hard ridge of arousal straining the button fly of his cutoff jeans. "Course, I need some help. From someone experienced in…projects."

She answered with a provocative thrust of her hips, and he groaned into the curve of her shoulder. "God, I love you, Prudy Randolph."

"And I love you, Case. With all my heart." She cleared her throat. "And speaking of projects, I just *happened* to run into Luke at the hospital and he just *happened* to mention…" She paused, feeling him tense. His head came up and he looked down at her, his eyes intense.

"Yes?" he asked tersely.

She made him wait, enjoying the look of frustrated impatience that came over his beloved face. "I'm warning you, Prue," he all but growled.

"Yes," she said softly. "Another miracle. I'm pregnant."

His shout of joy woke Buttercup with a start and had Chloe

giggling. "Hallelujah, let's celebrate," he said, kissing her long and hard.

When he lifted his head, she saw tears in his eyes. "Have I told you recently how much I adore you?" she whispered as she reached up to capture a stray tear with her fingertip.

"No, but—" He was interrupted by a strange sound that had his head jerking around a split second before a spray of water hit him squarely in the belly. He bellowed in outrage and Prudy laughed—a split second before their first "miracle" turned the hose on her mother.

And giggled.

*   *   *   *   *

Turn the page to preview Paula Detmer Riggs's
BABY BY DESIGN, the emotional conclusion to her
MATERNITY ROW *series, coming in September 1997*
from Intimate Moments.

Prologue

A paper end to a paper marriage.

It seemed fitting, Morgan Paxton decided as he tossed the letter from his wife Raine's attorney to the floor of the tent. All very neat and tidy, just the way he liked his life. No more ties. No more responsibilities.

No more Raine.

Closing his eyes, Morgan focused on the night in an attempt to assuage the sudden pain that lanced through him. Beyond the canvas walls of the tent, the booted feet of faceless men pummeled packed clay as the communal meal was prepared. The scent of spices that would be considered exotic back home in the States filled the air, mingling pungently with the acrid heaviness of campfire smoke and the occasional whiffs of camel dung.

Ah…the joys of being on assignment. Visiting foreign shores. Sleeping on a cot. Shaving without water. What more could a man want? Excitement, challenge, living on the edge. Morgan Paxton, news anchor extraordinaire. He had the world by the tail.

A bitter smile twisted Morgan's mouth. Knowing he

shouldn't, he slipped his hand under the pillow on the bunk
where he was sitting, to touch the dog-eared leather folder that
had been his constant companion for almost eleven years—
since Raine had sent it to him a few weeks after their wedding.
Inside, in one of the compartments, was their wedding picture.
He drew it carefully from its niche, the pad of his thumb caressing one corner where eleven years of handling had worn
away the edges of the photo. Not that he adored the woman,
or anything. Hell, no. According to Raine, he was too consumed with passion for his work to care deeply about anything
or anyone else.

The backs of Morgan's eyes burned as he studied the wedding picture. In direct contrast to her name, Raine was all
sunshine and sweet warm silk. As Morgan gazed down at her
precious visage, the photo lost definition and his memories of
her took over.

Raine. She had been the ultimate prize. A gentle spirit to
soften the hard corners of his personality. A caring nature that
forgave his faults and flaws, many though they were.

What had he given her in return? A child she adored, but
who had worn her out with his hyperactive ways and inexpli-
cable tantrums. A home and enough money to allow her to
give Mike the kind of constant attention he had required. A
husband fighting his way to the top, who had been gone more
than he'd been with her and their son.

Now, when it was too late, Morgan realized his mistakes.
Okay, so he'd made sure Mike had had a fat college fund—
his son would have gotten the first-class education Morgan
had secretly coveted—but did money make up for his not being there while his son cut his first tooth or took his first step?

Reluctantly, dreading the hard punch of guilt he knew to
expect, he shifted his gaze to the other picture in the folder,
the last photo of Mike ever taken. His son at eight, only a few
weeks before his death, smiling up at him, his blond hair
mussed as always, his brown eyes alight with mischief.

A miniature Morgan, everyone had said. The image of his
daddy, with Morgan's wanderlust and rebellious bent.

Mike would have been ten in a few weeks. Poised on the

edge of manhood. Probably would have been as tall as his mom by now. Close, anyway. Filling the house with his clutter and noise and energy. A house that had to seem terribly empty now.

Not that he would know.

It had been eighteen months since he'd been home. Eighteen months of trying to smother his grief and driving himself so fiercely he was teetering on the edge of massive burnout. A year and a half since Raine had asked him to leave and not come back. Having him there, seeing Mike in his every expression, was only exacerbating her grief.

"Yo, Pax, you awake?" His producer, Dave Stebbins, stepped into Morgan's tent.

"Yeah, I'm awake. What do you want?"

"Your presence, Oh, Mighty Star. In thirty minutes."

Morgan muttered an obscenity that had Stebbins grinning.

"A thousand bucks says you don't have the guts to repeat that on the air."

"Don't tempt me," Morgan muttered as the tent flap dropped, blocking Stebbins from sight. The man's footsteps receded, then blended with the muffled cacophony of camp activity.

God, but he hated war. The noise and smells and the waste. The pain. His own physical wounds had healed, leaving him with a few scars here and there and a constant dull ache in his shoulder, the one ripped apart by a Vietcong bullet a lifetime ago. Lord, but he had been young and innocent in those days.

Raine used to call him her proud lion. Undaunted. Undefeated. Her protector. Another sharp, agonizing pain ran through him at the thought. Instead of protecting her as he'd promised, he'd left her alone and vulnerable while he went off to prowl the world, looking for bigger and better stories to lay at the altar of his much-coveted success.

But hadn't that been what had drawn her to him in the first place? His fierce ambition. His drive to make his mark on an increasingly complex world? To reveal the insanities of war and oppression for what they were so the powers-that-be would be forced to make changes? In short, he had been a card-carrying idealist. A crusader for truth, justice and the American way.

Why else would a gently reared, brilliantly accomplished professor's daughter have been interested in a guy who'd quit school at fifteen in order to help his daddy turn out the best sour mash in Hanks County, Kentucky? Who'd joined the army at eighteen in order to evade the net of federal agents who'd hauled Zebulon Paxton off to jail for bootlegging?

By the time he met Raine Connelly, however, he'd been twelve years older, a lot more cynical and a great deal more polished. The ignorant country boy had still been there, all right, buried under the changes he'd forced on himself.

Because they'd met on a college campus, and because she was an American lit major, he made it a point to talk about books. Mark Twain was his favorite author, he'd told her, and *Huckleberry Finn* his favorite book. Because Huck reminded him of himself, he'd admitted with one of his engaging grins.

Though he'd bedded his fair share of willing women by the time he met her, he'd felt like a virgin the night he first kissed her. Trembling inside that he would make a mistake and drive her out of his life forever. Instead of catching the plane to Tahiti, where he'd planned to spend his much-needed vacation, he'd stayed in the little Oregon town of Bradenton Falls, where Raine had been attending college.

Every night for three weeks he'd told himself he was "leaving first thing tomorrow." And every morning he'd found another reason to stay one more day. No matter what words he'd used, however, the reason was Raine. Her smile. Her twinkling eyes. Her bright wit and clever mind. And most of all, her total acceptance of the man beneath the image. More than anything, he wanted to please his gentle princess who thought he was special.

But now...

Maybe he should just let her go, he thought, staring down at the laughing face of his bride. Free her to find her happiness with another man. A man who wasn't wandering the globe more than he was home. A man content to live a quiet, ordinary life. A man who could give her the security and serenity she now claimed to need.

A better man than Morgan Paxton.

On the other hand, a selfish bastard like Morgan Paxton would fight to keep her. Fight like the very devil, no holds barred, because to lose her would be like ripping a part of himself away. The best part.

A cynical jerk like Morgan Paxton would use any weapon, devise any strategy, to make her love him again.

Because he was too much of a coward to even contemplate living the rest of his life knowing he'd held sunshine and joy in his hands and then, like the ignorant, ill-bred country boy he really was under all the polish, been too stupid and too clumsy to keep his lady safe and happy.

Night after night, as he'd lain alone in a strange bed in some distant part of the world, he had comforted himself with plans for the new start they would make. The time he would take special pains to cosset and cherish her.

He'd been so sure she'd just needed time alone to heal.

Give me a chance, Raine, he pleaded silently. I swear I'll make it up to you. Please.

His only answer was silence—and the hard, steady agony of guilt.

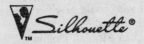

**Special Edition and Intimate Moments
are proud to present**

Janet Dailey Award winner
RUTH WIND

**and three new emotionally gripping
tales of love…**

The Forrest brothers—as wild and untamed as the
rugged mountains they call home—each discover a
woman as special and true as the Colorado skies. But is
love enough to lasso these hearts…?

Lance Forrest—left town
years ago, but returns to Red Creek in
MARRIAGE MATERIAL (SE#1108, 6/97) to a
son he never knew…and finds an unexpected love.

Jake Forrest—lived his whole life by a code of
military honor…until that honor failed him. In
RECKLESS (IM#796, 7/97), he comes home to find
peace…and discovers a woman for his heart.

Tyler Forrest—has raised his son, alone, in the quiet of
the Colorado mountains. But then his solitude is
invaded by the most unlikely woman…who thinks he's
HER IDEAL MAN (IM#801, 8/97).

THE LAST ROUNDUP…
Three brothers travel the rocky road to love
in a small Colorado town.

Available at your favorite retail outlet.

Intimate Moments is proud to bring you an unforgettable miniseries.

BEVERLY BIRD

The Wedding Ring

Wrapped in the warmth of family tradition, three couples say "I do!"

LOVING MARIAH
(Intimate Moments #790, June 1997)
Adam Wallace searches for his kidnapped
son...which leads him to the Amish heartland
and lovely schoolteacher Mariah Fisher.

MARRYING JAKE
(Intimate Moments #802, August 1997)
Commitment-shy Jake Wallace unravels the
ongoing mystery of stolen babies and helps
Katya Essler learn to believe in love again.

SAVING SUSANNAH
(Intimate Moments #814, October1997)
Kimberly Wallace needs a bone marrow donor
to save her daughter's life. Will the temporary
nanny position to Joe Lapp's children be the
answer to her prayers?

INTIMATE MOMENTS®
Silhouette®

Bestselling author

JOAN JOHNSTON

continues her wildly popular miniseries with an
all-new, longer-length novel

The Virgin Groom

HAWK'S WAY

One minute, Mac Macready was a living legend in
Texas—every kid's idol, every man's envy, every
woman's fantasy. The next, his fiancée dumped him,
his career was hanging in the balance and his future
was looking mighty uncertain. Then there was the
matter of his scandalous secret, which didn't stand a
chance of staying a secret. So would he succumb to
Jewel Whitelaw's shocking proposal—or take cold
showers for the rest of the long, hot summer...?

Available August 1997
wherever Silhouette books are sold.

Share in the joy of yuletide romance with brand-new
stories by two of the genre's most beloved writers

DIANA PALMER

and

JOAN JOHNSTON

in

LONE STAR CHRISTMAS

Diana Palmer and Joan Johnston share their favorite
Christmas anecdotes and personal stories in this
special hardbound edition.

Diana Palmer delivers an irresistible spin-off of her
LONG, TALL TEXANS series and Joan Johnston crafts an
unforgettable new chapter to **HAWK'S WAY** in this wonderful
keepsake edition celebrating the holiday season. So
perfect for gift giving, you'll want one for yourself...and
one to give to a special friend!

Available in November at your favorite retail outlet!

Only from

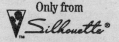

COMING NEXT MONTH

#799 I'M HAVING YOUR BABY?!—Linda Turner
The Lone Star Social Club
Workaholic Joe Taylor was thrilled when his wayward wife returned to him—and pregnant, no less! Then he realized that Annie had no idea how she got that way, at which point joy quickly turned to shock. What a way to find out he was about to become a father—or was he?

#800 NEVER TRUST A LADY—Kathleen Creighton
Small-town single mom Jane Carlysle had been known to complain that nothing exciting ever happened to her. Then Interpol agent Tom Hawkins swept into her life and, amidst a whirlwind of danger, swept her off her feet! But was it just part of his job to seduce the prime suspect?

#801 HER IDEAL MAN—Ruth Wind
The Last Roundup
A one-night *fling* turned into a lifetime *thing* for Anna and Tyler when she wound up pregnant after a night of passion. And now that she was married, this big-city woman was determined to see that Tyler behaved like the perfect Western hubby—but that involved the one emotion he had vowed never to feel again: love.

#802 MARRYING JAKE—Beverly Bird
The Wedding Ring
As a single mother of four, Katya yearned for Jake Wallace's heated touch, for a future spent in his protective embrace. But the jaded cop had come to Amish country with a mission, and falling in love with an innocent woman was not part of the plan.

#803 HEAVEN IN HIS ARMS—Maura Seger
Tad Jenkins was a wealthy, world-famous hell-raiser and heartbreaker, and Lisa Preston wasn't about to let her simple but organized life be uprooted and rocked by his passionate advances. But Tad already had everything mapped out. All Lisa had to do was succumb…and how could she ever resist?

#804 A MARRIAGE TO FIGHT FOR—Raina Lynn
Garrett Hughes' undercover DEA work had torn their marriage apart. But now, after four lonely years, Maggie had Garrett back in her arms. Injured and emotionally empty, he pushed her away, but Maggie was determined. This time she would fight for her marriage—and her husband—with all she had.